# OUT *of* REECH

# ADAM J. BEARDSLEE

outskirtspress
DENVER, COLORADO

Outskirts Press, Inc.
http://www.outskirtspress.com

ISBN: 978-1-4787-3902-9

Outskirts Press and the "OP" logo are trademarks belonging to Outskirts Press, Inc.

PRINTED IN THE UNITED STATES OF AMERICA

*For Aaron and Avery, the two people on this planet*
*I so badly wish had a chance to meet.*

*Aaron, although your star shone far too briefly,*
*it remains the brightest in my sky.*

*Avery, believe in yourself as I do,*
*and your accomplishments in life will be plentiful and vast.*

*I love you both immeasurably.*

## Acknowledgements

First and foremost, had it not been for the continual love and support of my wife, I wouldn't have gotten beyond the first page. Her patience, insight, and overall interest in the passion I held for my story is what helped me trudge through the frustrating times when writer's block blanketed my mind. She helped fuel my want to complete the biggest intellectual feat of my life, and it was her approval and pride throughout the process that I sought most. With that, I thank you from the very bottom of my heart, Brooke, and look to you for all of the same as I tackle my next endeavor.

Secondly, I would like to thank all of those who read my draft version, and provided feedback that made this novel something better than it ever had a chance of being without those comments. In particular, I'd like to thank Christina Cutler, who so graciously offered her brilliant mind and eyes to these pages that, over time, had become blurred in mine. Her ability to capture my oversights is what helped prevent readers of this novel from closing it after only the first few chapters.

*T*he sounds of birds echo around me; their beautiful songs help cloud my frantic mind. Some of joy, laughter, even argument. It's all there—a myriad of scenarios playing out above my head. There are friends meeting for dinner, cheers for the home team, perhaps a couple's quarrel brought out for everyone to see. I can't imagine what it would be like to fly.

I remember when my mother gave me a parakeet on my seventh birthday. I named her Pippy, and—in the green mind of a seven-year-old—thought that I was doing a great job of taking care of her. In truth, it was my mother who cleaned her cage, and kept her food and water dishes full, but my mom still gave me all the credit. God bless that woman. The only time that I truly did try to care for that bird was when I attempted to set her free from my second-story bedroom window. Unbeknownst to me, her wings had been clipped. I watched in terror as Pippy plummeted down to that rock garden, which ultimately claimed her life. Maybe it was for the better, what with being locked in a cage—much too small to call comfortable in the eyes of anything with wings—for eight months. What I know now is that for all the months that I rattled her cage, in mostly failed attempts at coercing her to sing, she undoubtedly loathed my very existence. To her, she was a prisoner *and I was her captor. I was seven for Christ's sake. What did I know about holding something, or someone for that matter, in captivity?*

The car made a hard right, fishtailing on to Elliott Road that led off the beaten path in Holly, Michigan, assuming there actually was a beaten path in the small town. Fall colors enveloped the road, blotting out the sky. The sun shone bright, but with the dense cover from the trees, all that remained was an ambient light that could only be appreciated if one were sitting in a smoky den surrounded by first editions of Poe.

Gravel sank into the soft soil as the car came to a stop. The driver looked in the rearview mirror, assuring himself that no one had followed. He noticed a blank, cold stare in the eyes of the hardened man staring back at him. He held himself at eye contact for a time, then directed his attention to the key in the ignition and turned off the car. He had driven far enough into the tunnel of trees to be lost in the shadows, indiscernible to passersby who might peer into the shadowy and colorful cave. Before today, the driver had spent many long nights playing out this scenario countless times in his mind, each time inventing more detail, to assure the success of his journey back north.

The driver began to exit the car, a 1994 white Chevy Celebrity. His feet worked like tampers as he stood on the rarely trodden earth, pummeling the dirt into the packed down embodiment of his size 11 wide. Black gloves hid his meaty hands, and a pair of jumper cables clawed at the ground behind him.

*I wish I were flying right now like the birds, soaring high in the blue sky, far above.*

The trunk of the car opened with a grinding sound that could only be produced through the presence of rust.

"You move, you die," the driver said. The sound of a gun cocking could be distinguished among the few other manufactured sounds cramping the airwaves.

Jacob Reech lay amidst old newspapers, clothing, and other meaningless junk that littered the roughly sixteen cubic feet void in which he had been stowed. Surely by now he had soiled himself. Rest areas and gas stations allowed for the driver to relieve himself or to grab a bite. Each time he emptied his disgusting bladder, a vague smirk pierced its way onto his face as he imagined the utter discomfort he knew Jacob was experiencing. The driver had won the battle over his conscience long ago.

"Help! Somebody!" Jacob called out in vain. He could almost hear his voice land on the rustling leaves and branches above, only to die out and flutter back to earth, mimicking so many of the dying early autumn leaves around him.

"No one can hear you. Now shut up," the man said,

sounding filthier than a stagnant swamp burping up methane. "Have you pissed yourself yet?"

"Help! Please! Can anyone hear me?!" he called out again, as a sick and twisted terror continued to consume him.

"I said shut the hell up!" the man said sharply, then punched Jacob in the stomach, proving his insides truly did have a threshold for suppressing vomit. He started to gag and cough while writhing in pain. The driver had made his point to stay quiet, and the brass knuckles that he had sewn into the outer lining of his gloves had added an exclamation point.

*I think he may have cracked a rib. Is that blood on my face, or am I crying?*

The sound of a second pair of footsteps became apparent a moment later. They were different than the pummeling sound Jacob had heard from the driver's big work boots. He had seen the black work boots only one time while he had been stowed in the trunk. Even with a duffel bag snugly around his neck, his eyes scoured their dark environment for any shred of light offering insight to the outside world. For the entire ride he'd lived in relative blackness, but at one point, a sign of hope emerged. Light.

*There's a hole in the bag! If I can just move this thing a little bit*, he thought as he maneuvered his jaw, as though trying to eat away at the canvas of the bag. Eventually, the tedious adjustment paid off.

He saw the boots through a pinhead-sized hole in the bottom corner of the trunk while the driver was pumping gas. The metal trunk was beginning to succumb to the rust which had first started eating away the bumper two years earlier. With the bumper now entirely gone all that remained of the rust was the hole that provided Jacob a single ray of light, and thankfully, he thought, a reliable source of air.

The sound of the second set of footsteps originated from a completely different style of shoes. The second pair sounded like dress shoes. No tread and a higher, more plastic-like sound.

"Here ya go," the driver said, as he handed the well-dressed man the jumper cables. "He won't cause a ruckus. We already been through that."

The sound of the work boots trailed off; all the while no new sounds came from the man apparently standing over the still open trunk. Jacob heard another engine scrape to life—a truck. The transmission called out in pain as the driver put it in gear and drove away.

The man in dress shoes placed another bag over Jacob's head. It was denser, blanketing out any residual light that teased his retinas. He could almost see more with his eyes clamped shut.

"Let me go! Why are you doing this?!" he pled with a muffled voice.

No answer.

"Where's Audrey? Have you hurt her? I swear to God, if you did anything to her! Anything...," he warned.

No answer. The well-dressed man ignored Jacob's delirious rant, and began to unwind the jumper cable cord that spanned fifteen feet. There was a faint smirk on his face. One of power. Control. Authority.

The beginning of The Movement was nearing.

Jacob could hear the car door open. Shortly after, the hood of the car heaved skyward. Then, the car screamed back to life. Something was dragging behind the man as he walked about. Shortly after, Jacob heard the dress shoes approaching the back of the car again, but this time he noticed a much more rapid gait in the man's stride, as if anticipating something.

The well-dressed man had affixed the cables to the car's battery while at the front of the car. He had done this many times throughout his life, even doing a stint of work with an auto service company back in the late nineties.

Unnerved, all Jacob could do was to listen to the electricity surging through the cables as their owner brushed opposing teeth against one another. He realized full well that he was in serious danger.

*He's doing that on purpose.* The thought materialized out of nowhere. *He's toying with me.*

Panic began to hover at the forefront of his mind. He was becoming numb with fear, his body radiating it.

With no warning, the well-dressed man clamped one set of cable teeth to the car's metal trunk above Jacob's covered head.

"No! Come on, please! You don't have to do this. What do you want? I'll give it to you. Please! Just stop!" Jacob yelled.

A gloved hand grabbed Jacob's shoulder, startling him, and the well-dressed man, with a mechanically altered voice, whispered, "What I want"—he paused— "is already in my possession."

At that moment, the many birds in Jacob's mind sang no more.

*Chapter 1 — September 14, 12:07 A.M.*

The single 40-watt bulb flickered as a man wearing a white coverall suit bumped his head against it for the second time since entering the room. It was his third visit to the room in the last three hours. Each time, he'd anticipated the same outcome—that his efforts would be fruitless yet again. He had no idea that his masterpiece was about to work for the first time since he started experimenting just over two years ago.

The room the bulb lit measured roughly five feet wide by eight feet deep, and was sectioned off in the man's basement, a steel workbench spanning one side of the entire room the only discernible object in it.

It was dank and came with a smell similar to that of a wet dog. A sad window mourned from one side of the room. Countless layers of discarded newspaper articles had been taped over it, preventing any light from entering. For years the newspaper held the sun's brilliance at bay, absorbed it, and over time had grown yellow from devouring its radiant beams. Essentially, the daylight that forever beat against the window was in fact a prisoner of the external world, never to be paroled into the confines of this unknown room it persistently sought.

Bare cinder block and mortar yawned at one another as they too yearned for a better life, one full of color, vibrancy, and purpose. That dream, however, would never come as long as the house was owned by the man now occupying the dreary room.

The suit he wore looked similar to a Haz-mat technician's. The only difference was that his suit was entirely homemade. Both cuffs and ankles were wrapped in duct tape, fusing the respective industrial rubber gloves and boots to the suit. A zipper had been sewn into the lining of the neck that included a hood with a makeshift Plexiglas face-shield. More duct tape was affixed to the face-shield, allowing no air in or out. Something which appeared to be a vacuum hose used for cleaning pools jutted out from the back of the suit's hood, and led to two small fixtures mounted to the wall adjacent to the door. The hose was separated into two nearly identical lengths, each connected to one of the fixtures, allowing the man to breathe.

As he inhaled an internal valve brought new, fresh air into his lungs. The same valve would then be forced closed from the pressure of his exhalation. There seemed to be enough slack in the hose for the man to move around as he needed, without threatening the integrity of the breathing system he'd so ingeniously created.

He slowly continued moving toward the workbench, and raised a gloved hand to steady the hanging light as the shadows from the recent jarring danced about. Not for an instant did the man's attention stray from what was on the workbench in front of him. He had knocked his head on the light many times, always forgetting that the suit added about four inches of height.

On the workbench, in a modified Petri dish, was a clear liquid that was emitting an orange gas. The gas was funneling into an attached surgical tube and collecting in a glass beaker. The beaker was not covered because the gas was heavier than the air, and simply gathered at the bottom of it, swirling as new gas poured in.

The man held a second glass beaker in his hand, this one much smaller than the one housing the orange gas. He inspected it. Nothing visible was inside. The man focused again on the container filling with gas, and a smile slid across his mostly hidden face. This was it, he knew. The time had come to test his masterpiece yet again.

As he saw orange gas begin to spill over the edge of the beaker, he put a clamp on the surgical hose, preventing any more gas from spewing into the now full beaker. He held the small one up to the light with a pair of tongs to assure there were no stress cracks in the glass, and slowly placed it inside the other beaker, vanishing as it entered the orange gas.

At the same moment, he started a stopwatch, and waited for sixty seconds. After one minute of exposure with a foreign object, the gas had turned opaque, its efficacy wearing off. He grasped the beaker again with the tongs, but this time pulled it out and set it on the workbench.

He studied the vessel in awe, the stopwatch still ticking, as he saw the fruits of his labor appear before his eyes.

Fingerprints. Precious fingerprints.

He admired them, watching as they seemed to protrude from the glass beaker with exacting precision. He found their unique curves beautiful and sexy, almost excited by them.

They were not visible before putting the container in the gas, and now they jumped from the glass canvas as if crying out for attention. His smile had turned into a teeth-filled grin reminiscent of a mad scientist.

One minute and thirty seconds had elapsed on the stopwatch.

The man looked at the beaker, then at the stopwatch. One minute forty seconds. His grin grew wider with anticipation.

Again his eyes found the beaker. One minute fifty seconds.

Before his eyes, and at precisely one minute and fifty-five seconds, the fingerprints began to diminish in intensity. By two minutes, not one fingerprint remained.

The man cheered out loud, knowing that his audible elation would not fall on the ears of a single soul aside from his own.

The cinder block and mortar cheered along with him, their psyches jubilant from the unexpected show of excitement. They wanted to celebrate with him, as a dog pines for the attention of its master. But he failed to acknowledge either of them. His attention was transfixed on that damn workbench and those beakers. They hated those beakers with a passion stronger than the bond that held them together.

He unzipped a portion of the suit, reached inside, and removed a pen that he used to finalize his lab notes, paying particularly close attention to the exact measurements of elapsed time for a given concentration of his experimental mixture. Once complete, he left the room as carefully as he'd entered, taking care not to bump the light hanging from the low ceiling.

At just after midnight, the man went to sleep, content that he had entirely disintegrated a set of fingerprints, leaving absolutely no remnant of their existence behind.

The disease, he knew, was progressing, and its grip on his life would be put to the test yet this morning.

E very star in the early morning sky seemed to wink at a man as he took a bite from his apple and pondered the very reason for their existence. He rested at the side of his barn after spending much of his early morning clearing away brush around his cornfield. While chewing, he wondered what each star fueled, and could not get past why God would go to all the trouble of creating them if not to harbor some form of life, or some other reason for their existence. He took another crunchy bite; a piece larger than expected came away in his mouth, and he adjusted it the same way an alligator firms its grip on fresh prey.

He pondered again why God created such a vast universe, teeming with the wonder of so many things unknown, if only to put life on Earth. *Why all the stars?* he thought. They're akin to mosquitoes in that they seem to serve no purpose. They don't provide a reasonable source of light at night. The Moon offered that. They did, however, give us constellations, he realized, but soon waved off the thought. So what else?

Then it came to him.

Maybe God created such a vast universe with countless stars to encourage all humans to do the one thing that transcends race, gender, age, and language, and allows each human to relate equally to the one standing on either side. *God*, the man thought, *simply wants us all to wonder about the unknown.*

Leaves rustled on a tree to the man's left near the edge of the cornfield; the morning sun was finalizing its preparations for ascent. The man nonchalantly glanced toward the tree, and in the same motion, tossed his apple core toward it, in a failed attempt to hit its trunk.

Before the core came to a stop, a figure dropped from the lowest branch of the veteran oak. The two caught each other's gaze and held it for a time during which no words were spoken.

Finally, the farmer broke the awkwardly long silence.

"How'd you find me?" His voice was firm.

"You're a fool to think I wouldn't," the man from the tree responded.

"It's been seventeen years," the farmer said.

"On the outside. More like seventy to me." The uninvited visitor began to approach the farmer. "You think a name change and an address in a different country would ever stop me from finding you?"

"Do we really need to do this? You're out. Why jeopardize your freedom over something that happened almost twenty years ago?"

"Freedom? I'm not free. And I sure as hell am not going back in there. So do *we* need to do this? No. But *I* do." He continued approaching the farmer.

"You know, my wife's in the house cooking breakfast." He motioned to his farmhouse on the other side of the oak tree. "All she needs to do is call the police and they'll be here in less than three minutes. See, they really look after you in witness protection." The farmer's voice grew in confidence as he spoke the words, allowing the reassurance of help from the authorities to set in.

"Was," the man clarified.

"Was what?"

"Your wife. She *was* in the house."

The growing display of confidence vanished from the farmer's face, and his eyes flushed with fear and rage alike.

"What have you done, you sick bastard?!"

"Well, I haven't *done* anything. I've only just begun. But what I can tell you is that her days of cooking you breakfast *are*, in fact, done."

"I'll kill you, you son of a bitch!" The farmer rose with the speed of an African cat, grabbing the machete that was next to him, and ran toward the other man, who began to retreat. The chase led into the cornfield that lined the back of the farmer's property, and the two disappeared into the early morning fog.

Five minutes later, a man emerged from the corn-field carrying a machete; the loose debris from felled stalks covered him head to toe, but did not entirely conceal the immense amount of blood on his body. Blood, that is, of which not one drop belonged to him.

*Chapter 3 — 5:11 P.M., 7 days ago*

Jacob's cell phone began to vibrate. It startled him, but his nerves jumped with excitement immediately. He knew who it was. Right on cue. His fiancée, Audrey, always called him at ten minutes after five. The conversations home undoubtedly put both of them in a good mood, but today was even more exciting than usual.

It was date night.

"How was work?" Audrey asked, in a voice that could lift Jacob's spirits even on the toughest of days.

"Always better when I'm out. Good thing you didn't ask me two hours ago. Man," he admitted as he sighed, happy to be done for the day.

Jacob was a professor of writing at the University of Michigan. Well, at the Flint location, that is. That distinction was always there. One of his biggest pet peeves was when people felt obligated to add the "Flint" part to his job title, as though teaching Ann Arbor "geniuses" were any more difficult than their "dangerous" and "uneducated" counterparts—most of whom had fallen off the radar at some point in their lives. Yes, most of Jacob's kids were a little rougher around the edges than the ones in Ann Arbor. And yes, he absolutely adored the University of Michigan – Ann Arbor. But he also had a very special place in his heart for those who roamed the halls, and streets for that matter, of Flint. "Who cares where they came from?" he once said to Audrey. "They're all just kids, right?"

While he was still in college, Jacob did his student teaching at an inner-city high school. The papers that he read, and asked students to read aloud in front of the class, weren't the best from a grammatical stand-point. But that didn't matter to him. It was the act of writing that Jacob scored his students on. During that semester, he read papers from students who had lost friends, family, and neighbors to gun violence. They had seen, or been the subjects of abuse beyond what Jacob could fathom. His class quickly became a venue for these students to give their grief a voice, and to look at it on paper; to go blow-to-blow with it, and for a lucky few, conquer it. How could he give a student anything but an 'A' for a paper that discussed being pistol-whipped as a child while the boy who wrote it cried to the class as the words quivered from his lips. The class was not intended as a class in grammar, and Jacob made that very clear.

It amazed him how so many students, while deal-ing with various socioeconomic struggles, were able to keep 4.0 GPA's. Jacob doubted that he could do half of what these kids did every day of their lives. Most had jobs. Many had kids. Some, at the age of seventeen, were the sole provider in their family.

"Sure," Jacob once said to his colleagues, "I teach my students how to analyze and appreciate writing, but I also teach them about juggling life's responsibilities." He always felt good when he said that. His students adored him for taking such a stance.

He allowed his students to turn in papers at any time throughout the semester. He refused to force his students into embarking on a journey of self-belittlement by having to ask for a deadline extension. Most of the department's faculty despised his approach, saying that he promoted procrastination and laziness. Jacob, however, knew what he had created.

"We still on for tonight?" he asked Audrey.

"We better be! I'm starving. Plus, I hear there's gonna be one heck of a handsome man there," Audrey said, playing into their excitement.

The beginning of the semester was always hard on them. Jacob had much more paperwork to do at the office, and usually had a handful of students contacting him to see if their waitlist number had been approved.

Audrey was also a teacher. She had been teaching kindergarten at Holly Elementary for three years. On nice days, she would ride her bike to work. The two lived only a half mile away from the school. What she loved most about her job was that the kindergarten school day was over by one. She was an evening girl, always making room at night to watch a good movie, treat herself to an ice-cream cone, or dive into a sappy vampire book. In some cases, however, she indulged in all of the above. But as the years of teaching passed, she became more interested in business, and hoped to open her own diner called Bump that would focus on the nutritional needs of women during pregnancy.

"I didn't know Brad Pitt was in town," Jacob volleyed back, keeping time with the meter in which they playfully bantered with one another. It was cute, you had to admit. The two were lost in love. Maybe it was because the wedding was only four months away. They had just started the planning process, and were looking forward to spending the best day of their lives surrounded by those who cared for them the most. Two hundred friends and family members all packed into one ceremonial banquet hall in Brighton.

"Do you know what you want?" Audrey asked. It was an empty question. She knew that no matter what Jacob said, they would still mull over the menu for fifteen minutes. Still, it was a fun topic to chitchat over while Jacob drove home.

"I'm thinkin' burger-town. You?" he joked, knowing she would bite on.

Jacob and Audrey had made it a point to never give up their Friday nights. Fridays had always been date night, ever since they'd gotten engaged four months ago. Tonight, they were eating at their favorite restaurant, the Fenton Fire Hall.

"You were supposed to say 'me'!" she flirted, playfully annoyed.

"You didn't mention anything about dessert!" he joked. "I'll be home in about 20 minutes."

"I'll be waiting," she said in an overly sexy voice.

Jacob began to accelerate. Home. He wanted to be there.

"Nice one! See ya soon, babe. Fourteen," he said, then hung up. The term "fourteen" was one Jacob used as a code for the times he wanted to say those ever-important three words but couldn't, and after years of use, it became the norm. The number always landed nicely on Audrey's heart. She knew it was far from just a number, but rather the reiteration of a promise Jacob made over ten years ago. The promise that she was the only *one for* him.

The alarm sounded. A wispy digitized version of waves lapping against a beach filled the room. Almost 5:00 in the morning seemed early, but the task had to be done at an hour such as this.

A man removed the covers from his bed, revealing a fully clothed figure. The clothes were simple enough: dark sweatpants and a dark blue-hooded sweatshirt, coupled with black gloves and boots. There would be no need for a mask or weapon, as the people he was planning to burgle were out of town on vacation, the second of three yearly ventures north of the bridge.

Campers proved to be the optimal target because once a campsite was set up, a family would likely hunker down for an extended period of time, after spending much of the first day tiring themselves out with unpacking, organizing gear, and hammering stakes that seemed endlessly necessary to quell any fear of the tent turning into a tattered wind sock during their stay.

It had been nearly two weeks since his last haul. The urge had grown fierce within his body, his blood boiling for the adrenaline.

He rose from the bed and put his glasses on to check his watch, assuring its synchronization with his atomic clock that sat on his nightstand. That is, the atomic clock that he stole from his then best friend, Anthony Johnson, in college, when he committed his first theft. Ever since, the need to steal had grown stronger with every successful heist.

He and Anthony met during an intramural racquet-ball league put on by the local university in response to an increasing number of requests from the student body to initiate the league. Most requests were sub-mitted by those who had been influenced by the chair-man of the Wolverine Healthy Extracurricular Activity Team, or WHEAT, as it was commonly known.

The man now standing at the side of his bed set-ting his watch went to that first league meeting, where he and Anthony were paired by means of a rudimen-tary numbering system. After their first match with one another, they slowly became friends. Before long, racquetball games ended with a quick bite at the rec-reation center's deli, and not long after that, the two termed themselves best friends. The man with the watch eventually helped Anthony move to a larger apartment at the start of their senior year.

While the young man carried one of the many cardboard boxes into its new home, Anthony's atom-ic clock mysteriously went missing, never to be seen again by its rightful owner, and giving birth to a disease that would firmly sink its claws into the poor soul's life, eventually consuming him entirely.

The man worked in total darkness while preparing for the night's heist. His night vision was in perfect focus, and lamplight would simply assault his retinas and delay his departure. Also, the man knew, it was important for lights to remain off so neighbors would not see any activity come from his house in the middle of the night, and thus, not be able to testify in court should he ever be identified as a suspect. He had even gone so far as to turn off the motion light on his garage the night before. With no witnesses seeing signs of life from his house, the police would have no chance of establishing the all-important timeline. If ever inter-rogated, he would say he was at home sleeping with diarrhea from the takeout he'd ordered earlier in the night, the receipt and Pepto-Bismol still on his counter to further authenticate his story.

If he stuck to his plan, his alibi would be foolproof. He knew the key to continued success resided in his al-ibi. Too extravagant and the person sounded guilty. Too many holes and the police would likely continue dig-ging, but one that was easy enough to prove, common enough to be believable, and embarrassing enough to its owner, was precisely awkward enough to direct in-terrogators elsewhere.

He watched the news religiously. The news was riddled with crime, and each story gave him the reassurance that the scales were tipped heavily in his favor. His methods were far more advanced than those of the ill-prepared halfwits whose mug shots he saw plastered across the headlines each night. He also came to understand that the most common alibi was, in fact, 'at home sleeping'. But he wasn't just at home. He had diarrhea and a head cold. He would prelude each heist with the same order from the local Chinese restaurant, Golden Dragon: seven egg rolls with extra hot mustard.

He looked one last time at the atomic clock, paying homage to its pinnaclistic virtue in his reformed life, and crept out the back door of his house and into the night.

Tonight he would target Peter and Carol Walker, newlyweds headed up north for their honeymoon. This was the second marriage for each of them, and both brought a teenager to the relationship, each of whom was invited to camp with the couple.

He knew his haul would offer several items from the recent nuptials—some likely still in their box—from which to choose.

The house was a brisk fifteen-minute sidewalk jog from his house. In fact, the two houses were only separated by a pond and a medium-sized cornfield that nestled up to the backyard of the Walker house. With the added bulk of two duffel bags, however, and a trek directly through the cornfield, the jaunt took about forty minutes.

Finally, he arrived breathless at the edge of the cornfield, and knelt for a moment to regain his rhythmically controlled breathing. Before long, he was standing on the Walker's back deck peering in through the sliding glass door attached to the kitchen, through which he would soon enter.

Feeling confident about his chosen point of entry, the man took one more look around and began opening the screen door which had been left unlocked. Far too many people neglected to lock their screen door, and this proved advantageous for gaining quiet entry.

Step one was easy.

Step two, the man felt, displayed only part of his true brilliance. He spent countless hours perfecting his unique method of entry.

With the screen door slid entirely to one side, he set his duffel bags on the deck with a quiet thud and retrieved a small piece of metal about the size of a deck of playing cards. A magnet.

He covered the raw magnet with a thin cloth, and placed it on the glass door adjacent to the handle where the lock was located. After assessing the lock, he began making slow swipes with the magnet in different directions on the door, the cloth preventing any scratches from being etched onto the glass. The trick was to find the proper arc for which the locking mechanism followed and to slide the magnet just right, in order to gain that sought-after quiet—and, more importantly, untraceable—entry. After a few more attempts, the man heard the telltale *shunk* of the tooth disengage from the locking bar. He opened the door and stepped into the house, leaving his shoes on the deck.

As soon as he entered the house, he held his breath for a brief moment while he listened for the quiet, intermittent beep of a silent alarm.

No sounds rang in his ears. Feeling confident that there was no threat of capture, the man proceeded to the main hallway, never once looking at the various pictures hanging on the walls of the house. Each picture told a story that the man did not care to know. They were intangible distractions that had led to far too many close calls in years past.

He kept his eyes on the open space in front of him, constantly sweeping his line of sight to other areas, making sure that the house and all its muted objects remained perfectly still.

He headed toward the master bedroom where people typically kept their most treasured possessions, jewelry in particular. He stepped gingerly on each stair from habit, as many staircases squeaked if stepped on without care. He was almost at the top of the flight of stairs, hands gripping the railing on either side. In just a few more steps he'd be able to peer around the corner down the hallway to where the master bedroom would likely be located.

"Hey!" a voice pierced the silence. "What do you think you're doin'?" the voice continued.

In a nanosecond the man's heart fell from his chest to his feet as he realized someone was standing behind him. Out of reflex he spun around to see who it was, and immediately remembered he was not wearing his ski mask.

"Oh, hi," the burglar calmly said. "I'm Tom, Pete's friend from work. He sent me a text asking to check in on the house." He began descending the stairs slowly, but no longer caring about the squeaks. "Couldn't remember if Carol unplugged the curling iron and asked me to check it out. Ya know, to save them the worry on their honeymoon." He took another step down the stairs.

"Stop! Don't you come any closer!"

The intruder paid no mind to the proclamation the other man just made, and descended yet another stair, his face now revealed in the moonlight offered from the skylight above the staircase. He came to a stop.

The two men looked at each other for the briefest of moments, as the weight of the situation sunk into their minds, both construing their own synopsis.

"Oh my God," the man said as he saw the burglar's

face, realizing the full gravity of his predicament even more than the synapses his mind had created only a moment ago.

He turned as quickly as he could and raced toward the kitchen. The burglar, charged with an uncanny spike in adrenaline, followed in pursuit.

*The phone. I can't let him get to that phone!*

The chase seemed timeless, as though the rest of the world had been placed on pause while they ran.

The first man entered the kitchen and sped between the hutch and island toward the phone located on the far wall of the breakfast nook. One and a half steps later, the man felt the pressure of a punch land on his chest with the ferocity of lightning. He staggered from the blow, air bursting from his lungs as he recoiled in shock. Delirious with fear, his eyes found those of the man who'd nearly brought him to his knees in pain, and grew wild as they focused on the knife firmly grasped in the hands of the intruder. The blade appeared black to the man, until his gaze followed its pointed end to the floor only to see a small puddle of black liquid. Only then did he see the true vibrant red for the color it was, and hauntingly looked at his own chest. His hands grappled at the island as the horrific sight brought him to his knees. Before the rest of his body hit the ground, he was unconscious, his flayed heart pooling blood out from under him and his now liquefied life coasting along the cracks in the hardwood floor of the kitchen.

The intruder stood over the body until no movement remained, and went back to his point of entry. He opened both duffel bags and in one, placed the bloody knife wrapped in his ski mask. He grabbed seven Glade Plug-Ins from the other, the fragrant liquid replaced with the gaseous mixture he'd perfected a few days ago, the remaining whole of the man's true genius. He went back into the house and placed them in various locations throughout the areas he traveled, paying close attention to the kitchen. He put three in that room alone. The potency of the mixture had been increased to account for large-scale use. He then exited the glass door, used the magnet to relock it, and sprinted to the cornfield.

As he ran, he wondered who the man was that he'd killed. It was not the homeowner, he was sure of that. He was also sure that given the time of night and circumstance, it was likely that no one would find the body for at least a few days. *Unless, that is, the man had a family who was expecting him home, a family that he'd told where he was going.* He ran faster, realizing the timeline might have just been drastically shortened. The evidence, however, would be another story. There would be none. He took the murder weapon, and his print bombs would eradicate all of his fingerprints. *What about other bodily evidence? Did I get cut in the scuffle? Oh my God, the blood, they'll analyze it all.* He stopped to check his body for any defensive injuries and to vomit onto the ground before him, the adrenaline purging. His hands grasped his head, and he fell to his knees gritting his teeth in silence, but screaming louder than ever in his mind.

"What have I done?" he whispered to himself aloud; the words carried away in the wind, never to return with an answer. He climbed back to his feet, and the grimace on his face proved his mind had turned maniacal from the brutal encounter. He was no longer a kleptomaniac. He was a murderer.

Kyle Voelner stood at Professor Reech's office door, wearing what every college student wore on a Saturday morning—a collegiate hoodie, sweatpants, and the ever-present pair of tattered moccasins—Kyle's showing the wear and tear of a lion cub's chew toy. His wavy blond hair, however, was never in disarray. It was a bit too long to be considered popular, but remained styled to perfection nonetheless. Kyle had a way about flipping his bangs out of his eyes that seemed to draw the attention of nearly every female classmate within range of catching a drifting whiff of his daily—or more—shampooing. Professor Reech had once referred to Kyle as Matthew McConaughey in front of the class, not knowing that Kyle would secretly thank him under his breath for doing so. He reveled in the comment made by his teacher, as he could attribute nothing else to the influx of attention he received from his co-ed classmates that day after class. In particular, the attention he got from Calista, who he made it a point to sit next to whenever possible.

"Dr. Reech?" Kyle inquired politely as he knocked. He stood in front of the office door passing time by scrutinizing the far too simplistic, and by no means authentic, name plate loosely affixed to the adjacent wall. Even the screws were fake. Kyle found it odd. He expected the placard on the office of someone as influential in his life as Dr. Reech would at least be given the symbolic permanence of being securely anchored to the wall.

He shuffled his feet as he contemplated knocking again. He didn't want to upset Professor Reech. Maybe he was on a very important phone call. Kyle's patience, however, was not so contemplative, as his arm seemingly rose itself and knocked once more on the office door.

"Professor? Are you there?" Kyle adjusted his bag as he reached into it to make sure he had his term paper he intended to speak with Dr. Reech about.

Kyle was invited to Professor Reech's office to discuss his paper. Little did he know that his professor was so impressed with his submission that he was going to ask Kyle for a copy, along with his permission to use it as an example to future classes of how a term paper should be written. Kyle's term paper was exquisite in the eyes of his professor. It was the most confidently written paper that he had ever received from one of his students. This paper flew circles around the typical, droningly mundane submission riddled with far too many prepositions, articles, and modifiers thrown in just to meet the expected length. Still others neglected to even address the basic question of dissecting a work of Shakespeare, taking the opportunity to go off on a tangent wherever possible. Kyle's was different—more confident, assertive. Any paper, Professor Reech believed, that claimed such an unorthodox argument as Macbeth playing only a minor role in the Shakespearean masterpiece named for him had better be as confident as possible while delivering it to his auditorium-style class.

*"Okay. Who's next? Mr. McConaughey, how about you?" Jacob probed. His comment was met with uproarious laughter from the class. "Come on," he continued. "You'll do just fine."*

*Kyle strode down to the podium. The journey took longer than expected to descend the stairs from his seat to the stage. The stairs were deep, forcing Kyle to take two strides per step. He felt awkward, as though his classmates noticed his broken rhythm. He arrived at the podium a moment later.*

*"Thank you, Dr. Reech." He now addressed the entire class. "Before I begin, I'd like to admit something to the class." His pause was abnormally long, and the room fell silent. Jacob could see that the entire class was now engrossed in the speaker. It was brilliant really, to begin by offering an admission. Admissions were personal. Admissions meant gossip.*

*As planned, all talking ceased, all faces were forward, all pens and pencils were on their respective desks, as though the owners had no idea they even existed, cast aside in want of something more important. Kyle cleared his throat. "I'd like to start by pointing out with absolute certainty that most, if not all, of you will initially disagree with my thesis." A few students stirred in their seats, realizing the admission carried no gossiptual value. "However, I can only hope that my argument, and the way in which it is explained, is strong enough to sway the opinions of those of you I am now addressing."*

*An indirect focus of Jacob's Writing about Literature class was to provide students a venue of exploration regarding the all-too-nerve-racking topic of public speaking. Kyle's ability to speak publicly was on an entirely different planet than that of his classmates.*

*"So with nothing further, I'd like to present to you my argument entitled 'WORDS are a SWORD Whilst We LIVE with EVIL (An Analysis of the Power of Words in Shakespeare's Macbeth).'"*

Kyle Voelner swayed many minds that day.

Feeling the ebb and flow of frustration pumping within his veins, Kyle gripped the office door and rotated the knob, expecting the bolt to catch, preventing any such action. On the contrary, the latch heaved then clicked with surprising ease. The door swung eerily open.

Kyle was immediately confronted with an unfamiliar and unpleasant smell. Only the beautifully ambient rays of sunlight slicing through the air, from the office's solitary window, could even begin to mask the stench.

He covered his nose and mouth with the sleeve of his unwashed hoodie, which only added to the bacterial assault of his lungs, checked the hallway to either side, and slowly entered the odorous room.

"**H**ello?" Jacob growled.

"You still sleepin'? Man, I've been up for like, two hours!" Victor gloated. "Today's the day, my friend!" The elation in his voice was undeniable.

"I know. But, it's only 4:30 in the morning. Go back to bed. Call me when you can see the sun. Appointment isn't 'til nine anyway," Jacob commanded, and then hung up on his best friend; although still half asleep, a slight smile crept onto his face.

"Was that Vic?" Audrey stirred.

"Yeah. He's just excited. I don't think the adrenaline's worn off yet," he said as he shifted in bed to face his fiancée; her succulent lips were the last thing he saw before once again succumbing to sleep.

Jacob sat at a booth in a local diner waiting for his friend Victor to arrive. His cell phone lay on the table in front of him, but no call had come through all morning. Victor was now twenty minutes late. Jacob wanted to worry about his best friend, but reasoned that although twenty minutes seemed incredibly long, it was an entirely relative measurement of time. Blindly waiting for twenty minutes in a comfortable booth was not nearly as stressful as what his father went through in Vietnam.

Jacob's father never came home from Vietnam. He had learned most of what he knew of his father through stories his mother told him. He enlisted in 1974, the same year Jacob was born. His mother got pregnant six months before his father arrived in Vietnam, and only two months after his deployment, Jacob's father, Russell, was bound and gagged in a holding cage built from bamboo in a remote village overtaken by the Vietcong. He had been captured after a spontaneous firefight that neither the Americans nor the Vietcong initially expected to see that day. It started when Russell accidentally dropped his canteen while marching in formation in a high grass field adjacent to a rice farm. When it reached the ground, it struck a boulder protruding from the earth. The sound it made could be heard for at least a mile. The sound, as the Vietcong knew, was definitely manmade, and it was considered a far from welcoming one.

Immediately following the canteen mishap, two groups of Vietcong swiftly sent spotters to investigate the sound, and upon word of the finding of Americans, both groups enveloped the high grass path about a half mile ahead of the unsuspecting U.S. platoon. Hiding in the grass, the Vietcong waited patiently for the signal to open fire. The call came soon enough, and a barrage of gunfire rained upon the surprised Americans, who took the most casualties. Only a few were able to successfully retreat back to the safety of camp, which was about two miles away.

After the shooting came to a stop, the Vietcong approached the bodies. Jacob's father had been hit in both legs, preventing any coherent movement on his part. He could hear periodic screams and gunshots. Eventually, Russell saw a solitary soldier approaching him, gun in the ready position, pointed at his torso. He reeled with horror, realizing he would likely never meet his unborn child. In an instant, he gave life to the little human growing inside of his dearest Beth; soccer games played in his mind, graduation, a successful career, all shrouded in an angelic silhouette that danced behind his eyelids before his assumed pending death. The last vision he had was of his beautifully silhouetted toddler poking at his sides with a stick, attempting to tickle him, Beth smiling on from behind. The laughter was so vivid in his mind. He cherished the vision as only a parent could.

He came to as the tip of a hot rifle prodded into his rib cage. His eyes opened, and reality rushed back into his mind with tsunamic power.

No words were ever spoken while he was being dragged back to the camp of the Vietcong. However, he could see that only two other Americans were still alive, both secured to makeshift bamboo gurneys on either side of him. They were the last Americans he would ever see.

It's unknown exactly how long Private Russell Reech was held in captivity, but based on the length of his beard when the Americans won control of the village and discovered his body, the best guess is that he endured four months of solitary captivity, before starving to death—at least that's what the military told his beloved Beth. During those four months, and with two unaided broken legs, severely battered ribs, a broken nose, and a forearm riddled with burn marks, his father had likely spent countless hours contemplating what options he had, and did not have. Jacob knew that waiting about twenty minutes in ideal conditions for his friend to arrive was not a matter for concern at all.

Before long, Victor arrived. Jacob stood up, and took part in the customary greeting between two males that consisted of a masculine embrace ending with a fisted pump on each other's back.

"Hey, man! Sorry to keep you waiting," Victor said, as he took a seat opposite Jacob.

Victor sat before Jacob with a grin on his face. The yellow and green plaid flannel shirt that he wore matched the exultant expression frozen on his face. In high school, however, that grin had never existed.

Victor was the kid with an ever-present bombardment of blemishes scattered across his face. His freshman and sophomore years proved the most difficult. Each school day offered an onslaught of jokes about his skin. He once got in a fight with Bryan Hoover after school because of one particular comment that landed more harshly than so many others.

*As he walked home that day from school, Victor saw Bryan approaching him riding shotgun in his friend's car. Bryan got out, and acted as though he was going to apologize to Victor for being so cruel. "Here," he said to Victor, "I wanna give you something." Bryan unzipped his backpack and retrieved an empty jug of motor oil, and handed it to Victor. "You outta think about sellin' that shit." He started laughing hysterically as he looked back at his friends in the car. When he turned back to Victor, a fist landed square on his eye, and Victor tackled him to the ground.*

*Victor pinned Bryan down and landed blow after blow. Bryan got more than what he'd expected from his scrawny counterpart he so often used as a verbal punching bag. In each white-knuckled fist, Victor packed the ridicule of each comment, stare, and joke he had felt and heard by his classmates, and released them onto Bryan's face. It was reminiscent of when Ralphie beat up Scut Farcus. The fight ended about as quickly as it started as one of Bryan's friends pushed Victor to the ground, allowing Bryan to get up. The defensive punches that landed on Victor were minuscule.*

When the ridicule started in the 7th grade, Victor initially fought back with words, making fun of the kids who dared to jab at him, but that only fueled their fire. Then, he attempted to ignore them, but that was all but impossible. People yelling slurs directly into his ear on a daily basis caused him to cry himself to sleep most nights. Eventually, he just learned to accept it, making peace with the comments people made. A side-effect of bullying was depression, and no one other than Victor himself knew how often he considered the solace that suicide could bring.

But when Bryan Hoover placed that oil can in his hands, a volcano erupted from within, like so many of the pimples that Victor hated on his face. Still though, regardless of physical pain, Bryan landed the Hail Mary blow. As he rose to his feet with the help of his friend, he wiped his bloodied face, his left eye already starting to bruise, and looked at his friend standing to his right. "I think he dripped grease on me," he said, casting his physical pain aside in order to continue badgering his prey.

It would never stop. This was, and always would be, a part of Victor's life. He walked home that day fighting what seemed to be a losing battle with the demons wrestling in his mind. Oftentimes, depression took a resounding seat on a person's soul, but every once in a while, it would make brief, calculated visits. These visits to Victor's shoulders always seemed to happen at the worst time—while he was alone with his thoughts.

Depression never tried to creep into his mind while he was

with Jacob. If it had, he would be able to easily stave off the pressure it brought, throbbing with suicidal urges. But there was nothing brief about the visit on the day of the fight with Bryan.

The pressure to end it all loomed far greater that day than in times past. Maybe it was because this time he had a failsafe means just feet away.

Bryan fled back into his friend's car as Victor looked on with an impulsive expression frozen on his face. His mind became his true enemy.

Should I? It'd be so easy. So quick. I'm going to. No, don't. It's not worth it. They're just assholes. But I can't take it anymore, he toiled dangerously.

The train was just around the bend. The demons in his mind screamed louder than any train whistle he'd ever heard. It was like they were more powerful than the speeding locomotive approaching him.

Fuck it. I'm going to. I'll show them. No! Your family! I can't take it anymore. Find another way. There is no other way. They won't stop until I'm dead! I'm doing it! I don't care anymore! He was on the verge of something horrible.

Then, a gentle hand found its way to Victor's shoulder. He looked to the side, and saw Jacob walking beside him. Jacob's empathetic expression bellowed above the train and the demons alike, and caused the unwanted visions to dissipate like the smoke billowing out and trailing behind the metal beast now roaring beside them. Jacob was his only true friend in the world.

*He'd never say the words, but had it not been for Jacob catching up to him on Grange Hall Road, Victor may have decided to take one last fateful step onto the railroad tracks that meandered ominously toward his house.*

"Don't worry about it. It was just a few minutes," Jacob responded.

The waitress saw the second half of the two-party table sit down, and moseyed over to the two friends.

"Coffee?" she asked pleasantly.

"Espresso," Jacob said, eyeing Victor to make his point, the bags under his eyes filling in the blanks.

"I'll have a coffee with two creams, please," Victor ordered, not catching Jacob's drift.

"Sure thing. I'll have 'em right up, guys."

The two sat at the table looking at each other for a time before a word was spoken, the situation still sinking in for both of them. The silent excitement was broken by Victor.

"Can you believe it? I swear, you and Audrey'll have nothing to worry about. Trust me." His voice was happier than ever. The scars of ridicule disappeared from his face and left behind a look of true appreciation.

"No need to state your case. I believe you, and I thank you dearly." Jacob's eyes widened slightly to emphasize what he'd just said.

The waitress arrived with their coffee, and the two nodded their heads in unison to say thank you. She was a bit plump, but with her gorgeous blonde hair, perfectly tanned body, and chipper attitude, neither of them noticed. Both Jacob and Victor were happy that she was their waitress.

"I just can't believe it, Jake! I mean, what do I do from here, ya know?" His excitement boiled over.

"Well, the first thing you do is make your appointment this morning. I mean it. This is not something that you want to miss." Jacob's voice was stern, but friendly.

"I know, I know. I'm just glad that you're coming with me. It means a lot," Victor admitted.

Jacob sipped his coffee and looked at the swirling liquid in his cup. Shortly after, he met Victor's eyes once again.

"Well, it is pretty damn early." He smiled as he patted his friend on the shoulder.

"You ready to go?"

"Yeah, I guess. This is my second cup this morning, thanks to you," Jacob instigated, and then grinned.

They each left two dollars on the table, got up, and left the restaurant. Nothing was said, but they both thought of how much of a tip they had each left for just one cup of coffee. But the waitress just had that personality that made people want to tip heartily. However, only Heather the waitress knew if that personality was genuine.

"As you can see from the picture," the real-estate agent said. Victor and Jacob met with Carol Simpson four days ago to schedule a day of house hunting. Victor was looking to buy his first house. He'd been one of the lucky, lucky ones. He won the lottery six months ago.

Victor Flanten and Jacob Reech met in ninth grade during gym class. The two were drawn to one another through the raw necessity of finding a like minnow with whom to swim in the sea that was a locker room they were forced to share with the barracuda upperclassmen. The men among boys were all too proud of their pectorals and biceps, and they carried in their testosterone-filled bodies an unwarranted aggression toward anyone they deemed sub-muscular in comparison.

Since the first semester of their high school careers, the two had been best friends. Over the years they had studied together, pondered the goddesses that roamed the halls around them, and gotten into fights on each other's behalf. Nothing changed in college, except, of course, the size of their pectorals. They had even made good on a yearly road trip to Victor's parents' cottage in Tawas since graduating college.

"The kitchen has been updated," Carol continued. "All appliances stay with the property."

The listing was incredible. Upon entering the gated driveway, a lush garden could be seen nestled off to the side of an older pole barn. The previous owners obviously did not use the pole barn, as it seemed the only overgrown aspect of the nearly two-acre plot. The house was a two-story colonial, with Mediterranean blue shutters that accentuated a medium-gray siding. There was an attached four-car garage on the left side of the house. But the most noticeable feature of the property was at the very top, protruding from above the attic in white: a dome of sorts. Without ever pondering the object, Jacob could tell it was a residential rooftop observatory. He had read about them in a *Popular Science* magazine not too long ago. The interior of the dome housed a telescope for the private, convenient, and comfortable viewing of the night sky.

"What kind of telescope do they have?" Jacob asked, displaying his knowledge of the architectural oddity atop the house to Carol and Victor alike.

"You know, that's a good question. I don't know if it's even still in the house, but I can check with the homeowners to see if they're willing to include it in the sale as well," Carol answered.

Jacob looked at Victor, as if to say, "Hey, why not let her ask, ya know? What's it gonna hurt?" Plus, it simply wasn't Jacob's question to answer.

"That'd be great, Carol," Victor said. "Let me know what they say," he finished.

The inside of the house was even more amazing.

The first object to be seen was a rather large chandelier hanging from a twenty-four-foot ceiling. It must have had over a hundred individual bulbs on it, spanning five feet in diameter. Other than that, the house looked relatively normal. The magnificent chandelier appeared out of place.

"The chandelier stays with the house, too." She read their minds. "The owners have already moved to Virginia and took most of the other pieces of decor with them. The chandelier's too large for their new home. What you see in the house now has actually been staged by my company."

Jacob and Victor nodded their heads in unison, then looked at each other with raised eyebrows. The house was immaculate, and was a steal at three hundred seventeen thousand dollars. Even in the buyer's market that a struggling economy inevitably produced, that price seemed low.

Deep down, Jacob was thankful that Victor had not won enough money to ruin his life, only to change it. Victor's haul, in terms of lottery winnings, was a mere $1.5 million dollars. These days, that amount of money wasn't quite enough to drive a person to eventually swallow the business end of a pistol. No one should be given more money than what they can understand how to handle, which is why Jacob knew Victor was one of the lucky, lucky ones.

"We must not fail." The Voice came through the phone on the console of a dark, impromptu meeting room. In the room, there were three men sitting at a folding table huddled around a single phone. The Voice filled the small room with authority. "The Movement is much too important. Those who run this country have been lying to us. To their people. Yet, they label us as traitors." He paused. "For crimes far inferior to their own."

"We will not let you down," the three men said in unison, followed by silence.

"His name is Jacob Reech. A local. A meaningless professor. It is not him we need, but rather what he has." More silence. "Information that proves our cause."

"So we get him to tell us this information. Then what?" one of the men asked.

"Then what? Well, we rewrite America's history. And let me remind you, Frank, guys like you are a dime a fucking dozen. Leave the questions to me," The Voice firmly responded, then continued. "And it may not be as easy as getting this Reech guy to just tell us the information, like what Frankie-boy thinks. He may not even be aware of the information he protects."

Silence filled the room for a time; only the echoes of discarded thoughts bounced off the walls.

"So we infiltrate," another man said after a few moments, his voice deeper than the first man's. "I mean, let's just remove him from the situation. It's gotta be in his house, right, if not in him?"

"Infiltrate. Could be tough," The Voice pondered. "We can't create too much attention with this. It'd be a circus around his house. We'd have no chance of getting in there."

"So let it be," the third man finally spoke up.

"Let it be what?" Frank asked, cowering slightly from asking yet another question. The Voice let it slide, but the ensuing silence on the phone was as effective as if The Voice were in the room himself. A few moments later, The Voice made his point by restating Frank's question. "Let it be what?"

"A circus," the third man said, then paused briefly. "I have an idea."

Jacob took the box of old pots and pans he'd prepared for the garage sale and carried them down to the basement. He hoisted the box above his head and placed it on the top shelf of a musty closet. As he did, the bottom of the box caught on something flat lying on the shelf. He placed the box farther to the left, and reached to retrieve the item.

He pulled it down and stared at it for a moment. It was the envelope given to him at his grandfather's will ceremony. Dust had accumulated on it since he last looked at it over three years ago. He blew it off, and a cloud appeared in front of his face briefly before dissipating as it settled to the floor.

Jacob's grandfather had really played more of a fatherly role in his life. His grandfather was the one who taught him how to ride a bike, throw a football, and tie a knot. It was even his grandfather who listened to a young Jacob as he described Pamela Jennings, his first crush in middle school. The act of involving himself in Jacob's life was made by Jacob's parents separately. His mother, Beth, approached his grandfather the day her husband was deployed, saying, "Jacob needs a man to look up to. If Russ doesn't make it back, you're all he'll have."

His father also approached him as they had drinks two days before he was deployed. The two shared stories about family they recalled from years past, but Russell became serious at one point, asking his father to swear that he'd watch over Jacob if he didn't make it home. They hugged tightly that day. Jacob's grandfather could not allow himself to even begin to entertain the idea that his son might not come back from the war, but he vowed to care for Jacob regardless.

He looked at it for a moment before emptying the envelope; it contained just one small sheet of paper. Two short sentences were written on it, and they shot out from the note as he pulled it from the envelope.

JACOB, FRANKLIN HAS A SECRET.
NOAH WILL HELP YOU.

*Chapter 8 — 3:00 P.M., 2 days ago*

The blanket wasn't big enough, but they made do. Jacob and Audrey were enjoying an "outside day" as they called it. It really didn't matter what they did, so long as it was outside. This day, they found themselves at Four Ponds State Park, no more than two miles away from their house, enjoying a basket of homemade sandwiches, fruit cups, and crackers and cheese.

In the past they had enjoyed these types of days searching for asparagus, visiting the zoo, and even driving to the eastern coast of Michigan to marvel at the vastness of the Great Lakes. If not told one was standing on the beach of a lake, one could only think he or she was looking directly at the Atlantic Ocean.

Four Ponds State Park had caught their attention several times over the past few years, due in large part to its locale, as they, along with every other American, continued to watch gas prices skyrocket out of control. More importantly, though, was the fact that the park had a variety of activities to keep the two busy throughout the seasons. Every season offered its fair share of outside days.

Spring had wondrous blooms across an encyclopedia of wildflowers. Summer days were drenched in sunshine and blue sky, any one of the ponds from the park's name offering a place for sunbathers to stay cool. Autumn ambushed the eyes with the most vivid shades of fuchsia and yellow, trees seeming to close in on the many winding pathways laced throughout the park. The park became a wonderland of white in winter, where ice skaters and fisherman alike could co-exist among the four perfectly circular ponds, all of which graciously tempted those who set eyes on any one of them.

This day, Jacob and Audrey were enjoying a brisk walk through the paved pathways after they'd shared lunch on their blanket. Each pathway was lined as if it were a street, denoting the approved direction of travel. In addition, there was about a two-foot-wide section running along either side of the pathway for bikers to utilize—safety being of the utmost concern during these 'sue-happy' times.

"So have you decided what colors you want in the wedding?" Jacob asked.

"Not quite. What do you think? Should we go with violet or eggplant for the bridesmaid's dresses?" Audrey inquired.

"Wait, there's a difference?" He smiled at her.

They began walking up a steady incline that they always made sure to incorporate into these walks. After a time, their conversation was riddled with gasps for air, and deep, labored exhales.

"I guess…my only question is…what flavor cake are we going with?" Another smile crept onto Jacob's face. He was fully aware of the oncoming shoulder slap that Audrey would administer in three, two, yup, right on time.

"Ya know…you could be…a little more excited… After all…it's your wedding too, mister."

They were nearing the top of the steep hill where a bench had been placed to allow for a breather. The bench strategically overlooked the vastness of Four Ponds State Park. The scene seemed to be infused with the beauty only captured in postcards and travel guides.

"Wow, look at those colors, Aud. It's great, isn't it?" Jacob commented, his question more rhetorical than anything.

"Yeah. I wish it was like this all year. The colors, I mean." She gasped for air. "They're breathtaking." The chuckles that followed paid homage to her convenient pun.

Once the laughter subsided, they sat on the bench drinking water, in perfectly comfortable silence for a time. Jacob eventually stood and went closer to the ledge that was guarded by a stout wooden fence. Time had taken its toll on the integrity of the wood, and the stain had all been weathered away years ago. He looked across the expansive landscape, marveling at God's canvas. While panning the view, his eyes caught something in the sun. He saw what appeared to be two glints of light in very close proximity to one another coming from the opposite side of the pond in front of him. After his eyes refocused, Jacob could see that the glints were associated with a person at a picnic table sitting next to a bright green car. Binoculars. Probably a birdwatcher. This was a great time to view all wild-life. There were always people peppered throughout the park, doing a variety of different things. Amidst nature's beauty, Jacob brushed off the uneasy feeling he felt growing in his stomach, and turned back to Audrey.

Jacob's heart nearly jumped out of his chest at the scene in front of him. No more than two inches from his face, Audrey was holding her puckered lips, awaiting a kiss. She held her hands behind her back and lifted one foot off the ground, bending it at the knee.

"Geez!" Jacob gasped. "You scared me," he explained.

"I didn't know I was that ugly," Audrey replied, her puckered lips slowly turning into a playful frown.

"Come here," Jacob said. He wrapped his arms completely around her and kissed her.

"The zebra's down for a drink, mate," the man said into the receiver of the two-way radio he was holding. He had a thick Australian accent.

"In English, please," a voice came back.

"They just set up a picnic on the other side of Third." There was little accent in his voice this time.

Four Ponds State Park was nestled snugly on a 300-acre plot that most passersby would not even know existed unless looking for it on a map. Most of the park butted up to Interstate 75, where countless vehicles heading south added to the noise factor that any park tries to diminish. However, the way that the land sloped down from the Interstate, peppered with towering hardwoods and pines, played a major role in absorbing most of the daily rumbles that any expressway inevitably presented. Every now and then, however, a screech of tires would pierce through the air and could be heard by all.

The four ponds located in the park had each gone through the process of being named. Some people voted to pay tribute to the men who had a hand in building the park from the ground up. Others submitted suggestions—from the preposterous to the mundane. However, after many days of discussion, and review of all suggested names, the ponds were each given a name that would help visitors identify each pond, and assist in locating them on a park map. The ponds were named One, Two, Three, and Four. The DNR cleverly used this naming convention as a marketing tool for the park. The location of the ponds, similar to the numerical location on a clock, found its way onto the Four Ponds State Park logo, the tagline reading, "Add time to your day, from One to Four." The background of the logo showed a clock pointing to all four ponds at once. The only thing missing from the campaign, it seemed, was a Tim Allen voiceover.

"Are they both there?" the second voice came through again.

"Yeah. They been here for a while now," he said, as he smacked his gum obnoxiously loudly.

He sat at a picnic table at the top of a hill overlooking Third Pond. A pair of binoculars sat beside him.

"Keep your eye on 'em. If they start leaving, let me know."

"No worries. You got all the time you need. They set up about a five-minute walk from their car. Even if they get up and leave right now, you still have about ten minutes, including drive time, mate."

"Good. I'll keep you posted."

"Afternoon!" another voice called from behind the Aussie, startling him. The Aussie turned around and saw a park ranger approaching the picnic table.

"G'day," the man said, his accent thick as ever. The man was from Australia, but had long since adopted the American accent. However, over the years he came to realize that his Australian accent always came across as friendly and non-threatening. "What can I do you for?"

"Just making my rounds. I saw you from across the way." The ranger pointed over to the area where Jacob and Audrey now sat. "You're not the only one with binoculars out here." He chuckled. "Mind if I ask what you're lookin' at? I didn't see that you had any company and weren't eatin' anything."

"Right on. Yeah, I was just doin' a bit of bird watchin'."

The ranger began nodding his head slowly as he read the Aussie's face.

"Is that right?" He paused. "Why aren't you by any trees?" the ranger pondered out loud.

"I just came from that patch over there not too long ago. Thought I saw a warbler fly out of it, and wanted to see if I could spot where it landed. Locate its nest, you know?"

"Ah." Another pause. "And the two-way?" the ranger interrogated even further.

"Got a partner down by Two, who's also watchin'. We keep each other on the up and up if we see somethin' flying the other's way. Honest. Got my bird guide and logbook right here. Go ahead, have a look." He handed the books to the ranger. "You want me to radio my partner so you can ask him?"

Hank, as his name patch read, began looking at what appeared to be a purely authentic logbook for a bird enthusiast. Complete with dates, times, locations, sighting counts, and sketches. He didn't even look up from the books to respond.

"No need." Satisfied, Hank handed them back to the Aussie. "Sorry to bother you, sir. Enjoy your day." The ranger then began walking back toward his truck, but turned back after a few steps.

"Oh, one more thing."

"Go on."

"Warbler's don't typically fly to great lengths. She's probably nesting in one of those jacks over there." He pointed to a rather small plot of nearby jack pines where the Aussie had been originally training his binoculars.

"Thanks! I'll take a gander in a quarter-blink!"

With that, the ranger got into his truck and drove off.

The bird guide worked perfectly. Its rightful owner's body, however, had been placed in a thicket by a still swamp only six hours ago. No one would be looking for him either.

The Aussie did his homework, and picked a single 67-year-old man who had no living relatives and had never been married. A handful of casualties was a small price to pay in order for The Movement to truly begin, and the Aussie was more than happy to use a heavy fist wherever and whenever needed.

After letting out a contented sigh, he brought the binoculars back up to his eyes and saw that Jacob and Audrey were nowhere to be found.

Kyle entered slowly into Professor Reech's office. With his shirtsleeve over his nose, he took in the surroundings: wall-to-wall bookshelves with countless works spilling over the ledges, and a modest desk with the typical green banker's lamp on the right corner. A single window hovered on one wall. It was covered with a cheap ivory sheer, which was pockmarked with several random holes, offering a few lucky rays of sunlight to skewer the room; dust particles only became visible when floating into a laser beam of light.

Kyle was now standing in the middle of the office, facing the desk. The awful stench still wracked Kyle's olfactory sense. It smelled almost bitter. He didn't even realize he was doing so, but he started moving around the room, looking intently at a small red light peeking from behind a globe. A camera, Kyle thought. As he neared the red light, his nerves became more apparent in his actions. He kept looking back toward the door, as if at any moment someone was going to catch him. *Catch me doing what?* Kyle thought. Sure he may be snooping a bit, but he was invited here. It's not like he was breaking and entering.

The red light was almost discernible amongst the

piles of papers, trays, and office supplies. Kyle took a few more steps, more rapid now, and it wasn't too much longer until he realized what the object was, and the source of the awful smell. His shoulders dropped as he let the tension out, walked over to the shelf, and turned the coffeemaker off.

Kyle removed the cuff from his face and looked at his watch, as though it was going to tell him how long the coffeepot had been left on, and maybe more importantly, unattended. He wasn't late for his meeting, but where was Professor Reech, and why was the coffeemaker on?

Kyle headed around the desk, almost smashing his leg on an open drawer, and took account of what was located on the desktop: a green lamp, a printer, and a laptop computer that was open and turned on. He looked at the monitor and saw a picture of a woman wrapped in Professor Reech's arms light up the background of the screen. Kyle admired her looks for a few moments; her hair and gorgeous smile leapt from the screen. He also noticed that the computer had not been locked out from not being used for a period of time. Once a computer goes into sleep mode, the security program installed on every campus computer reverts back to the user's login screen. Professor Reech must have been here less than ten minutes ago.

Just before Kyle looked up, he noticed the corner of a piece of paper sticking out from under the laptop.

He quickly noticed the word 'dies' shoot out from the sheet on which it had been typed. He grabbed at the piece of paper and pulled out what resulted in a half sheet of standard printer paper. There were more words on the paper. In fact, it looked like a letter, of sorts. Kyle slid the paper to the other side of the desk, and sat in one of the chairs that was positioned in front of the desk. He saw that it was addressed simply to "Mr. Reech," and the last line simply read: "Go outside."

"Hey, what're you doin'? How'd you get in here?" a strong, but elderly voice called from behind Kyle.

"Uh, I have an appointment with Professor Reech," Kyle explained nervously.

"No, no, no. I saw him leavin' with his coat a few minutes ago." The janitor's voice overpowered Kyle's.

"Really, I do. I'm supposed to talk with him about my term paper." Kyle pulled the paper from his bag and held it in the air as though it were evidence in a class action lawsuit.

"Well, then you'll have to wait in the hallway for him, 'cuz I gotta lock this door. So come on, get your things, and let's go," his voice came with finality.

"Alright," Kyle said. He grabbed his backpack from the desk, and in one swift motion, heaved it onto his shoulder, taking attention away from the fact that he also took a single half sheet of paper off the desk, and clumsily shoved it in one of the many pockets of his bag.

*Chapter 10 — 9:00 A.M., Yesterday*

The phone on the dining-room table rang four times before a withered, but strong hand slowly emerged from beneath the tabletop, as if crawling from within a tomb. The effects from a life now spent in despair, loneliness, and sadness screamed from each time-hardened crease mapped into the hand. A wheelchair could be seen supporting the man as he sat.

"Hello?" a phlegm-filled voice strained. It sounded shaky, like something was wrong.

"Foley? Is that you?" a friendly voice responded through the receiver.

Foley took the phone away from his ear and looked at it, as if searching for the answer to an unasked question.

"Uh, yeah," Foley said, clearing his throat in an attempt to rid his voice of the gravelly debris still lodged within his larynx from the previous night. "Who is this?" he continued.

"Well, it's been about five years, but I was your favorite client, and I owe you one heck of an apology."

"Jake! Long time, my friend!" The gravel was gone in Foley's voice. A technique he had perfected. He could hide his true feelings, like his voice, perfectly when he needed. "How goes it?"

It had been three years since the accident. But it wasn't how much time had passed that plagued Foley, who was rendered paralyzed from the waist down after a FedEx truck pulled out in front of his motorcycle. Now what plagued his mind was how much of this lousy life he had left to live. For some reason, Foley felt that this day could very well be his last. A part of him, however, was just fine with that.

"Listen, Foley. I need to apologize for n…"

"Stop right there," Foley cut him off mid-sentence. "I'd be insulted if you apologized. Now come on, let's be serious. I've had a phone all these years too." He seemed content, fulfilled.

"That's nice of you to say, but I feel bad that it's been so long, ya know?" Jacob added.

"We're talkin' now, aren't we?" he pointed out.

"I guess you're right. Thanks for understanding. It means a lot to me."

"Jake," Foley said, his voice becoming serious. "Good friends will always be good friends." He paused. "Regardless of the circumstance."

Jacob had no idea just how happy Foley was to be speaking with him right now. No more than ten hours before his phone woke him up, Foley had actually held a gun to his own head.

Drunkenly sitting in front of his bathroom mirror

the night before, Foley contemplated the quick and easy solution that suicide offered. He appeared to himself a failure. A nothing. He had no family left, and would leave behind no nieces or nephews. It would have been a clean getaway for Foley. The gun would act as the vehicle, and the bullet as the gas. He looked at himself in the mirror, as though he held power over the face looking back from the polished glass. "You're nothing!" The bottle of Jack Daniel's still swirled from a recent swig. "Look at yourself! I wish you had died, you son of a bitch! What, is this what you want?" he said as he lit his seventeenth cigarette of the night, and placed the .38-caliber revolver under his chin, pointing upward. He squeezed the trigger and heard the click of an empty chamber. His eyes never flinched during his game of drunken Russian roulette, but rather remained locked on the monster in the mirror.

That same gun now rested on his left temple. This time, however, it was being held by someone else. A man Foley had never met.

"So, what can I do for you, old friend?"

"I need you to keep something safe for me. Some information."

Foley leaned closer to the table as the topic of the conversation became more apparent.

"What kinda info?"

"The delicate kind, if you get my drift. And believe

me," he continued, "the circumstances don't allow me to explain right now. I'll call you and explain in a couple days when it's safer. I just need to know that I can count on you."

"Safer? Are you in some kinda trouble?"

"Let's just say that I'm taking preventative action—from a hunch I have."

"Oh boy. Does Audrey know?"

"Negative. Can I count on you?"

"Yeah, of course. You guys doin' okay?"

"Yeah. No, we're fine. It's nothing like that. Now's just not the time to bring her up to speed, you know?"

"Up to speed on what?" Audrey asked, her voice coming from behind Jacob.

Jacob had thought that she was outside gardening. She *was* outside gardening. He had made certain of it! How long was she standing there? How much had she heard?

"Are you talking about me, Jacob?"

Jacob turned around to see Audrey innocently standing in the doorway. Her hair looked radiant in the mid-morning sunlight coming from the French-style patio door.

"Hey," Jacob said into the receiver. "I need to call you back." He began lowering the phone from his ear.

"Jake," Foley pled. The signal went dead on Foley's end.

ADAM J. BEARDSLEE

"Jacob. Answer me. Up to speed on what?" Audrey's hands were now positioned on her hips, and her smile began to fade.

"I was trying to wait to tell you until I had better news. I found out a couple days ago that my continuing education credits came up short. I might lose my certification."

"What? How?"

"Don't worry," Jacob said, realizing she had taken the bait. He played into his story even further. "See, this is what I was trying to avoid—you worrying. The department already agreed to work with me. They said that I can get the credits I need by attending an accelerated conference next week, instead of taking the actual classes."

"Why didn't you tell me when you found out?"

"Because I wanted to wait until after my meeting tomorrow with the Dean. He's going to fill me in on the specifics. I just wanted to tell you when I had more information. I didn't mean to keep anything from you, sweetheart. I just wanted to be able to answer all the questions you may've had, so you wouldn't worry."

Jacob's lie went over just fine, but his insides were now churning with guilt. He hated lying to Audrey, but reasoned that the truth—about the car outside their house at night and at the park—would worry her even more than his harmless lie. Jacob never thought to call the police to report the car. They lived in a residential area, where cars were allowed to park on the street at night. Maybe the occupants knew one of their neighbors, or were house-hunting in the neighborhood. Why would he even call the police anyway? The first time he saw the car, it posed no threat at all. The second was nothing to shake a stick at, as they could have just bought one of the many houses for sale on his street. It wasn't until the third time that Jacob even pondered other, less plausible reasons for the car to be parked in the same spot. At the park, however, Jacob felt the palpable onset of brief nausea as he wondered if the binoculars he'd seen the other day were being used to look at him and his fiancée.

The man holding the gun pulled it away from Foley's head, and another man brought duct-tape to his mouth. Foley didn't try to scream, thrash, or prevent himself from being bound. He simply looked into the man's eyes who, after taping his mouth shut, took away his last identifiable piece of self-worth: his voice. He knew it would soon be over. That is, until he saw the other man pull out a cigar cutter.

K yle arrived home more quickly than usual, the entire time thinking about the letter he took from Professor Reech's office desk.

*Should I have taken it? What does it say? Who wrote it? Does he have something they want?* These were all questions that plagued his mind as his car seemingly sped itself to his apartment located just two miles off campus.

He slammed his apartment door and heaved his backpack onto the dining-room table that served as a filing cabinet and poker table more than as an eating surface. Space was tight in his studio apartment; several areas, and furniture for that matter, had been multipurposed to maximize the close confines. He promptly muscled his way into the over-packed Eastbay collegiate bag to retrieve the letter he'd crammed into it only a short time ago. Eventually, after pulling out a variety of loose papers and power bar wrappers, he found the letter and pulled it out. With his eyes locked on the letter, he slowly sat down in his U of M beanbag chair in the shape of a football—different than his normal 'sigh-and-plop' method—and began to read.

*Jacob, do not mistake this for a joke. Your decisions from this point forward will map your foreseeable future. Follow my every word, and you will be fine. Deviate in any way, and Audrey dies.*

Kyle looked up from the letter to assure his senses he was in fact reading in private.

No movement. No sounds.

He took a deep breath, already immersed in the story unfolding before his eyes and within his mind, resembling the little boy reading *The Never-Ending Story*, and looked back down to continue.

*If you understand, open the top left drawer of your desk. When the drawer opens, a timer will be activated. You will see a set of car keys lying next to the timer. They belong to the green Mustang parked out front. The same Mustang you've probably been wondering about. Do I have your attention now? Good. Now take the keys, the timer, and this letter, leave your cell phone, speak to no one, and go outside.*

Kyle looked up again. "Holy shit," he said aloud, the words escaping his throat. Then, questions began erupting within his mind, some spewing out from his mouth.

*What kind of trouble is he in?* "Timer?" *How much time was on it?* "Green Mustang?" *Where did they tell him to drive? Where is he now? Is Audrey okay? Should I tell the police?* He placed the letter, as though it were as delicate as an ancient relic, on the table and sank deeper into the beanbag chair as he heaved a weighted sigh from his chest. Kyle stared up at the ceiling in nervous contemplation, and was met with a jolt of nauseous heat as he heard someone knock on his apartment door.

The traffic on US-23 South was not too bad for this time of day. After all, it was a Saturday. Most people were not working, and any weekend warriors had already headed up or down the state on Friday. The skies were clearer than most early fall days. The wind, however, was always present. Those who called Michigan home habitually used the terms *bitter*, *gust*, and *wind* to describe most air currents during this time of year; people from more temperate states had the luxury of choosing variables of words like *chill*, *breeze*, and *draft*.

Jacob gripped the wheel of the bright green Mustang, unknowingly gritting his teeth just as hard. It was the same car he saw periodically in the week leading him to this point. He had been driving for only fifteen minutes, but had not once stopped wondering who could be doing this to him, or why. His only thought was that the note seemed to threaten Audrey. He needed to know if she was okay.

He had heard stories of how, when adversity finds its way into a person's life and rips away all useful resources, that person instinctively reverts back to an oftentimes animalistic response to a given situation.

that were following him, but they all kept changing. He had no way of telling which cars were new, and which, if any, had been keeping pace.

*Who the hell is doing this?* he thought, as the speedometer plateaued at one hundred and two miles per hour.

Just then, a mechanical voice came over a speaker and said, "Do you *want* Audrey to die? Slow down, and set the cruise to seventy. Don't think I don't know what you're trying to do."

"Who is this?!" Jacob demanded.

A brief pause followed. Jacob waited for an answer, then repeated himself.

"Answer me!"

Still no answer. Then Jacob slowed the car as directed to seventy miles per hour.

"Good boy."

*Shit, they're watching me*, Jacob realized.

"One other thing, the next rest stop is about two miles away. Why don't you stop there and put your cell phone, you know, the one I told you not to take with you, on top of one of the vending machines. That's strike one, Superman."

"And if I don't?"

"You will." The voice paused. "Because Audrey here's counting on you to listen to me," he lied. He didn't have Audrey. She was at home worrying about

Jacob. But Jacob didn't know that. The lie worked.

"Leave her out of this! It's me you want, right? Let her go, dammit!"

Milking the lie, and growing more powerful at the same time, the man responded, "I think I'll hold on to her for a while. She makes good company."

Jacob saw the sign for the rest area. It was three-quarters of a mile ahead.

"Okay. The rest area is just ahead."

"Good. Now, look in your rearview mirror." He paused. "See that white van about five cars back? We're all nice and cozy in there. Like a big family on a road trip."

Terrified, and more level-headed now, Jacob spoke. "Okay, okay. Don't hurt her. Just tell me what you want me to do."

"That's what I like to hear," the voice said as Jacob pulled into the rest area. "You have one minute to drop off your phone and get back to the car."

Jacob looked in his rearview again, and saw the van idling in one of the parking spaces. As he got out of the car, his eyes hunted for a surveillance camera mounted on the building. He saw none, but kept his face held high in hopes that he missed one, and would be able to be identified on camera. He quickly walked to the nearest vending machine.

Once there, he did his best to act normal, and to

blend in. He set his phone on top of the machine while hunting for money from his pockets in order to purchase a water. He retrieved his wallet from his back pocket, pulled out two one-dollar bills, and fed them into the money slot. He looked around, and saw several faces moving about at the rest area. A family at a picnic table, a man walking his dog, and a slow-moving elderly woman walking up to the vending machine about twenty feet behind him all caught his attention. Jacob hurried to make his selection for water, and waited for it to drop to the reservoir at the bottom.

A moment later, he heard the loud tumbling sound of his selection being deposited. He bent down to grab the bottle, but fumbled briefly, struggling to grab it. Soon enough, though, he turned from the machine with water in hand and promptly headed back to the car. As he passed the elderly woman, he smiled cordially, nodded his head, and took a sip from the frosty plastic bottle.

As Jacob closed the door of the Mustang, he glanced at the elderly woman who was still at the vending machine.

"Drive," the voice said as soon as the door shut. "I said one minute, Superman. That's strike two."

Jacob drove off, watching his mirrors to see if someone was going to get out of the van to pick up his cell phone. He was almost around the corner of the on-ramp when he saw the passenger door of the van open.

The elderly woman bent down to grab her beverage from the reservoir, and noticed a yellow sticky note affixed to the bottom of the reservoir with writing on it.

The man from the passenger side of the van approached the vending machine with the pace of a cheetah. He saw the phone on top of the vending machine, but couldn't get to it with the elderly woman in the way. He waited for her to finish, pulling his wallet out too, in order to prevent drawing any attention from lookers-on scattered around the grounds of the facility.

He knew that there were often undercover police officers positioned at rest areas, to help cut back on drug dealing and the solicitation of sex, and decided to err on the side of caution while retrieving the phone.

"'Scuse me, sonny," the woman said as she smiled and began walking away with her orange juice. Her voice sounded wet and raspy, like her throat was a rock tumbler.

The man responded with a smile and nod, then faced the machine once again, placing his hand on top of it as he inserted his money. His hand was lying on Jacob's phone, and as his drink plummeted, he pulled his palm off of it with the phone buried in his grip. He pushed the reservoir door open and grabbed his pop.

The sticky note was no longer there.

Jacob called out once back at highway speed. There was authority in his voice. "Okay, now what?"

"Eager, aren't we, Superman?"

"Just tell me what to do."

"Exit 37. Take it and find the Park Blue parking garage on the northeast corner of the intersection at the off-ramp. You got that?"

"Uh, yeah. Park Blue off 37."

"Park on level 1. Then go to space 78 on level 2. Still following?"

"Park on 1. Space 78 of level 2."

"Good. Now, the other key on your ring opens the white Celebrity you'll find in that space."

"Where do you want me to go once I switch?"

"You're not driving. The key is to the trunk. I need you to get inside, throw the keys on the ground, and close it."

## Chapter 12 — September 14, 11:30 A.M.

L ost in bewilderment, Kyle stuffed the letter under his chair and tried getting up without making a sound—a task impossible to accomplish, of course, from his beanbag chair. He slid out of it like a chunk of a glacier slipping into a hungry sea. He rose quietly and approached the door, ever mindful of where the cracks lay in his floor.

Heart racing, he pondered a few things. *Did someone follow me here? Shit! Now they know where I live.What if they threaten me too?* Instinctively, his hand fell on a wooden Louisville Slugger he kept in the corner, calling it his 'just-in-case'. He had never thought there would come a time he would actually need to use it.

He gripped the bat in his left hand and the doorknob with his right. After a moment he flung the door open and readied himself to swing at the unknown person on the other side.

"Geez. I didn't know I was *that* intimidating," WRKI news reporter Lucinda Garrett proclaimed, as she stood unfazed in the entryway, her orange suit doing wonders lying against her glowing cocoa skin. As always, she looked scintillating.

"Oh. Uh, sorry, Miss Garrett," Kyle stumbled,

taken off guard, his adrenaline showing in his labored exhale. Feverishly searching for a viable explanation, he landed on one he considered a gem. "Some of the guys said they were gonna kidnap me and take me on a weekend trip to Windsor. I told 'em I couldn't because of my term paper. But ya know, that never stopped 'em before." He chuckled nervously.

"Lucinda. Please, call me Lucinda."

His bat was now entirely lowered. "Okay, Lucinda. Come on in." He held the door and stepped sideways, allowing Lucinda to enter his apartment. As she passed, he couldn't help but notice her perfume. Or was it her shampoo? Either way, he felt he now had a better idea of what heaven truly smelled like.

Lucinda approached Kyle about a week ago, asking to interview him regarding the dive team's recent qualification in the state championship and how the team planned to prepare for their unbeaten rival, the Leelanau Aqua-ducks.

Lucinda offered to conduct the interview at Kyle's apartment. No man had ever denied her entry into his dwelling. It was simple really. A little hair adjustment here, a crossing of the legs there—she had it all plotted out. Before long, Kyle would be begging to tell her everything he knew.

"Have a seat," Kyle offered, as he pointed toward his couch. She obliged, saying "thank you" with the nod of her head. The motion sent a new wave of "Heaven's Scent" in Kyle's direction, nearly tranquilizing him. *Is that coconut? Shampoo. Has to be shampoo.*

"Thanks for agreeing to meet here," she said as she looked around. "You have a nice place. Do you paint?" Lucinda asked.

"I'm sorry?"

"I noticed that painting over there." She gestured with her entire arm. At the same time, she strategically pushed out her chest. Her gaze was directed toward the painting, which offered Kyle the opportunity to stare at her for a bit. She knew he would take the bait and do some sightseeing when not in direct eye contact.

Her attack had begun.

"Oh. Uh, no. I picked that up at Pier 1," Kyle responded as he fought with his mind. *Calista. Think of Calista.*

"Too bad. I love sharing ideas about true art. It's a passion of mine," she flirted.

*Love. Passion. Jesus she's beautiful.*

"Anyway. Tell me what it's like to be underwater," she continued.

"Well, when I'm submerged, I'm free. It's a different world down there. All the stresses from above seem to dissipate as I go deeper." Kyle felt proud of the statement, as though he was only just realizing his pure love of diving.

"Powerful words. I can tell you truly love the sport. Or is it more than a sport to you? It's not the competition you yearn for, is it Kyle? It's being alone with yourself, to think and feel however you like. Am I wrong?" she countered, equally proud of her statement as she expected Kyle was of his.

"Actually, no. You're exactly right. It's incredibly quiet down there. It's my paradise."

He felt his mind begin to shift.

*"Have you ever had sex underwater?" she asked, playing with her pen, clicking it between her teeth.*

*"No, but I'd love to," he said, looking at her body in awe; her bra strap was almost slipping over the edge of her silken shoulder.*

*"Do you want to have sex with me underwater?" she responded, helping the bra strap make its journey south. The other followed a moment later. The bright pink bra loosened and began to descend down the front of her chest, exposing her to him.*

"Kyle?" she paused. "Kyle?"

"Huh?" he said, coming out of a daze.

"I asked you if you've ever had a scare underwater," she repeated.

"Oh, sorry. No. I've never had any problems."

His response was too quick. She was losing him. Time to up the ante.

"How many guys are on the team?" she said as she threw her hair over her shoulder, sending another waft Kyle's way.

"Uh, ten," he said.

"But I'll bet you, being captain and all, are the best. Right?" She pulled out the heavy artillery and crossed her legs, her skirt cinching up ever so slightly, revealing about an inch more thigh than what was previously visible.

"Actually, Lucinda, can we talk about something else?"

*Got him*, Lucinda thought.

"But I can only talk about it if I can trust that you'll keep it off the record."

*Interesting*, she thought, her mind wanting more.

"Kyle, my entire world exists because of trust and confidence. Believe me, you can trust me." And he could. Lucinda may have used her assets from time to time to get information, but had always held her sources in the highest of confidence.

"Um, I think someone on campus has been kidnapped." The sentence tumbled out of his mouth. "That's why I answered the door the way I did. I thought someone followed me back here," he embarrassingly admitted.

"Really?" she said, taken entirely off guard. "Who?" she finished, still hung up on the word *kidnapped*.

"I'd rather not say just yet. I found a letter that was addressed to a person I was supposed to meet today that was pretty scary. He, I mean, this person, never showed for our meeting. Just before you got here, I was contemplating whether or not to contact the police. The letter said not to, because, well, *his* girlfriend might be killed. It sounded like they had him drive somewhere, but I have no idea where," he said, inhaling deeply afterward.

"Okay. Let's slow down for a second. Is this person a student or faculty member?" Lucinda offered.

Hesitantly, Kyle responded, "Faculty."

"Do you have the letter here?" She paused for a moment, and then continued, "Kyle, you can trust me."

Kyle slowly reached under his chair and retrieved the letter and placed it on the coffee table in front of Lucinda. Like very few things in his apartment, the coffee table was in fact being used as intended.

"The reason I wanted to talk to you about this, is you may be able to help. I assume you are a bit more resourceful than I am," Kyle blurted out, not exactly knowing if the words he said matched the context. She was a reporter, not a private investigator.

Lucinda opened the letter and began reading faster than ever before.

"Dr. Reech is my favorite professor. What do you think I should do?"

"Where did you get this?" she asked as she dissected the paper with her eyes.

"The desk in his office. We had a meeting, and he

never showed, but his coffeepot and computer were both turned on."

"Did anyone see you leave?"

"Not that I know of." He paused. "Wait. The janitor kicked me out of his office. He said he had to lock the door. Saturday and all, ya know?"

"Did he seem like he knew anything? Could he have been in on this?"

"I don't think so. I've seen that guy cleaning halls since I was a freshman."

"Hold on. Kyle, why have you decided to tell me this?" Lucinda's voice was extremely inquisitive.

"I guess I feel like I can trust you. And, think that I should do something rather than nothing," he responded.

"Okay. Well, let's do this the right way. One option is that we could run a missing-person report on the news. That would keep your name out of it. Let's face it, Kyle. If he really was kidnapped, the public will eventually know about it."

"Is there another option?" Kyle asked.

"Well, you could take this letter to the police and let them do the job that they're trained to do. Or—and I hope you don't choose this option—you could do nothing."

"I see."

"I know how these things work, and I think the best option is to have the news cover this story, at least initially. You want to be very careful about the timeline too. Once this is covered on TV, everyone knows about it, so you won't be identified as someone who knows more than any other person, and that protects you, Professor Reech, and even his fiancée."

"Looks like I have some thinking to do."

"Tell you what, I won't say a word, but if you decide to get the news involved, call this number." She handed him her business card. "Ask for Calvin Sneed, the Executive Producer at WRKI. Don't tell him too much, just that you think Professor Reech was kidnapped and nothing more. He's going to ask you to call back. Do that and you should get me on the phone. If not, just hang up. I just want you to feel comfortable in doing what I feel is the right thing. You need to be the judge of that though. Okay?"

"Uh, Okay." Hesitation mixed with nerves filled his voice to the brim.

"Kyle, you can trust me. If you flip that card over, you'll see my personal cell phone. Call me any time," she said as she handed Kyle the letter, got up, and headed for the door.

Lucinda Garrett had just led a conversation which she knew nothing about. And she did so perfectly. Damn she was good.

"Okay. I'm here," Jacob said. His voice was less certain this time.

"Good. You have five minutes to get inside that trunk. Starting now."

"I'll suffocate."

"You'll be fine. 4 minutes 58 seconds."

Jacob turned the car off and exited it, surveying the parking garage as he did so.

It was Saturday in football season, and the lot was filled to the brim with cars. The game started almost two hours ago, and although the lot was packed, Jacob couldn't see one person.

He walked to the second level, and hunted for the parking lot space numbers. After a moment, he noticed they were painted on the ground, most cars covering their respective number, so Jacob knelt down to identify the closest one to him.

Space 53.

He kept walking up the incline. He checked again.

Space 66.

He was getting closer, and looked up the row to see if he could see a white car. He saw several as he checked his watch. Four minutes and fifteen seconds had elapsed since he left the car. *Forty-five seconds*, he thought as he walked faster. And then he saw it. The Chevrolet emblem stung his eyes as he saw it. Fumbling for the extra key, he checked his watch again. Twenty seconds. With one last look around, he inserted the key into the trunk's keyhole, and turned it. It opened with a creak that echoed in the spacious room. Inside, he found a variety of things. One in particular was a note lying on a small duffel bag.

He reached for it. *Put this over your head, and zip it*.

"*What?*" he said to himself, and then looked over his shoulder yet again. He looked at his watch. *5 seconds.*

"Shit!" He jumped in, oriented himself in as comfortable a position as possible. *2 seconds.* He groped for the bag with one hand as his other found the handle at the top of the trunk's lid. *One second.* He yanked the lid down and tossed the keys out in one swift motion. He heard it latch, and all light was extinguished around him. In total darkness, he hesitantly placed the bag over his head and zipped it snug.

As he lay there, he realized that if they were going to kill him, they would have already. They either wanted him to do something, or wanted something that he had.

In mid-thought, he heard the car door open, and felt it jostle as someone got into it. A moment later, the car roared to life and began to back out of the parking space.

*Chapter 13 — September 14, 6:00 P.M.*

Audrey's car sped out of her garage. She spoke with
Detective Patrick O'Reilly from the Holly Police
Department, on the phone as she drove.

"What do you mean he's not *technically* missing?"

"Miss Carlson, only minors are considered missing within hours of their failing to come home.
Adults are different. Jacob could have just gone for
a drive."

"Excuse me? Gone for a drive? Now you listen to
me, Jacob would never, ever just go for a drive. Do you
hear me?"

"Yes, ma'am. But there's nothing I can do until he's
officially missing."

"48 hours? Do you have any idea where he could be
by then, or what could happen?" Her voice was shaking
with panic and frustration alike.

"I'm sorry, Miss Carlson. My hands are tied until
then." He shrugged his shoulders helplessly.

"Well, I'm coming to the station. We need to talk
more about this."

"You're more than welcome to come out here."

Her car fishtailed onto the road and accelerated
down the drive. As it disappeared around the corner, a

man emerged from the bushes and entered her house through the back.

"It's gotta be in there," a man's voice came through the receiver of a two-way radio. "And don't mess shit up in there either."

"Yeah, yeah," the man in the house said, as though he were swatting a pesky fly from his shoulder.

"Seriously. The Voice'll be pissed. So don't fuck this up for me," the other man said. He felt as though the mentioning of The Voice would carry some authority, even though he held absolutely none.

"Ohhh, The Voice is gonna be mad!" he said sarcastically. Don't get your panties in a bunch about it, alright? I'm fine."

"Look for a safe or cabinet. Start in the bedroom."

"You don't want me to screw things up, right?"

"Correct. And sometimes you need a little kick in the ass, wouldn't you say?"

"Just let me do my damn job."

"Well, you better find something. I'll let you know if she comes home."

The man in the house hurried to the master bedroom. He entered the closet and began brushing clothes to the side, hoping to find 'the thing' he had no idea he was even looking for. Unsuccessful, he turned his attention to the drawers of the nightstands on either side of the bed.

Nothing.

He left the bedroom and headed down the stairs back to the main level.

"Anything?"

"Negative."

Immediately after he said that, he turned the corner and saw the screen of a computer glowing black on a desk. He smirked, and advanced toward it.

"I take that back."

"Whaddya got?"

"Maybe nothing, but he's got a computer in his den. I'm gonna see if I can find something there. E-mails, contacts, files, ya know, that '*anything*' you were just asking about."

"Well make it quick."

The man sat down at the computer and ran a query that displayed the most frequently accessed files. One in particular appeared on the screen.

"Bingo." He pressed the two-way radio button and spoke into it. "Think I got a file."

Whoever was looking at this file accessed it more than fifty times last month alone. He looked at the file name. *Comparisons.xls*. It was a spreadsheet.

"Get the damn thing and get outta there."

He closed the query and searched for the file by

name, and found it rather easily. He double-clicked the file and a password prompt appeared.

"Password. Password," The man said to himself, while pondering what it could possibly be. After a moment, he began typing one of the most common passwords used. He called out the letters as he typed them.

"P...A...S...S...W...O...R...D." When he pressed enter, the prompt disappeared, and the file became lost within the hard drive of the computer.

Audrey pulled into the Holly Police Department's parking lot and stormed into the front lobby.

"I need to speak with Detective O'Reilly. Immediately."

The receptionist, a young brunette, didn't say a word but pointed to a closed office door at the end of a short hallway. Audrey rushed over to it, and walked right in.

"What if he went missing this morning? What if he never made it to work? That's a possibility, right?"

"Hello, Miss Carlson."

"Right? You're a detective for crying out loud. Can't you just move back the time he was reported missing?"

"I would be happy to do that if I didn't value my job, which, unfortunately for you, I do."

Audrey shrugged her shoulders in frustrated defeat as the detective's phone began to ring.

"Please, have a seat," he said as he picked up the phone. He held the phone to his ear.

Audrey reluctantly sat in the seat across from the detective's desk. A part of her felt that answering the phone at a time like this was rude, but another part knew that he had to.

"Detective O'Reilly speaking... Yes... You did? Hold on, let me grab a pen." Detective O'Reilly looked at Audrey as he reached for a pen, uncapped it, and began writing on the pad in front of him. His eyes pierced Audrey's. The look concerned her as she listened to him continue.

"Where? Uh huh. And how long ago was this?" His voice now carried some of the same concern as Audrey's. She noticed the change in his voice and leaned forward in her chair.

Detective O'Reilly looked directly into Audrey's eyes as he spoke. "Okay, I'll get a car out there right away. You did the right thing by calling. Good-bye," he said as he hung up the phone, still looking at Audrey.

"Detective? What was that call about?"

The detective folded his hands and placed them on his desk.

"Unfortunately, it appears you were right about Jacob."

"What? How? Who was that?"

"Edna Cosgrove. She said she saw him at a rest area down by Ann Arbor. She found a note in a vending machine."

"A note? What'd it say, did she tell you?"

"She did." He looked down at his notes. "It said, 'Jacob Reech - Green Mustang - 2 pm.'" He looked back up at Audrey with a confused look.

"What else did it say, Detective?" She paused, still holding his gaze like a steel clamp. "Tell me now."

"The last thing he wrote was 'Call Holly Police - They have Audrey too.'"

Audrey's eyes went blank as they filled with tears. Her hands climbed to her face, covering her mouth in disbelief.

T he car stopped. Jacob could hear the familiar
sound of a railroad crossing, accompanied by a
distant whistle whose voice increased in volume each
time it spoke. The sound reminded Jacob of Holly,
even though he was miserable after being stuffed in the
trunk of God knows whose car, in God knows where.

Jacob absolutely loved Holly. It had a legacy. Too
many towns were losing their roots, their integrity.
Jacob appreciated towns that kept a historical district.
Holly had Battle Alley.

The car began moving again. Jacob wondered if
there were any cars next to him during the stop. If so,
he wondered if any were police officers.

Cramped inside the car, and almost accepting his
captivity, he began to let his mind wander.

All too often, Jacob thought, older towns were being plowed down and rebuilt, all because some 'Ace'
of an architect put together a winning *city renewal* sales
pitch to committee members. What Ace always left out
of his slide show was that the brick facade of the re-
newed city would be just that, a facade. A fake. French
words, if used strategically, could easily captivate an
unsuspecting room of board members. Ace always

promised to do the job right, and use only the most qualified of contractors and state-of-the-art materials. Keep in mind that "state of the art" does not necessarily mean the best. Modern state of the art meant that each building would be given a one-inch-thick composite, stamped to appear like authentic brick—the exact material that is being voted to demolish.

The car came to a gradual stop once again, and Jacob could hear the driver's door open. He also heard the frighteningly familiar sound of something being dragged across the gravel. *Not the jumper cables again.* Jacob passed out from the electrocution, but had every recollection of the agony he'd experienced during those quick 2 seconds before his mind went blank.

The trunk opened. Jacob's vision, still masked, let in no light. He noticed that sometimes, he didn't even know if his eyes were open or closed.

If the architect saw that the crowd was leaning toward passing on his proposal, Ace could always restructure the sentence to appeal more to the voters by promising that the project would create several new jobs for the town by using only local contractors. Either way, his pitch fell upon happy ears.

Sparks sounded above the roar of the engine of the car as the driver toyed with Jacob.

"Ready to talk yet?" the mechanized voice announced.

"I don't know what you want from me!" Jacob yelled.

Jacob loved a town with a legacy, every day allowing its townspeople to pay homage to a time when a brick was as solid as a brick, and to a time when a person didn't have to worry about being electrocuted for the second time that day.

"I need that file!" a stern, manly voice command-ed through the receiver of a two-way radio, his fingernails unkempt, adorned with residual dirt and grime and other unknown filth.

The man with the fingernails stood by a large win-dow in a chic hotel room. The view suggested the room was located on the tenth floor or higher. The room was furnished with a king-size bed, a full desk, and a sepa-rate living area apart from the bedroom with a couch and coffee table. No doors separated the spaces, but where one room stopped and another began could eas-ily be determined; the designer obviously, and aptly, attempted to decrease visual obstructions and at the same time, increased the perception of a larger space which a guest could call a temporary home.

"I know, I know. But whoever set up this security software is good, man." The response was from a voice filled with far less testosterone. "Hacking passwords takes time in the first place, but with the lateral en-cryption this guy's put on his hard drive, I can't crack anything in less than about eight hours. And that's if I'm lucky, Don."

The man in the hotel made a fist out of his free

hand and clenched with all of his might, his face contorting in hot rage.

More calmly now, "I thought I told you not to call me by my real name." A moment passed, and Don began unclenching his fist. "Lateral encryption?" he finished, his relaxed palm showing the marks of the recent assault from his fingernails. Bluish-purple crescents frowned from his hand as he let it lay slack by his side once again.

"Dammit! Sorry," the other man pled. "Anyway, this lateral encryption. It's something I've never seen before. It's, it's like a chameleon. Brilliant, really, but pretty high-tech. Almost outta my league."

"I know what you called it." The rage began to bubble again. "What I asked was, what is a lateral encryption?"

"Alright, alright! Man, you need to get laid or something," he said jokingly. His tone, however, suggested otherwise. "As soon as I enter a password incorrectly, your file here assumes the name of another random file on this guy's hard drive. Then, I gotta search for the correct one all over again, just to try another password. Happens every time. He's experienced. Probably got some background in IT. Other than that, I don't know what else to tell ya. It's just gonna take some time."

Silence.

"You still there?" the soprano voice called out.

"Tell me, *Frank*, that you'll figure out the password. Fast!"

More marks now appeared on Don's palm.

"It's not that easy, *Don*. Let me explain something to you, Mr. God Almighty. Under normal conditions, I can crack a password like this in less than two hours. My program runs about a million queries a minute, based on a 32-bit encryption. That's over a hundred million queries every two hours!"

"And? That sounds pretty damn fast to me," he shot back while still standing at the window.

"You're right, it is fast. That is, if my God-damned program would work! How many times do I gotta tell you? It's as good as useless against this encryption! I have to enter each query manually, then manually search for the file again each time I'm wrong. It takes me about four minutes per attempt. You can do the math from there. Or maybe you can't," he said, getting one last jab into his colleague's side.

"What other options do we have?"

"Right now, good old-fashioned trial and error. But," he continued, "there is one thing that's a bit sloppy."

"And? What is it?"

"Well, he created a security question, probably for fear of losing the file's location. He wanted to make damn sure he never entered his password incorrectly."

"And you know what the question is?"

"Yeah."

"Jesus, Frank." Don paused. "Would you like to share it with me?" he asked sarcastically.

"It says…" He now began reading from his notes he had generated of all of his previous attempts. In them was the security question that he'd jotted down the first time he saw it. "*What's the country you never sleep in?*"

"Any ideas offhand?"

"I didn't even graduate high school, and I hate geography. I Googled it, but nothing solid came up."

"Well, better start guessin'. We're not getting paid to come up empty handed."

A few minutes lapsed without a word being shared between the two men. Then, louder than before, the receiver sprang back to life on the coffee table at the hotel.

"Jackpot! Still can't get to that file, but I found an envelope in one of the drawers. Get this, it says, '*Jacob, Franklin has a secret. Noah will help you.*' I'm still working on getting that file, but that could be a lead."

"Well, we gotta find this Franklin guy. And find out who wrote that note."

Just then, the voice in the receiver blared out yet again.

"Gotta go, someone just pulled into the garage."

*Chapter 16 — September 14, 6:52 P.M.*

"I need everyone in here for a minute," Calvin Sneed, the Executive Producer of WRKI News, announced to the room, and headed into a conference room with walls of glass.

A few faces in the news center turned and raised their eyebrows at each other, before they heard the conference room door open again.

"Now!" he yelled, just poking his head out from the room this time.

Every person in the room leapt to their feet and hurried to not be the last one to enter. A few shoves could be seen and snide comments heard from challengers as they all scurried toward the conference room. Soon, the entire WRKI News staff was packed into the conference room; only the lucky few who'd arrived first had seats.

"We're no longer running the zoo video in the top spot," he said, almost feeling relieved to get it off his chest. "I just got off the phone with someone, who said that a professor at U of M–Flint"—he paused—"has been kidnapped. Professor Jacob Reech."

A few inaudible gasps and remarks could be heard over Calvin's trailing voice.

One hand, however, calmly found its way into the cramped and stuffy air.

"Question, Miss Garrett?"

"Were you able to validate the tip?"

"I called the university right after the call. It is true that Professor Reech didn't come in to work this morning, and he's not answering his cell phone," Calvin responded, nodding his head in appreciation for the show of manners Lucinda displayed by raising her hand. "So to answer your question, the validity of the call is warranted, but no absolute confirmation has been made. That's where we come in. It's only a matter of time before the other networks catch wind of his disappearance, if in fact he has disappeared. We need to confirm and be the first network to run the story by 8 o'clock tonight." He paused again, then continued. "Who's prepared to cover this one?"

A hand from the deepest corner of the room was the first to go up.

"I said 'prepared,' Donovan," he rebutted, still scanning the crowd as a few others lowered their hands in fear of receiving a comment similar to Donovan's. The only two hands that remained belonged to his best reporters, Nick Laslow and Lucinda Garrett. Their good-natured but all-too-real rivalry had proven to be the fire in each of their pants to best the other. As long as they kept turning out such great material, Calvin let them take their blows at each other.

"Calvin, I got this one," Nick said, his voice resolute. Nick had a slight southern accent that always seemed to have a gentlemanly flavor to it, even when he took a quick and venomous strike at one of his coworkers.

"Wait just a minute!" Lucinda interjected. "Nick's been swamped with that political sex scandal that's due next week. He can't afford to devote the time needed for a story like this." She looked directly at Nick and leveled with him. "This isn't just a story, Nick. I mean, come on. Kidnapped?" She directed her gaze back toward Calvin. "This could go on for a while. Not to mention get national coverage." She paused briefly, then addressed Nick once again. "Are you truly ready for a story that might come with a national spotlight?" she said, holding firm.

"I was made to be on national television," he said, then smiled and adjusted his blazer. "Hell yes, I'm ready."

"And there it is, Calvin. Nick here would damn near die to appear on national TV. Me? I don't care if it's local, national, or intergalactic. I would report the story the same way regardless of my audience."

Nick realized the trap he'd just been led into by Lucinda, and pulled the pin on his last grenade. Without hesitation, he flung it her way.

"Oh, please, Lucinda. How long do you spend putting on your makeup in the morning, before you appear on your not-so-important TV station? Admit it, you're just another pretty face, *acting* like a real reporter," he exploded, sending shrapnel out in all directions.

"Dammit, Nick. I'm more than just a pretty face. Don't you get it? I am some*body*, too!" she said, exaggerating a strategic portion of the word. She put one hand in her hair while striking her most sultry seated pose, and blew him a facetious kiss.

Not a word was spoken by Lucinda, Nick, or the other dozen or so people still occupying the room, each doing their best to hold back facial expressions and laughter from the bout between the two lead reporters that just played out. After a few moments of contemplation, the Executive Producer made his decision.

"Lucy, this one's yours," he said, then immediately continued while pointing at her counterpart, "Not a word, Nick. You'll get yours. Everyone out. I need to speak with Lucy for a bit."

With that, the room emptied almost as quickly as it had filled. After the door closed behind the last person, the conversation continued.

"Lucy, I need your best here. The guy I spoke with sounded extremely concerned. Scared even. Honestly, I don't think he'd told anyone else yet. I asked him to call back in 40 minutes so we could validate his claim.

That was 35 minutes ago. The next time this phone rings"—he pointed to the phone on the conference room table—"you will be the one answering it."

"Okay. Calvin, thank you."

"Don't come to me with a 'thank you.' Come to me with a solid story. Your little spat with Nick may work for zoo videos and sex scandals, but there's no place for it with a story of this magnitude. If he really was kidnapped, Luce, the nation will eventually see it on TV. And I'm thinking sooner than later."

"Understood, Mr. Sneed. I assure you, it'll be my very best."

Just then, the phone began to ring.

"Uh, Calvin? If you want my best work, I'm going to have to ask you to leave. I keep all communications with my sources entirely private."

The phone rang a third time. Calvin stood there, perplexed for a moment.

"Calvin, do you want this guy to hang up?" she said, then shooed him with her hand.

"Watch it," he mouthed to her, then swiftly left the room.

On the fifth ring, she picked up the phone.

"Hello?"

"Is this a private line?"

"Yes, entirely." She paused, then finished her thought. "You can trust me."

"Okay. Lucinda, what should we do? I don't want to run too much on the news, ya know? In case the kidnappers think Mr. Reech told someone. I mean, the kidnappers specifically told him to take the letter with him." There was a brief, but discernable pause. "I think he left this letter knowing I would see it." He paused as an epiphany hit him hard. "Lucinda, I think he's asking for my help."

"Let's not get ahead of ourselves, Kyle," she said, almost whispering, her back to the rest of the newsroom, which likely had all eyes on her. She so badly wanted to turn around, but couldn't allow herself the guilty pleasure. "Tell me again when you found the letter."

"Saturday. Just after eleven."

"So it's been about…" She did some quick math in her head, then went on. "…8 hours since he left his office after reading the letter. There is no way for you and me to know where he could be by now."

"How long does it take to file a missing person's report?"

"Gosh, I think after 12 hours, Kyle. For adults," she clarified.

"That's in like, less than four hours. Should we call the police to confirm?"

"Kyle, that's 12 hours from the time a person goes missing. No one probably realized he was missing until about 5 o'clock in the afternoon. So technically, he's only been missing for a couple hours at best. The police won't be able to give us any information for at least another 8 hours or so when he officially becomes a missing person."

"I see."

"Kyle. Are you sure you don't want to share this with the police?"

"Absolutely. If Professor Reech wanted them to know, he would have already contacted them. Apparently, he took this very seriously, and I am not going to make a decision for him."

"Okay, okay. Well, what do we do from here? Do you want to do what we talked about?"

"Yes. And Lucinda, it may not just be you there. I would imagine Audrey would call family members, and people would start talking, ya know?"

Kyle had thought about contacting Audrey, but feared the act would open a risky door that he could not shut.

"Yeah. No worries. I'll be the one the kidnappers tune in to, if they're watching the news. Once we run the initial story, it'll be a lot easier for you and me to speak."

"Sounds good. I'll be in touch."

"Alright. And Kyle? Be safe, okay?"

"You too."

The two hung up, and Lucinda Garrett calmly left the conference room and went back to her desk, saying nothing to her colleagues, all of whom were transfixed on her, wanting the juicy details. They would not get any information from Lucinda. Not now. Not ever.

*Chapter 17 — September 14, 7:43 P.M.*

"I don't give a shit what we *want* to know, Andrews. What *do* we know?" Detective O'Reilly spouted as the two spoke outside the rest area on US-23, where Edna Cosgrove found the note from Jacob Reech.

"Okay. Well, uh, we know we have someone who says he thinks Reech was kidnapped. Operative word 'thinks.' We also know that Reech has not been heard from in about 9 hours. He was last seen on a campus surveillance camera leaving the university in a green Mustang at 10:52 this morning. And, we have an Edna Cosgrove who says she found a note from him stuffed in that vending machine over there," he said as he pointed to the small brick building located among a slew of tall oak trees.

"Good. The facts, Michael, are what's gonna help us with this one. And it's a fact that we *know* far less than what we need to. That's not acceptable." He paused, hand once again finding its way to his goatee. "Put a trace on his credit card, and get all roadside cameras at all southbound off-ramps and interstate junctions to the state border. If he's still on the road, we need to know which one he's on. If he's not, we need to know where he got off. And when."

"Understood. I'll keep you posted."

With that, Officer Andrews went back to his cruiser, as the detective continued exploring the rest area for more evidence that Jacob may have hidden.

Audrey stirred in bed as her eyes fought to remain closed after a long and emotional night.

Or was it morning? Hell, she didn't know.

She threw back the covers of her bed. The flowery pattern of her comforter, complete with wispy pinks, yellows, and greens, was revealed as an avalanche of tear-soiled tissues cascading over the edge of the bed to the floor. There were just as many tissues already on the floor from phase one of the previous night.

Phase One, consisting of Audrey sitting at the edge of her bed crying while looking at Jacob's picture, lasted for about an hour.

Phase Two, simply put, was an extension of Phase One, except Audrey had changed positions. She now sat quasi-upright in the middle of the bed, slunk over like a forgotten bag of groceries. She had gotten cold and decided to migrate to what warmth she could find within the covers, desperately searching for the comfort she missed so badly from Jacob. Phase Two had not yet come to an end.

Audrey didn't even notice that she'd stepped on the snow pile of tissue, as she groggily searched for the bathroom door. *What time is it?* she thought, as her hands padded at the bathroom vanity for her pink glasses.

Audrey's style could not be mistaken. Her wardrobe was riddled with flowery, loose-fitting dresses, scarves, jean jackets, and all sorts of chic mid to upper-calf boots. The accessories only began there. Her wrists were rarely visible, feverishly adorned in a series of bracelets, and multicolored, and multi-materialed, bands. Simply put, she defined eclectic bohemian.

As she stared into the mirror, she could barely recognize her reflection. She had gone so long with Jacob by her side that she felt a sense of inadequacy as she opened the linen closet to get more toilet paper. It was on the top shelf. Only Jacob could reach the top shelf. It was true; the smallest things were what she missed most. She was out of tears, but still managed a congested sob.

Audrey shut the linen closet door, defeated, and headed for the bathroom on the main floor, first stopping by the bed to get her slippers. Only then did she notice the soiled tissues from the previous night. She quickly looked away from them, doing her best to suppress her emotions. Simply looking away did not work. The image of the tissue pile was still there, as if emblazoned on her retinas. As she closed her eyes to rid herself of the image, the pile of tissues remained as bright as ever, playing off the backdrop of her eyelids:

the negative of a photograph. *I miss you so much, Jacob. Please be okay. I need you.* Her thoughts were written on her face just the same. It appeared that she had aged a decade in just the last few days alone. It was amazing how extreme stress left its mark on the human body.

She reached the landing of the stairs adjacent to the front door with her eyes half shut. Today, optimism did not exist; glasses were half empty, every journey led uphill, and yes, her eyes were half shut. Just as she began turning the corner from the landing, a deafening bang startled her, nearly bringing her to her knees.

The sound, as her vanquished mind heard it, reminded her of the piñata at her fifth birthday party held at her late grandmother's house. Her grandmother had surprised her with the piñata as the pinnacle of encore presents, each given just as she thought there couldn't possibly be another. She had the method perfected, like a pop singer returning to the stage for the clichéd "last song." With Audrey's grandmother, however, the encores seemed to never end.

Audrey remembered the way the broomstick felt in her hands the first time she gripped it. It was blue at one point in its life, but now wore the marks of frequent use, stained into the once-shiny finish; two marks in particular, positioned at the top and roughly one quarter of the way down the shaft, paid homage to Nana Betsy, as she was the only one who actually used the broom for its intended purpose. Audrey knew not what sugary treasures were packed inside the oversized and brightly colored papier-mâché frog, but simply that there would soon be a shower of color-fully wrapped goodies to share with her friends. She remembered gripping the broomstick with all of her might, her body full of torque, and focusing all of her energy on the floating frog, swinging fearlessly in front of her blindfolded head, and completely missing her target. The momentum of the swing sent her awk-wardly forward and off balance; her head was the only thing that ever touched the piñata before she came to an audible halt on the cold concrete floor. The broom-stick was no longer grasped within the seemingly tight grip of the five-year-old. As young Audrey reluctantly removed the folded handkerchief and looked around at her peers, she saw the glee-stricken faces of her friends and their parents, many pointing at her as they laughed, some even holding their stomachs as though the spectacle would kill them. Sprawled on the con-crete, and full of shame and embarrassment, Audrey's eyes continued panning the crowd, eventually landing on her grandmother. Nana Betsy's endearing smile, and the slight tilt of her head atop a wrinkled neck, as if to say, "Oh, everything is going to be just fine, my dear," was what picked her up off that cold concrete floor. That look of endearment was still emblazoned in Audrey's mind to this day, as what she saw in her grandmother—Nana Betsy, rather—even after her passing over ten years ago.

She found herself instinctively heading for a near-by window, brushing the heavy curtains to one side, and looking into the daylight for what seemed the first time in eternity. *What time is it?* she pondered again.

The sight that Audrey squinted to comprehend was that of chaotic pandemonium. Her first thought of the scene was how closely it resembled an army of ants scurrying about immediately following the destruction of their mound by a curious adolescent. Today, like when she was five, Audrey hated the *ants* devouring her front lawn. She wished they would simply vanish.

*Chapter 19 — September 15, 9:49 A.M.*

"We're coming to you live from the house of missing person Jacob Reech," one of the reporters said, an African American woman of approximately twenty-five years. Her skin was immaculate and blemish free, adorned with a glowing mocha tone; shining ribbons of black hair decorated her face and cascaded down and around her neck. She was painfully beautiful—a deity's goddess. "Also living here," she said as she pointed over her shoulder to the modestly colored house directly behind her, "is Jacob's fiancée, Audrey Carlson. Miss Carlson has remained inside this house since her fiancée failed to return home from work Saturday afternoon."

After refocusing her eyes from the onslaught of natural light, Audrey could now see and hear much of the scene playing out in front of her. She kept the curtains open only enough for her eyes to navigate within the thin sliver of light now snooping around her room. These few rays of light were the only visitors she had allowed access to her home since Jacob failed to return from work Saturday.

Peppered across her lawn and along the street curb were countless news vans and media personnel equipped with their weapons of choice; video cameras, pencils and steno pads, audio recorders, microphones, and even a few 35 mm cameras were chosen to inflict as much damage as possible. Each barbarian held his or her weapon in hand and hoped for a chance to interview Audrey, or at the very least, to see movement from inside the house, in order to build some sort of exaggerated and speculative story. Audrey was aware that there would be a media presence at her house. She had no idea, however, of the pandemonic circus it would become.

Audrey noticed one reporter immediately from the bright red business suit she donned, standing directly in the center of her lawn, a flawless ruby yet to be mined, shining brightly amid a quarry of innocuous stone.

"The only verifiable outside contact that Miss Carlson has made was her call to the police to report her fiancé missing. The details of that call have not been shared with the public, but WRKI News has confirmed its existence." The reporter put a cupped hand to one of her ears and nodded slightly. After a brief moment, her hand reunited with the other on the microphone and she took a deep breath in preparation for once again addressing the viewing public.

From the window of her family room—*ironic*, she thought, as she felt no more a familial presence in the

room than a homecoming queen felt unpopular—
Audrey recognized the woman in the red business suit
as the reporter who broke the story about the under-
ground gambling ring in the back room of a local soup
kitchen. An elected official went to prison for it, and
the soup kitchen closed down for good.

*Holly Mayor, Corbin Oliver Weinstein, had been running
for reelection, and was losing. He had become a different man
since the landslide victory which led to his first term for which
he was serving at the time of his arrest. He had put on a sloppy fifty pounds, all of which resided in his now jolly stomach.
His voice had become raspy over time from a mixture of ciga-
rettes and projected public speaking. His hair, or what was left
of it, had all but given up the hope of more voluminous and
shiny days, and he had developed a limp that almost looked
manufactured due to the dramatic arm-swinging he injected
into his adjusted stride.*

*The arrest of Mayor Weinstein happened as a result of an
anonymous tip leading authorities to the local soup kitch-
en, Sue P's Soups. Some people still speculate that the soup
kitchen's owner, Sue Padillo, was the anonymous tipster, and
that the kitchen was becoming more of a burden to her than
a hobby, and a political scandal was the perfect guise to hide
behind, allowing her to fade into true retirement down in
Florida. Once the police obtained a search warrant, which was
not difficult based on the extremely detailed anonymous tip,
the floodgates of evidence opened.*

*The mayor had been soliciting the homeless into an illegal gambling ring, operating under the appearance of an "up and coming" casino. Takers were given fifty dollars to come and play, and they were told that if they gambled all fifty dollars, they would receive another twenty-five dollars to take home; all monies, however, were those of taxpayers. Preposterous as it was, it became the carrot at the end of a rather short stick for which the homeless could grab.*

*Once the gambling began, Weinstein would have one of his men bring around voter registration paperwork for each person to fill out. Weinstein knew he was targeting a demographic that would not vote on their own accord.*

*Through his deceitfully executed plot, the mayor gained his patrons' confidence and approval. All he asked for in return was their vote. After the trial, the headlines cleverly referred to the imprisoned mayor as the Cash COW—a play on his frequent and fraudulent doling out of taxpayer dollars, and how his unhealthy lifestyle correlated to his very initials.*

"I've just been informed that a trusted source for WRKI has spotted Miss Carlson's mother in her car leaving the local supermarket. It is suspected that she is en route to the house. We'll be here for her arrival, and will have it live. This is Lucinda Garrett reporting for Channel 4, WRKI News."

Audrey also knew that since the story aired, the reporter in the red suit had been trying tirelessly to erase her assumed name, "The Queen of Clubs."

Jacob's disappearance was just Lucinda's way of trying to uncover something morally good. Something, she hoped, refreshing. The town was ready for a story to end well, and this reporter wanted every piece of the action she could get. It wasn't too hard either, because despite her name, most every man wanted any portion of her he could get his hands on—or simply his eyes for that matter. Men were her fan base. Men were her demographical audience. Men, as Lucinda Garrett so confidently knew, were her weapons of choice.

*Chapter 20 – September 15, 7:17 P.M.*

"What'da we got, Andrews?" Detective O'Reilly said to Officer Michael Andrews.

"Looks like a double homicide. Appears to be Charles and Ann Freeland. Married twenty-two years. First marriage for both. No kids. No priors. Both clean as a whistle." He stopped to breathe.

"*Appears* to be? They haven't been ID'd yet?" the detective examined.

"The wife, yes. The other body we assume is the husband, but no one's been able to confirm as of yet. PD's tried to contact the husband, but nothing so far," the officer clarified.

"Could it be Jacob Reech?"

"Not likely, I don't think our John matches Reech's description. This guy's huge. Wait'll ya see him. Well, parts of him," Michael said as he pulled the rather large yellow tarp back, revealing what remained of the victim's body.

Detective O'Reilly pondered the scene for a moment, unaffected by the horror splayed across the ground in front of him—the visual toll of years of crime scenes ever-residing just behind his eyelids.

"Why the mutilation? You think we're dealin' with

a crazy, or did this guy have an enemy?"

"Both. Get this, if this is the husband, he was entered into the Witness Protection Program back in '91. Charles Freeland testified against some no-name thug for drug trafficking through the use of minors. That thug was also an illegal. No papers. No nothin'. Got him deported back to Australia where he served a full 15-year sentence."

"Either way, whoever that no-name thug is, he needs to get a name real fast, Andrews. We need to find this guy," he said, still looking at the crime scene strewn across the ground in front of him; his hand massaged his goatee—a clear sign of thought. "My God, he's strong. Look at this," the detective continued as he pointed to the severed leg. "He sliced his leg off in one hack!" They both considered how strong a person would have to be in order to accomplish such a feat, especially cutting through the femur, the body's most formidable bone.

"What did he do to the wife?" The detective paused as he looked around the scene. "And where is she?"

Officer Andrews motioned with his head. "Kitchen. Duct-taped a bag around her head, and cut off both of her hands. Coroner will have to say whether she bled out or suffocated. He's on his way. Should be here any minute."

"Sick bastard." He paused for an abnormal amount

of time, still rubbing his chin. "Mike, pull four people from the department and assemble a team. We need to be smart and fast with this one."

"You got it," Michael assured, and started to walk away.

"Find out if anyone else had a restraining order against him, or if he was an accomplice in any other case. I can't have this guy picking off any more families." He shouted so Officer Andrews could hear his words.

Michael's response was a simple hand wave above his head, confirming he'd heard Detective O'Reilly's every word.

As he drove off, another department vehicle came from the opposite direction. As the two cars passed, the driver's greeted one another by putting a hand out the window and offering a wave. The second car came to a stop and coroner Harvey Bloomfield, a frail, white-haired man, emerged from inside.

A paperboy tossed a stack of newspapers onto the sidewalk at the corner of a party store, making a loud *smack* as it collided with the concrete. The heavy stack of papers nearly made him lose his balance on his bike, but he corrected just before crashing into a nearby sign. The street was all but empty at this hour. Every shop was either just opening, or still entirely dark. The newsstand, however, had been open since 5:00 am.

A burly, bearded man of about fifty years emerged from his newsstand with a cigarette hanging from his mouth. He was one of those people who never let it leave his lips, bright cinders flaring with each breath the owner took. He grabbed the stack of newspapers and began heading back inside.

"I'll take one of those," a voice said from the bench not too far from the newsstand.

"What's that, a paper or a cancer stick?"

"Both, if you're offering."

"Yeah, sure. Just, uh, gimme a buck and we'll call it good."

"Quite a bargain," he said, handing the man the money.

"Need a light, too?"

"Nope. Got that from the paperboy," he joked, as he lit the cigarette and began opening *The Holly Chronicle*, a local paper published twice weekly. The front page was nearly covered with a grainy photo depicting a ghostly figure's distraught and barely identifiable face. A caption below read: *Reech's fiancée, Audrey Carlson, peers through her window at the media on her lawn*. The man looked at the photo, read the caption, then began reading the article written by staff writer Janet Grummel titled "Out of Reech, but in Our Hearts."

The man took a long, deep puff from his cigarette as he read about the security camera last showing Jacob Reech driving away from campus in a green Ford Mustang. He caught himself thinking that those who owned the green car would likely repaint or disassemble it now that authorities knew of its existence and involvement in his kidnapping. The first mistake by the police, he believed, was to tell the general public the make, model, and color of the vehicle they were looking for. Sure it might generate a few leads, but more times than not, it prompted the kidnappers to hide the car even more, or ditch it altogether.

He flicked his cigarette as he finished the story and threw it on the ground. As he stood, he stomped the discarded butt, extinguishing its flame. As the man walked away, he scuffed his left foot to wipe the residual ash from the bottom of his dress shoes.

Audrey found herself fishing through the remaining scraps that inhabited her pantry. She hadn't gone shopping since before Jacob went missing. Sure, her mother had brought over precooked, tinfoil-wrapped meals for Audrey to eat, but no one ever thought to bring over actual groceries like canned goods, boxed pasta, fresh chicken breast, fruits and vegetables, and flour and sugar. Audrey found coping to be easier while cooking. Since Jacob's disappearance, Audrey seemed to do her best at emptying her pantry in order to cook whatever she was able. Often, she wouldn't even eat what she cooked, it was simply the act in which she found comfort. But, none of the staples of her pantry were present, and she was approaching the point of desperation. She had to get groceries. The need to cook was quickly becoming too strong to ignore. That meant she had to get out of her house.

Her attention, as of late, had never once been focused on anything other than Jacob. But, as nothing other than habit could explain, Audrey grabbed her coat, shoes, keys, and shopping list from her refrigerator door, and stepped outside for the first time in what seemed an eternity.

Audrey looked at the grocery list. Items ranging from asparagus to zucchini had periodically made it to that list. A precious few even exhibited the quirky and seemingly neurotic handwriting of Jacob. The two's relationship had blossomed beyond its years as they grocery-shopped together for the first time more than six years ago.

Jacob once told Audrey that a person could tell so much about someone by grocery shopping with him or her. It was, in Jacob's mind, the best first date a couple could go on.

"You know, Audrey. I've always wanted to go shopping with a"—*Jacob did the quote sign with both hands*—"potential love interest."

"Well, I hope all of your questions are answered on my receipt."

*They spent the next two hours strolling up and down each aisle—each with their own cart, and own pocketbook—of the confines of a local Super-Center. Over the course of their date, Jacob and Audrey periodically caught themselves stealing glimpses of each other. As the date continued, their carts filled, and the aisles served as a canvas for each to take mental pictures, placing them deep within the vault of romance partitioned in their respective minds.*

*On the way home after loading bag after bag of groceries into the now cramped trunk of Jacob's Oldsmobile, their date continued.*

"So, d'you find everything you were looking for?" *Jacob started.*

"Most of it. You?" she replied.

"Yeah, I did. Along with a lot of intel." *He smiled, and raised his eyebrows several times.*

"Oh yeah? Like what?"

"Like what? Like, for starters, that I had no idea you ate microwave pizzas, or so many candy bars! It's interesting really how someone so fit and slim could have such a healthy appetite for the unhealthy."

"Not bad for someone whose sole purpose is to scrutinize other's shopping habits. I do have one piece of advice though."

"What's that?"

"Next time you're on this very same date with another"—*she now made quote marks with her hands*—"potential love interest, don't tell her that you plan to learn a lot from her choice in groceries. She may just decide to fool with you."

*For dinner that night, the two ate microwave pizzas, candy bars, headcheese sandwiches, and pigs' feet, all of which were either the unhealthiest or most disgusting things either of them had eaten in their adult lives. But, as both would agree, the night could not have ended more perfectly.*

Audrey pulled into the Super-Center, her car idling in a parking spot. It was early, and she didn't think she had been followed by any media since she'd left her house. She turned her car off, and sat in the driver's seat for a time to gather her thoughts before she ventured into the public arena.

As her hands fumbled to pull the keys from the ignition, Audrey noticed a sight she had come to see far too often. Parked at an adjacent Coney Island restaurant—if one could actually consider the establishment a restaurant—were two police cars belonging to the local force. They were parked nose to tail, and the driver's window was rolled down on each vehicle.

Without realizing what she was doing, Audrey found herself driving her car, approaching the idling cruisers. Only when she was on her final approach did she come to the realization that she was in fact driving her car directly at the two police cars, entirely disregarding the parking lot driving lanes. She was traveling perpendicular to the painted aisles of each parking lane. Luckily, it was early, and the lot had not yet begun to fill.

Her car came to a stop once again, and she exited the vehicle without shutting it off.

"Hey!" Audrey yelled at the police officers.

From the look on the officer's face in the car closest to her, he knew exactly who she was. He took one last bite of his Coney dog, wiped his mouth with a steam-dampened napkin, and got out of his car.

"May I help you, Miss Carlson?" the man said,

waving off the other car, which in turn drove away.

From the moment the man got out of the cruiser, Audrey recognized who it was. Detective O'Reilly now stood directly in front of her, with his hands in the pockets of his departmental jacket. His name appeared on the left breast, and simply read, DET. O'REILLY. His emblazoned badge seemed a bit more sophisticated than other officers' that she had recently seen.

"Miss Carlson?" he repeated. "Are you okay?"

Without warning, and with the speed of a snake striking its prey, Audrey slapped the detective across his right cheek. Caught off guard from the unexpected assault, he stumbled back, hands bursting from his pockets to help steady himself.

"You do nothing to find Jake!" Audrey fought the tears that scratched at her eyelids.

"Miss Carlson, do you have any idea what we do on a daily basis? If not, I suggest you calm down."

She slapped Detective O'Reilly again. His cheek was now painted with a ghostly handprint from the recent trauma, caused by his inflamed blood vessels working to repair the damage, the cold air only accelerating the process.

"Don't tell me to calm down! Your cops do nothing but sit on their asses, drink coffee, and eat hot dogs. I see them! Don't lie to me, Detective!"

"Now hold it!" Detective O'Reilly was visibly

shaken and his voice came with more authority this time. He took a moment to regain his composure. "Yes, Miss Carlson, you're right. I'd be lying if I said my officers aren't frequently seen at local diners and cafes. But let me ask you, how many times a day do you eat? And of those times, how many are from the comfort of your own home, or at a time that suits you?" Detective O'Reilly had his hands in his pockets again, and returned his voice to a speaking tone. "You see, Miss Carlson, to you, eating is something you take for granted. For my men, my *good* men, it is a luxury. They don't have the chance to eat at home because they are working around the clock to find your fiancée, and they can't do their job on empty stomachs. I think you'd agree that they must eat, would you not?"

"Well…" Audrey paused. "Yeah," she finally finished.

"Okay. Well, I am sorry that you don't notice the hard work that they do when you are bundled up so comfortably in your bathrobe, lying on your couch eating whatever it is that you eat, but if you'd like, I could arrange for a ride-along from say, 8 pm to 8 am? Of course, if you do this, you may just have to eat a meal in the parking lot of a local diner or café. Now, if you don't mind, I have a job to do." He turned and walked back to his car.

A brief moment passed.

"Detective, wait," Audrey pled.

The detective turned around, knowing what would come next. This hadn't been the first time an emotionally drained loved one had done this to him. It was a part of the job, but, more importantly, Patrick O'Reilly knew, it was vital for each person to reach this point in a missing persons investigation: the point where they were truly at their wit's end, and simply couldn't take anymore. The only option left was to lash out. Patrick O'Reilly knew from experience that once this threshold was passed, a person could only move up. Bottom line, he understood and held no grudge, but didn't plan to open up entirely for Audrey right here and now. She needed to bask in this process for a little while to fully understand how many people were aiding in the search for Jacob.

"What is it, Miss Carlson, do you need to smack my other cheek now?" Detective O'Reilly played into the moment a little bit. This had to be done sometimes. There was no harm in it, and everyone would end up better off anyway.

"Of course not. I shouldn't have slapped you in the first place. I'm sorry," she admitted, and then continued, "I'm just so tired, and don't know what to do. I've never felt so helpless before."

"The truth is, Audrey, there's not a lot you can do right now." He called her by her first name. That was personal, and Detective O'Reilly hoped it would prove to her that he truly cared. It was one of the few things a person could do that was an unspoken sign of sympathy during a time such as this. "All you can do is keep hoping," he finished.

Audrey once again caught Detective O'Reilly off balance. "Tell me, do you think Jacob's alive?"

"I don't think this is something that we should be talking about, Audrey."

"Don't dodge my question. I'm a grown woman, and I want to know what the lead detective thinks about my fiancé's condition. Now, please answer my question, Detective O'Reilly." Her voice held firm as it began to shake with emotion.

"There's really not a lot of evidence yet. And the last thing I want to do is guess at something like this."

"Please, just give me what you can. Do I need to beg, Detective? Literally get down on my knees? Would that help?"

Patrick now knew what she was after. She didn't want to hear what he really thought, or what evidence they didn't have. She didn't even want to hear about what potential leads they were following. She was after one thing.

"Yes. I do think that he's alive."

Audrey removed a wadded tissue from her jeans pocket, dabbed her eyes, as if composing herself, and hugged Patrick right in the middle of the grocery store parking lot.

"Thank you. And, tell your officer who's been outside my house since Saturday night that he's needed elsewhere. I can handle myself, and would feel better if he was helping to find Jacob."

"Okay. Consider it done. I'll reassign him as soon as I get back in my car." He paused. "Now, why don't you go home and get some rest. I'll call you with an update as soon as I have one. Promise, okay?"

Audrey let out a labored sigh. "Alright. And Patrick?" She paused. "Thank you for making me feel like the world isn't completely falling apart around me."

"Aside from eating hotdogs and drinking coffee, it's my job." He winked at her, annihilating the walls he had so recently put up, and completing his goal of building the spirits of the grieving woman now standing before him.

She smiled at him, got back into her car, and drove home, looking forward to placing herself in a soft bed, and placing her worries—at least for the next few hours—on the shoulders of a friendly detective. As she entered her house, she took her coat and shoes off, and before heading upstairs, she placed the shopping list back on the refrigerator door. Funny, she thought. Her raging appetite had been satisfied.

A search party had been assembled a few days following Jacob's disappearance. Originally, it consisted of close friends and family, but had grown into something much larger than anticipated. Unfortunately, some of the party members were there only because of the media buzz, but no one cared too much; curiosity still aided the search. The party began combing the wooded lots adjacent to Jacob's neighborhood. There were about forty volunteers who continued to diligently search for any sign of Jacob. Audrey, lost in a highly emotional and potentially delusional state, actually removed herself from the search and took the time to notice just how many friends and family had shown up to help in the search for her Jacob. It made her oddly happy; reassured

Some volunteers were on foot, searching area woods for "signs of Jacob." Audrey had seen the posters, and she knew what people were thinking, and expecting. That Jacob was dead, and that they would soon find his body. But, the people remained politically correct in their word choice. It didn't matter to Audrey. She would never lose hope.

Victor and Kyle found themselves paired together

ADAM J. BEARDSLEE

in a car to post notices in area businesses, on countless telephone poles, and storefront doorways. The
only place Jacob's face and name weren't plastered,
it seemed, was on the side of a milk carton. As they
continued to meander through Jacob's neighborhood,
the grim reminder of a spiraling economy filled their
retinas.

A regional recession was always apparent, no matter how hard people tried to hide it. No master list
of who was hit the hardest ever existed, but the truth
was always right there in front of those who called the
neighborhood "home." In this particular subdivision,
like most others, the clearest division between the affected and the flourishing was the state of the lawn
care. Peppered sporadically within the neighborhood
through which Kyle and Victor drove were lush, watered lawns, vibrant with life. Much more alive were
these lawns than the sparsely watered lawns that were
brittle with dehydration—a typical first sacrifice when
money was tight.

Soon though, they came to the entrance of the
neighborhood, pulled out, and headed to the next
closest one, which was about a five-minute drive from
where they were now.

Victor was driving, and began to swerve slightly,
as he fished for his ringing phone buried deep in his
pocket.

"Hello? Hey. Yeah, we're searching for Jake right now. Since four, why? Right. I understand. I guess just do what you gotta do, ya know? Alright. Bye."

A short time passed.

"Sorry about that, Kyle. My cousin's trying to get out here to help, but can't get out of class. He's in college. Good kid. Just needs some direction. His folks, my dad's sister and her husband, were never really there for him. He's been on academic probation for the last two semesters, and if he misses any more classes, they'll kick him out of the program. Funny thing is, he skips class because he's too damn bored to listen to the professor. He's so smart it's dangerous, ya know?"

"Yeah, I've been there myself," Kyle said. "That's too bad, though. Where's he go anyway, OCC?"

"Yeah."

"Really? What's his name? I got a lotta friends that go there."

"Brendan."

The screech of the brakes on the dry pavement sent chills down Kyle's unexpecting neck, and pierced his eardrums. The deer that Victor almost hit continued walking along, entirely oblivious to the near collision of fur on metal.

"Jesus! You okay?" Victor asked.

"Yeah. Man, that thing came outta nowhere!"

"These damn things are everywhere out here.

Well, we're almost there anyway. You wanna just gas up here?" Victor pointed to a small gas station at the corner up ahead. "We can ask to put Jake's picture on the door."

"Sure. Sounds good."

"Vic." *A man's voice sounded into Victor's phone receiver.*
"Hey."

"Are you with that kid?" *the voice asked.*

"Yeah, we're searching for Jake right now."

"Has he been with you the whole time?" *There was a thick Australian accent to the voice.*

"Since four, why?"

"He's no good, Vic. Believe me."

"Right."

"Vic, are you hearing me? You gotta lose the kid. I think he might be up to something."

"I understand."

"You want me to make him disappear?"

"I guess, just do what you gotta do, ya know?"

"Consider it done."

"Alright. Bye."

"O'Reilly," the detective said as he turned on the speaker of his desk phone.

"Detective, it's Warren. Just responded to a call about a murder."

"Jesus. Another one?"

"Who this time? And how bad is it?"

"Well, the homeowners just got home from their honeymoon. They say it's their friend who was watching the house while they were gone. Daniel Carter. Looks like a single stab wound to the chest."

"You need me to get out there?"

"No, I got it under control. We're taking pictures of everything. They say that nothing's missing except a murder weapon. To me, looks like a robbery gone bad."

"Alright. Just radio if you need another car out there."

"Will do, and one last thing: the wife said she found some Glade Plug-Ins in several outlets. Swears on everything holy they're not hers. Want me to bring 'em in as evidence?"

"Yeah, why don't ya. I'll take a look at 'em. Better safe than sorry."

"I should be there by six. By the way, there's not one single fingerprint in this house. Not even the homeowner's. Is that even possible?"

"That can't be. They gotta be there. Andrews, find me some goddamned fingerprints!"

Detective O'Reilly turned off the speaker phone

and disconnected the call. His hands found their way to his head and massaged his hair and face. Two murders and a kidnapping in the same month were quickly filling up his calendar.

Τhe computers made a quiet, but audible hum as their owners looked at the screens. Periodic keystrokes hollered as they formed words on an electronic page.

It was late, but deadlines kept no time.

"So why'd you get into reporting anyway?" Nick said, looking up from his computer.

"For fame and fortune, why else?" Lucinda replied sarcastically, without allowing her eyes to leave the screen.

Nick sat back in his chair, taking a break from his article. He stretched his arms, as though they'd been stuck in the same position for a month, and shook the sleep from his hands.

"Seriously. Was this your 'Plan A'?"

Lucinda looked up from her screen. "If you must know, my plan was to find a career, rather than a job. You can fill in the rest how you want."

"Between you and me, reporting wasn't even on my radar until '08. Saw a piece on the AIDS epidemic in Africa. It really got to me how many kids die there every day." He paused. "It's like the news in America is a form of gossip. I mean, seriously? Why am I reporting who had sex with whom?"

Lucinda stopped typing and relaxed a bit in her chair. "Because it's the governor having the sex."

"So what? So it's news? Come on. Yeah, maybe the guy's a player. Does that mean he's not a good governor?" he scoffed.

"He's scum," Lucinda countered.

"I don't think 'no consensual sex with willing women' is on his job description. You wanna know why it's so important to people?"

"Oh, please enlighten me," Lucinda humored.

"Because they want to gossip about it. News, to the public, isn't to be informed, it's meant to ruin people. Anyway, I decided to get into this to bring some importance back into the news. A school shooting? That's important. An epidemic threatening the nation? People need to know about that. But a damn sex scandal? They can find that at their local theater."

Lucinda paused before responding. "That surprises me. You don't seem the type. I mean, you seem to take anything that comes your way."

"I gotta pay the bills. Doesn't mean I agree with it."

"Touché," she said, then promptly continued, inquisitive. "So why'd you give up so easily over the Jacob Reech story?"

"You buried me. As soon as I said 'I was made for TV,' I was sunk. Anything after that was just the last grenade I had to toss your way. But I'll get the next one, you'll see." He smirked; both of their faces glowed from the soft white light of the screens in front of them.

"Why do you come off so cocky then? It doesn't fit your story," Lucinda probed.

"I don't know, I guess I just feel like it'll help me fit in, ya know? That's what people want to see, right?" he said, then continued, "Or, maybe I'm just screwin' with ya to break down some of those walls you have up."

Lucinda sighed. "In your dreams, anchorman." She continued typing.

"Yeah, well. I gotta get out of here." He got up from his desk and swooped into his jacket. "Got beer at my place. Interested?"

"Did you not hear what I just said?" She didn't even stop typing as she scowled the words.

"Figures," he said, and turned to walk toward the door. As he neared it, he couldn't hear Lucinda typing any longer. She was watching him. A slight smirk crept onto his face as he left the office they shared.

*Chapter 24 — September 16, 11:58 P.M.*

Jacob sprang to life as a hand smacked his face.

"Wake up," a mechanical voice said. "Who's Franklin?"

Disoriented in the darkened room, Jacob took a moment before responding.

"Franklin?" He hadn't been sleeping, but his voice still sounded groggy and raspy. Maybe it was from all of the yelling for help he'd done while held captive in that trunk.

"Who is he?" Another slap assaulted his other cheek.

"I don't know what you're talking about. Please, stop," Jacob pled, exhausted.

His eyes gathered their focus and explained to their owner as much of their surroundings as was possible in almost total blackness; he was in a small room nearly void of all objects. He could tell he was facing a wall, though. It was about two feet in front of his face. There was no paint on the walls, no decor; just cinderblock and mortar.

"Your grandfather's letter. It mentions a guy named Franklin. Who is he?" The Voice continued to probe, unscathed by Jacob's plea.

"Yeah, I've read it," he admitted. "But I don't know a guy named Franklin. I swear." Anxiety leapt from his voice. *No more jumper cables. Please.*

"Well, your grandfather did, and it sounds like Franklin was pretty damn important."

Jacob interjected, "What do you want from him anyway? If you just explain to me, maybe I can help you."

The mechanical voice came from behind Jacob, and closed in on his cheek. He couldn't see him, but could feel and smell his breath radiating onto his cheek as he spoke.

Jacob could barely see in the darkness of the room, and he was tied to a chair. Sight and touch were no longer senses he could use. His stomach howled. He last ate, it seemed, more than a day ago. There goes taste too. All he had left to rely on were scents and sounds. All of his focus challenged the two senses to provide as much detail as possible. Each piece of data, Jacob locked into his wary mind for recollection at a later time.

"Let me give you a little briefing, asshole," The Voice said. His breath could gag a maggot. The smell of old coffee with the pungency of escargot assaulted one of the remaining two senses Jacob was able to use as The Voice continued. "You work for me now. Your payment will not be in money, nor is that what I want from you." He paused. "It's Franklin that I want, and when you give him to me, your payment will be Audrey's life."

"Where is she, you son of a bitch?!" The chair feebly wobbled in place as Jacob strained to release himself of his binds.

"Relax yourself, Superman. She's fine. All she's doing right now is buying stock in Kleenex." It sounded like he was smiling while he spoke.

"You bastard," Jacob said, realizing The Voice had been lying to him while being held captive in both cars. He'd thought they had her. He would have done anything to keep her safe. "If you even touch her..." He stopped mid-sentence, not exactly knowing how to end his futile threat.

"Don't worry, I won't touch her. I'm not in it for that. But, one of my men just might be. We can find out if you like."

The thought nauseated Jacob and a grimace briefly exploded onto his face, before melting into an expression of utter obedience.

"No. I'll do whatever you want me to. Just leave her alone. Please." *Oh, God! I'll kill him.*

"I figured you'd say that. But that's good. Now we can be friends. I like having friends, don't you?"

No response.

"I asked you a question, friend. My friends know to

answer my questions, because if they don't, I get mad. And when I get mad, I get impulsive. I hate not being in control of my own decisions." The crisp sound of a knife being sharpened echoed in the small room. "So, let me ask again. Do you like having friends?" His voice was terrifyingly calm.

Hesitantly, Jacob responded. "Yes, I like having friends."

"Wow, we're getting to know so much about each other already. I think we're going to be friends for a long time. Audrey too."

Jacob remained silent, realizing he held absolutely no power in the situation. He heard the man walk away from the chair and open a door. It didn't sound like a regular door, though. There seemed to be an absence of a latch, but he heard a faint click.

"You go ahead and hang out here for a while, and think about our friendship. Someone will bring you some food. Eat it. If not for me, for Audrey, cuz when I come back, I need your mind energized."

The door clicked shut and Jacob was once again all alone, consumed by darkness.

The ground felt cool, overtaken by a shade tree in the near distance. It was covered in a deep bluish grass about four inches deep. Some of the blades had collapsed on themselves from their own weight. Others showed the marks of recent foot traffic, like the walking path that appears throughout a golf tournament. A sprinkler system watered the grass early in the morning, and the droplets had all dried or descended to the ground at the base of each botanical spire.

The soil beneath the grass was extremely fertile, dark brown and full of moisture and healthy organics. This was the soil that any homeowner would wish to have on the lawn. There was a suitable mix of pebbles, stone, and rock dispersed throughout it, allowing for not only the filtration of water, but also providing a sturdy foundation on which the soil could comfortably reside.

Birds hopped across the ground, plunging their beaks into the lush soil as they hunted for the fat and healthy worms that chugged within the tunnels of their thriving community below. One could argue that if given a mouth, each worm in this soil would use it to bare a smile more noticeable than their ringed clitellum. Diving deeper into the ground, however, the sight of worms became less frequent. Rocks impeded on them and obstructed the extension of their network of tunnels, like a subway system meeting a cast-iron wall. The soil too, began to surrender to loamy clay piled atop an old wooden box about six feet in length.

The wood was warped in nearly all places, but it still appeared somewhat structurally sound. Inside lay the bones of a person still dressed in a blazer and pants, though they had lost most of their color from the ground creeping in over time. Tucked beside one of the skeletal arms, however, was a sealed Mason jar that contained a single document. If viewed by one man, the document was invaluable in preserving the nation's history, but if viewed by another, it could be used to rewrite it.

Officer Andrews looked at the screen, making sure he was certain of its content before he called Detective O'Reilly. Shortly after his thorough examination, he picked up the phone and dialed his boss's number.

"Detective. Got something in the Jacob Reech case."

"Let's hear it."

"Got a green Mustang, same year as in the surveillance from U of M, pulling into a parking garage in Ann Arbor."

"You sure?"

"Affirmative. Pulled in yesterday around noon."

"Were you able to get a shot of his face?"

"No. Only got a view of the passenger side."

"Find out if there are any other cameras inside the structure. We gotta confirm it was him."

"Already did. There aren't."

"Shit. They're having him switch cars. I need a report of every car that leaves that facility for the next eight hours of film. Every single one, Andrews. Got that?"

"Yes, sir. I should have it on your desk by the end of the day, Detective."

"Good."

Frank began to feel inadequate in his ability to log into the file. Not only was his brain aching from thought on what seemed to be the millionth attempt, but his pride was now in jeopardy too. His frustration continued to fester as Don challenged him to his limits. He could almost feel Don's voice radiating on the back of his neck, even though his voice was held at bay on the other side of the two-way radio.

He had tried everything he knew in his countless attempts to combat the lateral encryption he'd encountered for the first time while at the house with Don.

*What's the country you never sleep in?* he pondered yet again, as he directed a blank stare at the note he'd written with that password hint scribbled in blue ink.

"What could it be?" he said aloud from his dining-room table, which served as more of an office desk than eating surface. Strewn across every square inch of tabletop were geographical reference books opened to various pages. All had been used to search for the eluding answer to the riddle required for entry into the file that would hopefully allow The Movement to truly begin.

Original attempts at the password consisted of the basic country names that Frank knew offhand, but over the past few hours he had better educated himself, and was searching for a possible deeper meaning of the needed passphrase.

In his possession, he held a report of all travel itineraries that the owner of the house had ever visited. They weren't that hard to obtain, actually. Living in the age of heightened security had its upside as well. After hacking into the TSA's website, he found a database of names, Social Security numbers, and home address at the time of travel.

Frank knew now that whoever lived here had traveled to many countries throughout his or her life, many of which he didn't even know were countries in the first place. That is, until he had begun his research.

He looked at the list with frustrated eyes.

"Damn it!" Franked blurted. He knew time was now of the essence. He needed the content of the file in less than a week, and he felt like he had made no progress at all. He noticed destinations of Ireland, Scotland, Australia, Germany, Aruba, and even South Africa, all of which the homeowner had traveled to in the past fifteen years.

Frank had considered that the passphrase perhaps led to a memory of a vacation where there was little sleep to be had. He'd already tried all of those countries, and failed each time. He cast the useless list to the floor.

"Garbage," he mumbled, once again finding himself back at square one.

He sat back in his chair and looked at the ceiling, thinking again of the passphrase hint.

*What's the country you never sleep in?* There had to be something he was missing. He was clearly aware that his knowledge of country names was by no means vast, but realized that based on the way in which the password hint was written, there was a clear and finite number of entries that could logically align with the expected input: the name of a country.

In all of the books scattered across the table, Frank was able to find that there were only about two hundred different countries in the world, and even with various case-sensitive versions of each country, the number of entries still seemed to be far fewer than many passwords he had cracked over the course of his long and illustrious career.

Frank was never much to look at. Growing up, he spent most of his time as a basement barbarian, rarely venturing to the bathroom for a routine shave, or a brisk cleaning of his teeth. As an adult, nothing had changed, except for the understanding that his life revolved around an uncanny ability to gain access.

He had worked for many people, some extremely

desperate, and some extremely powerful. Certain jobs required that he gain access to secure facilities and safes, while others required the hacking of websites and computers. The computer always proved to be the easiest adversary for Frank to conquer over the years.

*What's the country you never sleep in?* He thought of each word individually this time, paying close attention to the solitary meaning behind every one.

"Who is *you?*" he said to himself aloud. "The homeowner. Has to be. It's his computer for cryin' out loud."

That led nowhere. His eyes focused on the rest of the sentence. He repeated it after reading it.

"*Never sleep in.*" He thought for a brief moment, then continued to dive deeper.

"Maybe a country he's never even been to, therefore never slept in?" He'd already dismissed the notion that the answer was simply a country's name due to the shallow pool of possibilities that would present. Anyone who was as brilliant as to create the never-before-seen lateral encryption would undoubtedly be wise enough to create a password trickier than one with about two hundred, or two billion, possible entries given their variations and use of special characters.

"Well, then what is it to not *sleep?*" Frank pondered if the word *sleep* referred to the literal definition of shutting one's eyes for rest, or if it pointed to the more lurid definition of 'having sex.' He considered it.

Nothing.

Frank's head was throbbing from the deep intellectual dive he was in. He couldn't remember the last time he'd thought this intensely about something so seemingly simplistic. In his line of work, rarely did he ever have to think too hard about anything. Most of his jobs required the knowledge of computer code, which to him was a more simple language than English to understand.

Without warning Frank shot up in his chair, a rush of answers pouring into his exhausted mind. He remembered his conversation with Don during his first attempts at the passphrase. *With the lateral encryption, the owner wanted to make sure that he never forgot his password.* He began to smile, feeling that he was close.

The way the lateral encryption was set up didn't take into account who entered an incorrect password, it would always assume the name of another file embedded deep within the computer's hard drive. Frank began to realize that the owner of the computer would have to go through the same process as he had for the last week just to find the file if he ever forgot it. An epiphany shot into his mind and onto his face.

"He couldn't *afford* to forget it! That's it!" he gloated.

Grabbing his two-way radio off the only opened spot on the table, Frank raced for the door.

Detective O'Reilly looked down at his speedometer and let an ironic smirk creep across his face. He was speeding in his off-duty Impala, and after noticing it, caught himself looking around for a police car lurking in wait of a speeder passing by. All policemen know that most people speed; even the men and women of uniform put a heavier foot on the pedal from time to time. He eased up on the gas and smiled after realizing he had just gotten away with breaking the law; no matter how minute, it felt good.

Speeding wasn't the first, nor would it be the last law the detective would knowingly break.

The smirk slipped off his face as the thought of Jacob Reech ransacked his mind. He was beginning to think that Jacob was dead, and felt guilty for allowing the thought to cross his mind. He couldn't help it though. Years of experience had told him that after someone had been missing for three days, the likelihood of finding that person alive fell off the proverbial cliff. *Poor Audrey*, he thought; the smile had been wiped clean from his face.

Without warning, his police radio blared to life.

"2301, we have a report of a B and E on Clondike.

What's your 20?" the radio croaked.

Detective O'Reilly sighed and picked up the receiver. "2301 is homebound. Have someone else handle this one. How 'bout 4602?"

A moment passed.

"2301, uh, 4602 is already at the scene, and uh, you're gonna want to see this one. Some kind of container was left at the scene. Deputy says it's like the last one. We may have a serial robber on our hands."

Piqued with interest, the detective responded, "Alright, I'll be there as soon as I can. I'm just gonna grab a bite real quick from home. I'm only a few minutes away. I'll be at the scene in no more than twenty."

"10-4, 2301."

Frank jiggled the modified bobby pin one last time in the lock at the back door. He could hear the mechanism disengage from within the lock's housing. Soon after, he was standing in the mud room of the house.

He hadn't brought anything with him other than a blank jump drive to copy the file to.

"You in?" Don asked, again through the two-way radio.

"Yeah. I should be out in less than ten minutes."

"Perfect."

Frank headed directly to the den located across

from the kitchen and powered up the computer. It looked as though he was the owner of the house by how naturally he navigated within and around its rooms. Once the computer was turned on, he sat in the chair, cracked his knuckles and neck, and started the all-too-familiar process once again. First priority, find the file on the hard drive. He had learned to start by searching for files that were modified within the last month, to minimize his search of the most recent files. One of those files had to be the one he was looking for.

After a few minutes of tedious searching, he found it. Auto-saved the same day he last tried to gain access to it. He selected the file, and a confident grin materialized onto his face.

Patrick turned onto the dirt road where he lived and drove on the opposite side of the road for a time, in order to avoid hitting the plethora of potholes and ruts that had been carved into the gravel over time. He could see his house about five hundred yards up the road on the right. His backyard butted up to a thin tree line, and beyond that was a cornfield.

His radio blared to life once again.

"Detective, it's Andrews."

"Any news from the parking garage?"

"Yeah, but you're not gonna like it. Football game

ended just after he got there, cars were spewing out of it, Detective."

"Damn it! Um, tell ya what. Contact Ann Arbor PD and tell 'em to get to that garage. Maybe Reech tried to leave another message like he did at the rest area."

"Will do." He paused. "What do you think they want?"

"Hell, I don't know. Ransom seems most likely, but Reech isn't wealthy by any means. He's perfectly average."

"It just seems like a heck of a lot of planning, don't you think?"

"Yeah. Tell ya what, see if you can find any enemies he may have. Could be a disgruntled student of his. Run the backgrounds of all his male students for the last two calendar years. Let me know if you find any red flags. Gotta go, just got another robbery call back on Clondike."

"Alright, I'll have something for you by morning."

The front of his house indicated zero female presence, as there were no signs of frilly décor or potted plants and shrubs, just barren grass meeting a solemn brick foundation. He wondered how long his night would be now that he would be investigating the breaking and entering. The thought led him to consider what sort of food remained in his kitchen that he could pack, as an unknown night stared him in the face. Then he remembered. Leftover lasagna. It was almost three days old, but would be perfect for this night.

Since this appeared to be the same guy as the last few times, he would likely get quite a bit of heat from far above his head to bring this guy down, especially now, since the simple breaking and entering had led to murder.

Frank began typing in the passphrase, saying each word as he typed.

"*What's…the…country…you…never…*"

"Frank, you there? Frank!" Don's voice erupted from the desk where Frank had set the radio. The sudden onslaught of noise startled the hacker to his core.

"Jesus, man! Yeah. I'm here. What is it?" His eyes never left the screen as he responded. He wanted to make sure that he did not lose his place in the passphrase because every keystroke represented a required character, even the spaces. All he saw on the screen, however, was a string of black dots, each symbolizing an entered character.

"A car just pulled into the driveway. You gotta get out of there, fast!"

"How long?"

"Thirty seconds. Tops."

On Don's end, there was radio silence following his last transmission. Frank was already on the move.

"*…sleep…in?*"

He pressed the ENTER key, and a file appeared. With time running out, he knew all he could do was hide. His eyes scanned the room and fell on a closet as his best option for concealing his presence. He got up from the desk and hurried over to it, and began stuffing himself inside. As he turned around, he noticed the computer screen was still shining brightly on the other side of the room.

He ran back to the computer, turned off the screen, and then heard the front door open. He was only about ten feet from the front door, and had no option but to crouch behind a fake plant near the corner of the den.

Chapter 28 — September 17, 5:06 P.M.

The lightweight door opened once again. Jacob had no idea how much time had lapsed since a man brought him food. It was amazing really, how darkness thwarted one's ability to keep accurate time.

Jacob could hear that another chair was being scraped across the floor, nearing him. A mechanical voice sighed as it plopped down into the seat.

"I hope you've thought about what it means to be a friend." He paused to let Jacob absorb the comment. "We know you're not telling us everything, Jacob. The phone call with your lawyer friend. You were going to tell him something. I believe you called it 'preventative action.'"

The statement racked Jacob's already wary mind even more.

"You tapped my phone? Jesus!" He paused. "How long have you been watching me?"

"Long enough. And take it easy, we didn't tap your phone. But we did pay your friend Speedy a little visit at his house. I think it's safe to say he's represented his last client."

"You killed him?!" he yelled. "What is so God damn important that you'd kill him for?" Jacob argued.

"In a word, knowledge. In more than one word, because you were going to tell him something that would help further hide what we're looking for."

"So what the hell are you looking for? Tell me so I can help, dammit!"

"The Washington Cipher. It points to a location that holds what's likely the largest flawless diamond the nation has ever seen. No living person has ever laid eyes upon it, but as soon as we find his cipher, it'll be mine."

"Why is this so important to you?"

"I'm glad you ask, friend," The Voice said, sounding excited to talk about the topic. It was his passion, his life, his everything. "The cipher will help decode a language that was used by the Society of Cincinnati in the late 1700s. I believe my great-great-great-grandfather created that language for George Washington, and helped him hide the diamond."

"How can you be so sure?" Jacob asked, oddly intrigued, given his circumstance.

"A few years ago, I found a document written in code. I believe it marks the location of the remainder of Washington's personal wealth that my grandfather translated into code for him. Washington was estimated to be worth about five hundred million dollars. We believe that number is about two hundred million short and is proven in this letter. He concealed its location in this code. Washington never went back to claim it by the time he died. Now, it's the rightful property of my family."

"How far back does your grandfather's document go?"

"I figured out the numbering system in the code. The document, if I'm right, was written in 1791."

Numbers, especially in terms of years, were always easier to decode than letters. He knew the first character had to be a 1, and then worked out other possibilities based on the document being written in the seventeen or eighteen hundreds. Once he had two characters, he was able to identify a pattern and fill in the remaining blanks for numbers zero through nine. Simple work, really. Especially for a man as devoted as The Voice.

"Why do you think he wrote it in code?"

"I think someone else also knew of the diamond. I think he feared for his safety."

"So why do you need me? What the hell do I know?" The sense of historical fascination was no longer in his voice.

"Not you, Mr. Reech. Your grandfather. He knew the location of the cipher and we think he gave you information as to its location."

"My grandfather never told me anything about this. I'm telling you the truth."

"I believe you. And I like how our friendship is progressing. But you need to hear me when I say this. Audrey's life depends on you figuring it out."

Jacob heard The Voice get up and leave the room. He sat in perfect silence for a time, as a new realization set in. He thought about his grandfather.

*What is it that you knew, Grandpa?*

The only thing Jacob knew that carried any secrecy from his grandfather was a file he was asked to protect. Jacob was asked to protect the file with a password, and to tell no one. That was all. When Jacob looked at the file, all it contained were numbers across several tabs of a Microsoft Excel document that made absolutely no sense to him.

He thought deeper, doing his best to remember the conversations he'd had with his grandfather before he passed. The two had always had such a great time together, but the recollection of those times was foggy now. All he could think of was the letter he'd found in his closet. The few words in it, however, carried no fog at all.

*Jacob, Franklin has a secret. Noah will help you.*

He pondered the sentences even deeper for a few moments.

Nothing.

He turned his attentive mind back to the file with which he had been entrusted. The numbers, thousands of them, made no sense. Or did they?

Jacob thought intently on how the numbers and tabs could possibly be related to an overall message.

*Were they years?* he thought, but soon rejected the idea, as he remembered seeing numbers of five and six digits in length.

His mind perked as he dove a layer deeper into his frontal lobe and considered the idea of each number representing a letter.

*Possibly*, he thought. *But then what about the colored cells?* He theorized their significance, but got nowhere with the idea.

"Damn it!" he said to himself, the frustration radiating. He thought of the note once again, and then directed his mind back to the file.

*Maybe they're connected somehow.* He pondered it briefly, and nearly felt himself jerk in his seat as an entirely new thought sprouted in his mind like well-fed bamboo.

"Hey! Hey! I have a question!" he screamed. After a few moments, the lightweight door opened.

"I think I may remember something, but I need a computer," Jacob said.

No response came.

"Jesus, you want me to help or not?" Jacob complained. "It's about the origins of the Society of Cincinnati. I just need to learn about them to know if what my grandfather told me is related to your grandfather's code. Honest."

The Voice responded wryly. "If you're lying to me, I will bring you Audrey's head in a garbage bag," he said as he shut the door again.

After a moment, Jacob heard some muffled rustling come from another room. It sounded like wires were being unplugged. Before long, The Voice came back into the small room, placed a laptop in front of Jacob, and untied his hands. His legs, however, remained tightly secured to the chair.

"This is only temporary. And let me remind you that you have no idea where you are located. Even if you reach out to anyone, they won't know where you are, but they will tell the police, who will then tell me. Get my drift?"

"Yes, just give me a few minutes. I need to see if someone was a member."

"Who are you thinking was a member?" The Voice inquired.

Jacob challenged the question. "Are you honestly an expert in the historical membership of the Society? If not, let me just validate something, then we can talk about it." The display of power raged inside Jacob's body, his veins nearly bursting with adrenaline.

"You just better watch how you talk to your new friend," The Voice said. "You can have all the time you want, but why don't I just keep you company."

"Suit yourself," Jacob said, as he began searching the Society of Cincinnati. He found a website devoted to the Society, and clicked on the "History" link that led to an article explaining the establishment of the Society of Cincinnati. He read it to himself as the man sat behind him.

*Founded in 1783 at the close of the Revolutionary War, when the leaders of the nation stood before the dawn of a new America. The foundation of the Society strictly focused on supporting the efforts of the men who helped secure the independence of our great nation.*

As Jacob read he heard the faint *blat* of a two-way radio come to life in another room. Still facing the wall, he heard The Voice exit the room to retrieve the radio.

As soon as the door latched, he quickly logged onto his home computer remotely. It's amazing the types of programs that could be purchased for phones, tablets, and computers these days. Hell, even cars could help a person stay connected. Or, as some would see it, prevent them from being disconnected. Everyone and everything was 'on the grid.'

"Any news?" came from the other room as Jacob pounded the keyboard faster than ever before.

He located the protected file on his computer's hard drive and saw that it was already open.

*Someone's in the file. They're at my house. Audrey.*

He quickly entered the passphrase and the file filled the screen.

"I gotta get back in there to check on him," The Voice came from the other side of the wall.

A thought sparked in Jacob's mind as he thought of the note from his grandfather. He knew this man wanted to know who Franklin was, but Jacob had no idea how to help. That is, until his epiphany proved fruitful. He thought again of a portion of the note from his grandfather. *Noah will help you.* The connection made perfect sense now.

Jacob worked with the file for a moment and before he knew it, a message appeared on the screen. One he had never seen before. His jaw nearly touched the floor as he plastered the image onto the canvas of his mind.

The footsteps were getting closer.

Jacob began hitting keys and hammering the mouse pad, changing as much as he could of the file to further mask its message, capitalizing on the unforeseen power he knew he held at his fingertips. He saved the file, and closed out of it.

The lightweight door began to open.

Faster than ever, Jacob logged out of his home computer, and quickly clicked a button to clear the browser's history as the footsteps entered the room and approached him from behind. He closed his eyes, fearing the man saw what he had done, and also hoping that the other person in the file had not seen the message before he changed it.

No reprimand came from The Voice, and Jacob continued the conversation they'd started before the man left, his adrenaline still bubbling just beneath his skin.

"So this Society was founded in 1783. That's before your grandfather's document. You sure you translated the code correctly?"

"Who was the member you were looking for?"

"A guy with the last name of Hughes. My grandfather mentioned his name a few times. Only by last name, though. Always talked about being educated by Professor Hughes. Maybe there's no connection, but thought I'd give it a shot."

"Well, the clock's tickin' on Audrey, so you better find something here pretty fast."

A gloved hand appeared in front of Jacob; the light from the screen illuminated the hand as it grabbed the laptop from the table.

"I'll take that. Next time you need to look something up, you can ask me to do it for you," The Voice said, as he once again left the room.

The sound of the door clicking echoed in the foyer as Audrey dropped her keys into the handmade clay dish she and Jacob bought from a vendor on their Spring Break vacation to Jamaica in 2008. The dish depicted a series of fish eating the one in front of it, each one descending in size from the very large to the incredibly small. The most interesting aspect of the dish, however, was the artist's ability to make the smallest fish appear as though eating the much larger fish in front of it, and completing the circle, was entirely natural; the unique use of colors proved to be the source of the clever optical illusion.

Audrey set her purse on the hutch next to the fish dish—its name affectionately given by its owners and stopped to admire it. It seemed as though a lifetime of memories was packed into the superheated clay from which the piece had been crafted. Her eyes welled, and her throat constricted as she heaved a weighted sigh from her shoulders.

Out of nowhere, something covered her eyes from behind, and was followed by an abrupt jerk, sending her to the ground. Her head, covered in a modified Crown Royal bag, hit the ground with a force she was not expecting. Luckily, the bag did not make it around her entire head, and fell off as it, too, recoiled from striking the ground.

In the blur of panic, Audrey saw a figure. She was certain the figure was male, and began to scream and kick wildly. The man said nothing as she connected with a few of her flailing defensive attacks. After a brief scuffle from one of her better-landed kicks, her assailant grabbed her shoeless feet and slammed them on the wood floor. Her heels took a beating she knew would be excruciating, but the expected pain was almost nonexistent at the moment, masked by wild fear.

She began clamoring up the side of the cupboards to her feet, not wasting strength on screaming, as she now realized that the man was holding a knife. Another kick landed in the man's crotch, buying her a few extra moments. She took full advantage and rose to her feet completely. She turned to the kitchen counter, looking for something to defend herself with, but her hands met only the smooth surface of the countertop before the man once again grabbed her. This time, he bear-hugged her, squeezing so tightly she could feel her chest depressing inward. She wondered how long her ribs could withstand the vise-like pressure before breaking. Her hands still grappled for a weapon. Anything. Finally, they gripped something and instinctively heaved it toward the man. He deflected the soft bottle of hand soap like it was an annoying fly. Her other closed fist came to the man's face as she tried to stuff a scouring pad into his eyes—a fruitless effort once again.

The man, only angered more by her attempts, slapped her across the face. It stunned Audrey for a moment, and she could feel her cheek begin to throb.

"Stop it!" the man growled.

Audrey's face contorted as she held back her tears; one, however, still escaped over the dam of her lower left eyelid. The solitary tear sprinted freely down her face and neck, absorbing into the collar of her wool sweater.

He was leaning over her at the edge of the sink, knife in hand, and fury in his eyes.

"No one needs to get hurt. Just be quiet, and do what I say," he commanded.

Audrey paused, looking him in his eyes, then reluctantly, she nodded her head in defeat.

The man then took a step back from her as he lowered his knife. He looked out the kitchen window over Audrey's shoulder to see if any passersby had seen the attack. He was relieved to see the landscape barren of humans.

"Okay. Now, go stand over there in that corner, facing the wall." He pointed his head in the intended direction.

"What do you want?" Audrey calmly pled.

"No questions." Audrey hoped he would continue talking, so his focus would not entirely be on her. "Just..." As the word left his mouth, Audrey swung her right arm as fast as she could from her side upward toward the man's face. "...keep walki..." Something collided with the man's lower jaw and sliced up through his cheek. Another devastating blow came a millisecond later, but this time from above, falling on the man's back as he bent over in pain from the initial blow. He never said anything. Audrey briefly looked at his silent, unconscious body lying on the kitchen floor as she dropped the granite sample. She had given Jacob such a hard time about not returning it to the Stone Cory store where they planned to purchase their new countertops.

Her years as a college softball pitcher had just paid off, and she would be ever thankful for Jacob's procrastination, as it might have just saved her life.

As she exhaled the adrenaline from her lungs, she heard the strike of a lighter and looked up only to see a second man leaning against the doorway, lighting a cigarette.

"Not bad. You play ball in college?" the second man asked rhetorically. He knew she wouldn't answer, nor did he expect her to.

A guttural moan, filled with terror, leapt from her throat, as her heart dropped to her feet; her teary eyes caught the taunting glint of a Taser in the man's other hand. She started to lumber toward the opposite kitchen door. The bones in her legs felt as though they had been replaced with soft rubber as she struggled to run. Before she could even take two steps, she winced as two claws bit into her back. A moment later the shock of electricity raged through her body. The man stood over her as she writhed on the floor, jaws clenched shut. He put the cigarette in his mouth and slowly began turning the dial up on the Taser.

As she lay there on the floor, Audrey heard the phone begin to ring. She hoped it was Detective O'Reilly calling with good news, but she would never find out. Two incredibly long seconds later, Audrey lost consciousness.

Detective O'Reilly hung up the phone after the fourth ring. He didn't want to give Audrey an update through an answering machine. As soon as he hung up, however, his phone started to ring.

"O'Reilly."

"I don't think it's one of his students. They all check out," Officer Andrews said as he sat in the swivel chair while on the phone with Detective O'Reilly. "Matter of fact, only one male student in the past two years had anything less than a C. Can't be him, though.

Died in a skydiving accident last summer out in Vegas."
The words sent both of them into silence as they challenged their minds to find something of use from the
seemingly dead end.

"Well, at least it's good that we can rule them out.
That puts us ahead of where we were," O'Reilly eventually posed. "How 'bout Ann Arbor PD?"

"Green Mustang was still in the parking garage,
but it was clean as a whistle. Couldn't find anything
that resembled a message Reech may've left," Andrews
said, scratching his knee. "If he did try to drop an SOS,
either someone else picked it up before PD got there,
or it wasn't as effective as the first."

The way he said the words sounded as though he'd
intently considered every angle, every option, and every possibility before sharing his ultimate assessment
with Detective O'Reilly. O'Reilly picked up on his attention to detail, but remained silent yet again, as the
two probed their twenty-plus years of experience for
an answer. The *plus* portion was really all that Officer
Andrews brought to the impromptu "think tank."

Andrews was fairly new to the force, graduating from the Academy in June of 2011, when he was
hired by the Holly Police Department. What years of
academic experience the man sitting before Detective
O'Reilly didn't have, he made up for with real-world
credibility. He was in a gun fight this past spring.

Detective O'Reilly knew that many officers spent their entire career tacking on hours in a cruiser, and gaining seniority for only doing a quarter of what they'd been trained to handle. Most of the time, after years of desk-related monotony, an officer's skills began to vanish into thin air. Or, they absorbed entirely into his gut.

Andrews and Officer Warren, somewhat his senior, both shared fire in an open baseball field with two drug dealers. The gunfight began after a foot chase, and as the two suspects turned simultaneously with guns drawn, Andrews and Warren alike gained years of proverbial experience. During the crossfire, Warren emerged as a true leader, taking control, and helping the rookie that Andrews was. Still is, technically.

"Damn. They're getting him lost in plain sight. We're losing more traction than we're gaining on this one. He could be anywhere by now."

"Any chance you think he may be heading for the border?"

"No, not with him showing up in Ann Arbor. They would have had him take 69 or 75. Port Huron, or Detroit."

"Right." *File, save as:"Boss_Knows_Best.101"*

"We're just going to have to wait until something, or someone, brings us something useful."

Detective O'Reilly had no idea, however, that that lead would never come.

Kyle dropped his bag on the couch after diving practice and plopped down beside it. After a moment, he remembered what Victor had said about his cousin. Intrigued, he sat up, opened his laptop, and began looking up all students with the name of *Brendan* at OCC. He could only find one, but he seemed to be a stand-out student. A member of the debate team, and enrolled in some advanced courses. It couldn't be Victor's cousin. After searching at length, Kyle couldn't find a shred of evidence confirming that Victor's cousin attended OCC.

He switched gears and decided to look up Victor's parents. He knew his dad's name from meeting him during the search. He opened up a Google search and typed it in. Apparently, his dad was a pretty big football player in college. He played for Notre Dame. Kyle clicked on the link that took him to Notre Dame's athletic website, where he found a biography of Charles Flanten that filled the screen in collegiate colors. On it, he read something that startled him. *The only child of Jane and David Flanten, Charles didn't always play football.*

"Only child? Why would Victor lie to me about that?" He was lost in bewilderment, but another word escaped from his mouth a moment later. "Shit!"

He picked up the phone and called his girlfriend, Calista. On the third ring, she answered.

"Hey, babe!" Calista said in her usual chipper voice.

"Okay. Don't be mad," Kyle replied, taking caution as he said the words.

"What do you mean?" Make that wood-chipper.

"I know I've been acting a bit weird the last few days, and I'm sorry."

"Uh, okay," she said, even though she hadn't noticed a change in his attitude as of late.

"I should have told you this sooner, but you know how Professor Reech is missing? Well, I kind of know something about that."

"What?! Kyle, are you serious? What do you know?" she interrogated.

"Well, there was a letter on his desk that I found when I went there for our meeting. It's pretty scary."

"Kyle, you have to tell the police! I can't believe this!"

"No, see? That's just it. I can't. Professor Reech's best friend is Victor, and I think *he* may be involved in his kidnapping."

"Why do you say that?"

"Because he just lied to me in the car about having a cousin who goes to OCC. He said that right after he got off the phone with someone."

"So what? Maybe it was his girlfriend, and he didn't want you to know what color panties she was wearing."

"Victor? Girlfriend? No."

"Come on, Kyle."

"No, seriously. There's no reason for him to lie like that."

The two talked for some time. Kyle filled Calista in where he could, holding back no information this time.

"*The* Lucinda Garrett was in your apartment"—she emphasized her name, as though even to her, Lucinda Garrett was irresistible—"and you didn't tell me?" she prodded sarcastically.

"It's not like that. She was there to interview me about *diving*. I told you that."

"Yeah, well, you conveniently left out the fact that Lucinda Garrett would be seducing you," she said as she punched him in the arm through the phone.

"Stop it, no she wasn't. Anyway"—he changed the subject as quickly as possible—"I think Victor may have Professor Reech. Or know where he is. You know, he did buy that house recently. Maybe there's something there that could help."

"And you know where the house is, I assume?"

"Holly. I'm gonna go there tomorrow. See if I can find anything."

"You most certainly are not doing that!"

"Cal, I'm doing this. Like I said, Professor Reech is asking for my help. I have to."

A silence overtook their conversation. "God, why am I so smitten by you?" She paused. "I'm coming with you."

"Not a chance, Cal. It's too dangerous."

"Kyle, it isn't me that I'm worried about. And by the way, I'm no damsel. I can handle myself."

Contemplative breathing filled either side of the phone for a few moments, until Kyle broke the silence.

"It doesn't matter what I say. You're coming either way, aren't you?"

"You know me better than I thought."

The two hung up and Kyle heaved a sigh as he pondered potential reasons for Victor's lie. After a while, and with no fruitful epiphanies, he left to grab a bite to eat.

"Here. Read this over for me, would ya? I've been staring at it all night."

It seemed like a repeat of the last night Lucinda and Nick found themselves cooped up in the same office. It wasn't quite as late as last time, but the computers still registered their mark of illumination on the face of their owner.

"Sure," Lucinda said, as she got up from her seat and headed over to Nick's station. "What part?"

She looked at Nick's face, which wore the brand of the stereotypical puppy dog.

"All of it?" Lucinda responded.

"It's only two pages. It'd help me out a lot."

"I'll have a cappuccino." She didn't even look at him as she seated herself and leaned in closer to the monitor. "Medium."

"You got it," Nick said, not missing a beat. He headed over to the office vending machine to retrieve her request.

Lucinda began reading the draft of Nick's story about the governor's sex scandal. She made quick time of it, as Nick knew she would. The story hadn't yet caught too much attention as it was merely an accusation at the time. Nor would it ever. Nick's story detailed the fact that Governor Walker was not even in the same state as the woman during the time frame in which she claimed they were intimate.

The story made her rethink her statement about the governor being scum. She was actually rather impressed with the piece, though she would never admit it to Nick. His head was already bigger than what his neck could support.

"Care if I join ya?" Nick said, as he returned to the desk. He handed her the cappuccino as her payment, and held one of his own in his other hand.

"Oh, please sit, my knight," she said sarcastically.

"Come on, be nice. You didn't think I had it in me, did you?"

"What, a shred of dignity? No, I didn't."

"Ha ha. No, I went out and got some damn good material. You know, Governor Walker's career may just be saved because of my article," he gloated.

"Okay, cue the over-inflated ego."

Nick stood above Lucinda as she sat, and her perfume danced within his nostrils.

"Damn. D'you fall in a vat of perfume this morning, or are you trying to ward off animals?"

Lucinda turned around and stood facing him with an offended look on her face.

"Listen, asshole. If you don't like the smell of it,

don't breathe! Matter of fact, do me a favor and don't."

She never had a problem holding her ground with him, or any man for that matter. She stood confidently in front of him, prepared to not move a muscle until he apologized.

After a moment, their shoulders lost their tension, and they both leaned in and kissed each other as though they were long-lost lovers reunited for the first time in years. The passion for the moment and for each other filled the room of the darkened office, as they became lost in the grasp of each other's explorative hands.

Lucinda's fingers scaled up Nick's back and into his hair. Nick's hands followed her curves down to her hips and he pulled her close.

"You're so beautiful," Nick managed between kisses.

Her fingers dug deeper into Nick's scalp, enticing him to the core. Without notice, her hands left his head and attacked his blazer, casting it to the ground. Nick picked her up and laid her on the ground, and they tumbled together, still locked mouth to mouth.

Before they knew it, Lucinda bared only her bra and skirt, with Nick on top of her, the passion growing with every kiss. Nick's hands were all throughout her hair, and in one motion, he pressed himself tightly against her.

"No. Nick," she said, then kept kissing him. He

didn't argue at all. At her next opportunity for a breath, she continued.

"I can't. I'm a virgin," she said, sitting up as though the admission would be the end to their encounter.

"Who said anything about sex? You read too many 'sex scandal' articles," he said, and then continued kissing her just as passionately as before.

"Wait. That doesn't bother you?"

They were sitting up together now. Lucinda's skin shone as silken as ever.

"Does it bother you?" Nick asked.

"Well, no, of course not."

"Then it doesn't bother me." His statement came with a finality that gave Lucinda butterflies.

The tables had turned. She wasn't familiar with these grounds. She had always been an object to men. So much so that she had learned to deal with it, and most times, use it to her advantage. But Nick, she realized, was far different. She could see he wasn't intimidated by her. She thought deeper and realized he never had been. The man sitting before her had endured so much of her ridicule that she now felt ashamed, even though most of that ridicule was left unspoken. She pondered his last statement, then made a decision; one she'd never thought possible, especially with Nick.

"Do you wanna come back to my place?"

"Only if we can stop and get a movie on our way."

The butterflies crowded her stomach, as though they were made of lead. This could be it, she thought. The man she had waited so long to find might finally be looking her in her eyes, rather than through her clothes.

Kyle pulled into the parking lot at the local grocery store to pick up a quick dinner. It was late, and tonight he was thinking pot pies. The cheap ones were his favorite, and he usually ate four at one time: two turkey, one beef, and one chicken.

He stared into the frozen pantry's frosted glass door for a moment, and after briefly contemplating how many of each flavor pot pie he desired tonight, he opened it, grabbed for the usual, and gently tossed them into his handheld shopping basket, each slapping on top of the other as they landed.

He let the door close that he was holding with his left shoulder and was startled when he saw a man looking at him from the opposite end of the aisle. He didn't recognize the man, but the way he was standing at the edge of the aisle made Kyle uneasy. He was standing still, arms to his sides, looking directly at Kyle. At first, Kyle thought the man was looking at someone behind him, so he turned around to see, and to his surprise, he was the only other shopper in the aisle. Also odd about the man was that he did not appear to be shopping at all—no grocery cart, no basket, no items in his hands, and he was not even looking at the fully stocked shelves to either side of him.

He was simply staring.

The standoff lasted for what seemed about a minute to Kyle, but was actually about five seconds—a good five seconds. Then, without warning, the man slowly disappeared into the next aisle, and out of Kyle's sight.

Again, and as though expecting a different result, Kyle looked over his shoulder behind him to see if someone else had seen the eerie spectacle.

No one.

*Light blue shoelaces?* Kyle thought as he shook his head, realizing just how many strange people there were in this world, and continued shopping, all the while making every effort to only shop in the aisles to the left of where the man had gone after their encounter.

Kyle was already in the pop aisle headed for a 2-liter of Orange Faygo when he realized that the cottage cheese he needed was in the very last aisle, on the opposite side of the store. The side, that is, where the odd man ventured.

With that thought, Kyle felt foolish. He couldn't believe he was even giving some whack-job this much time and space in his mind. *And for what reason?* he thought. This was nothing like the time he had seen a couple dressed entirely in black leather, shopping at this very store.

The woman walked, while the man wore a dog collar and crawled on the ground behind her, as though he was her slave. Or dog. Periodically after passing the couple in the aisle, Kyle heard the faint sound of a dog barking, and couldn't help but wonder if the man-slave was the root of the noise, or if a shopper brought in an actual dog. He remembered laughing at the thought. *What if a shopper did bring their dog into the store? Would the dog bark at the man-slave, or would the man-slave bark at the dog?* He chuckled again as he recalled the experience.

That day, Kyle was the one staring.

He rid the strange man from his mind, and continued to the dairy aisle, found his cottage cheese, and headed for the checkout, not only content with the items in his basket, but also with his surroundings.

"He's just coming to the checkout now," a snarly voice blurted from a two-way radio receiver.

"Good. I don't want him getting home," Victor's voice came back. "And make it quick, Liam. No mistakes, and not so much God-damned blood this time, okay?" he finished.

"The guy had a machete. What'd ya think I was going to do, ask him to put it down nicely? I do this work for you, Victor, and I do it well. If you want someone else, feel free to shop around," Liam shot back.

Kyle Voelner would be Liam's eighth murder victim; the third for his work for Victor. Kyle was just a kid. This would be easy, Liam knew. It would also be easy to keep it clean.

*The man in the cornfield three days ago was a different story. He was a behemoth, and stood toe to toe with Liam for a while before succumbing to the vise-like force of his thumbs pulverizing the man's eyes. The man began to scream and grab for his eyes immediately after Liam had poked at them, but his hands landed on nothing, just empty sockets. He staggered in panic, the machete no longer in his hand. Liam, feeding off the rush of the battle with the man, retrieved the machete from the ground, held it above his head, and came down with the might of a samurai, lobbing off the farmer's right arm at the shoulder, in much the same fashion as a grizzly bear lazily clears the dead twigs from a thicket before lying down. Afterward, the man became wild with fear. Liam could almost hear the frantic man's heart throbbing from within his chest. Liam then coiled his body, holding the machete like a baseball bat, and swung at the man's left thigh. The blade made easy work of the largest bone in the human body, and lodged half-way through the other leg before coming to a stop. The man was brought to the ground from his weight resting on the leg that was no longer attached to his body. He was no longer screaming. He was crying.*

*"How are you crying with no eyes?" Liam laughed, still charged with adrenaline. "Here, let me help ya." Liam didn't even realize he said the words as he climbed on to the writhing man's torso.*

*"No!" the farmer pled.*

*But Liam had already reinserted his thumbs into the holes where the man's eyes once saw the world, and began scratching at his brain that resided not too far behind and above their sockets.*

Liam saw Kyle exit the grocery store from the seat of his car. He had only been waiting for about six minutes for his prey to leave the store, and emerge back into the wild. This would really be easy, Liam thought. Like a cheetah chasing a wounded wildebeest. Kyle reached his car, got inside, and began driving off, like any other evening. He was oblivious to his looming doom, the autumn night setting in, swiftly blanketing the sun's rays from having any luminous effect on the world around him. Once he turned onto the main road, Kyle opened the 2-liter and took a long, labored chug that became audible as the carbonation burned his esophagus. He exhaled hard and loud to quell the burn.

Kyle lived about a five-minute drive from the store, and was located off one of the many side roads that periodically extended from the main road, like capillaries branching off the artery to which they were connected.

As he steered into a curve, he realized that the vehicle behind him was progressively getting closer, its high-beams blinding Kyle.

"Asshole," Kyle said out loud, soon realizing it was a truck from the roof-mounted headlights. "Jesus, man! What the fuck?" Kyle yelled as he felt the jarring tap of the truck against Kyle's rear bumper. Rubber began to screech as Kyle regained control of his car, his blood racing through his arteries, fueled by adrenaline and fear.

His mind raced, pondering his options. He considered slowing down to let him pass. No. This guy was not interested in passing. He thought about turning into a random house, as though it was his own, hoping the man would continue on his way. No. He'd be trapped if he did that. Then, he made his decision. Speed up, and try to lose him. If he got far enough ahead of him, he could turn onto a side road and turn off his lights, disappearing into the night. *Sure*, he thought. *That's feasible. My car is faster than a truck, and is definitely more maneuverable.*

Kyle stomped on the gas pedal, and his car chugged down a big swig of gas, modeling the way Kyle recently slurped down his pop that was now rolling around on the floor of the passenger side. He came to an S-curve and sped through it, cheating into the opposite lane to minimize how much he had to turn his wheel. His dashboard read 80 miles per hour. Amidst everything, Kyle felt for a brief moment that he was a NASCAR driver, riding high on the straightaway and dipping low into each curve. He could feel the g-forces pulling at his body. The adrenaline grew with each slowing curve, and speeding straightaway. He looked in his rearview mirror, and saw the lights falling behind as he reached 95 miles per hour. A small smile grew on his face, in acknowledgement of his pending victory.

He continued speeding through the night, putting distance between him and the truck in pursuit, and soon came to the realization that in the middle of the next S-curve, he could turn onto a side road, and quickly turn off his lights. Before the man behind him caught on, he would have already passed him, thinking that he was already beyond the second curve. Only when the driver couldn't see Kyle's taillights would he even think to slow down, let alone turn around.

Kyle turned onto a side road, and shut his lights off.

Five seconds passed. Then five more.

Then, without warning, Kyle's heart jumped from his chest as he saw a set of high-beams turn onto the same road he was on, and shined on a distant yellow sign that Kyle had no trouble reading.

It read, DEAD END.

With his mind now on auto-pilot, Kyle grabbed for anything in the car that could identify him—his wallet, dead cell phone, and backpack—and ran into an adjacent cornfield, disappearing into its sea of stalks.

He ran for about five seconds straight in, then turned left, and ran against the grain for another ten seconds. He slowed to a gingerly pace as he stepped across a few more rows, making sure not to disturb the stalks in an attempt to mask his trail.

What prompted him to take such precaution was an episode of *CSI* he recently saw, where the suspect was on the run from the police. The suspect was able to elude four officers and held up in his hiding spot for an additional hour. Eventually, though, the suspect was caught. Kyle never thought about the "getting caught" part when he decided to retreat into the cornfield.

He stopped, and could hear the gravel being thrown from the screeching wheels of the truck as they came to an abrupt stop. Kyle panted for a moment to catch his breath. He was in great shape, but the adrenaline, mixed with fear, was taking a toll on his breathing pattern. He held his breath after one last big gulp of air, and listened.

He heard no running, as he thought he would. There was no speaking to help identify his pursuer's location.

Kyle panicked. Was the man at his car, investigating what he could to learn more about him? His mind reeled as his brain fought to remember what the car looked like before he got out and ran.

Kyle knew a friend who had a photographic

memory in high school. That same friend always seemed to get perfect scores on tests, as all of his notes were captured in his mind to be developed at a later date, and upon his need for the information. Kyle had put his friend Kevin through various tests to see if it was true. Even a person's best friend is often the biggest skeptic. This was true for Kyle and Kevin, until Kevin was able to rename every single card in a deck that Kyle had just shuffled and displayed for his friend briefly, one by one. Afterward, Kyle was a believer, and painstakingly tried to develop the same ability as his friend—or skill as Kyle saw it. He believed that if someone was born with an ability, that ability could also be learned, attributing that belief to the vast power of the human brain. Through the remaining years of high school, Kyle's memory got sharper. More crisp. His rate of recollection grew with every test he put himself through. Growing with it was his confidence to tackle more complex memory tests. The one test he'd never put himself through, however, was recalling visual information while under great stress, such as his current predicament.

His mind's camera was grainy, and slower to develop. Only snippets of the overall picture were coming to him. The steering column. The DEAD END sign. The car's exterior.

*No!* Kyle thought. *Inside the car.* He redirected his

mind back into the car once again.

The picture was clearer now, but still underdeveloped. The upholstery now appeared in his mind. Then, the clock: 10:23 pm. He made note of that, and discarded both images, his closed eyes squinting to focus his mind even sharper.

Just then, the photo developed in full. Kyle could see everything now. The seatbelts, the heat vents, door handles, his own legs in the driver's seat.

He turned his head, as though it would help pan the interior of the car, and more images shot in front of him: the car mat, the 2-liter bottle of pop, a white piece of paper on the passenger floor.

His blood seemed to melt the veins that housed it as the fear amplified in his body.

The receipt. Another image shone on the rear of his eyelids. He saw himself take the receipt from the cashier and briefly look at it. And at the point where the receipt was closest to his face, the image seemed to pause. He paid with his debit card, and his full name was clearly displayed on the receipt. His closed eyelids clenched as the realization set in.

Then, he heard soft footsteps to his left, and the images vanished into the night as his eyes shot open.

Frank sat at the computer, lost in thought as he pondered the information in the file. The screen had gone black about ten minutes after he initially sat back down in front of the computer following the scuffle with Audrey. That was over five hours ago, and Frank hadn't moved. He was out of options. The Voice was counting on him to find this file. If only it were as simple as finding the file. Now, he had to make sense out of the seemingly nonsensical data residing within it. Aware that his paycheck, and maybe even his life, depended on what was in this file, he reentered the passphrase and once again saw the contents of the file he'd spent so much time trying to access. He felt like he was back at square one.

He forced his eyes to grow wide with focus as he scoured the screen yet again. But nothing had changed since first laying eyes upon it. It was a spreadsheet, as he expected from the file's name, with a dozen or so tabs at the bottom. Each appeared to be the abbreviation of a state. He saw tabs like "Nev.," "Minn.," "Tenn.," "Mich.," and "Cal." among many others of the same format. He clicked through several of them, but all he saw were numbers and different colored cells.

Countless columns and rows of numbers.

He clicked on a cell in the "Mich." tab. There was a random number formula. He clicked on another. Then another. The same random formula.

*They're all random*, he thought, as he massaged his jaw from the recent blow from the piece of granite heaved by Audrey. *What does that mean?* He clicked on other tabs to see if the same remained true. It did.

"Dammit," Frank said, the words escaping his mouth, protesting the fact that he was no further ahead now than when he began trying to hack into the file in the first place.

He explored his Excel Savvy for a moment, and then attempted a variety of queries to try to make sense of what was on his screen. As he was doing this, Don came back into the room.

"So I got into the file."

"And?"

"And nothing. I'm working on it."

"Well, what is it?"

Frank pondered for a moment before answering.

"I think it's coded."

"What do you mean?"

"Well, why would this guy go to all the trouble of hiding and protecting this file, if all it contained were randbetween formulas?"

"Randbe-what?"

Frank shook his head, waving off the question. "There's something in here, but it can't have anything to do with these numbers."

"How do you know?"

"Uh, because I know how formulas work." He calmed himself, then continued. "The numbers will change every time the file is opened, so they can't mean anything. There's no consistency. Not even predictability."

"So what does that mean?"

"It means there's something else in this file that I'm not seeing yet. I'll figure it out. By the way, where's the girl?"

"Trunk. Still out cold. I'm gonna drive it to Howell, put her in the van then head back to the house. Gonna be tough keepin' two people apart in the same place."

Frank didn't respond. He was in obvious thought.

"Hmmm, 'two.' What did that letter say that was addressed to Jacob? Ya know, the one from his house?"

"Something about Franklin and Noah."

"Yeah, dammit, what was it?"

The two thought about it for a moment until Frank remembered what it said.

"Noah will help," he said, charged with new excitement. "Holy shit, that's it!"

Frank directed his attention back to the computer screen, and with a few clicks that Don was unable to follow, something profound materialized on the screen.

"Ta-da!" Frank looked at Don, who was dumbfounded, but at the same time awestruck. Seeing Don's confusion, Frank elaborated on his brilliance. "What did Noah board?"

"The ark."

"Right, the ark. As in Arkansas. And how did the animals board?"

"Is that the 'two by two' you're looking for?"

"You got it! Two pixels by two pixels."

On the screen, the file appeared scrunched, like it was an aerial photo of harvesting fields taken at twenty thousand feet. Something as clear as day screamed from the zoomed-out page. The colored cells. In particular, the dark blue ones, which formed a message that both Frank and Don could read without hesitation.

The figures 38 8 43 N and 88 2 34 W appeared on the screen.

"Those are coordinates," Don said, feeling smart.

"Bingo."

Don paused. "Call The Voice. The Movement is about to begin."

Kyle's eyes were wide with fear. He held his breath, fearing his assailant would hear him exhale or see his breath in the cooled air the evening offered.

Another footstep.

Kyle's hands turned to fists, readying himself for a fight. Before he could hear another footstep, he heard a button click, then click again.

*Shit!* he thought. *He's got a flashlight!*

The man stopped pressing the button and shook the flashlight a few times to jar the batteries. The shaking created a loud clacking noise, and offered Kyle the much-needed opportunity to better conceal himself from the coming light.

Under the blanket of the noise, Kyle dropped to the ground and located a patch of high grass. He realized he was practically at the edge of the field, but decided to hunker behind the grass, not having the time to weigh his options to run or hide, against one another.

He heard the button click once more, and a beam of light slalomed through the stalks of corn.

Kyle could almost feel the heat of the beam spilling onto his back. He watched in horror as the light panned the field—first left, then back toward Kyle's location. The beam was bright. He was close.

Another footstep.

Kyle couldn't determine if the steps were getting closer to him or not, but knew he could not stay in his current location for too much longer.

More footsteps.

He picked up his head just enough to look over his shoulder, and saw that the beam of light was trained in the opposite direction, and the man was slowly walking away from him. He exhaled for the first time in what seemed an eternity, finding some comfort in the growing distance between him and the other man. After a moment, he turned his body to face the man, whose flashlight continued to shrink into the field. As he turned, his leg snapped a twig on the ground.

*Fuck!* he cursed himself and held perfectly still yet again. The beam of light stopped moving.

Kyle slunk down just as before. His heart beating even faster this time.

Without notice the beam spun around and shone in his direction, followed by the sound of stalks breaking.

*He saw me!* The reality plagued his mind, and his only option left was to run.

He jumped up and sprinted out of the cornfield; the other man lumbered behind him.

Kyle exited the field and raced toward his car. He

never looked back, but kept watch of the beam of light erratically dancing on the ground out in front of him. For the only time in his life, Kyle's own shadow scared him as it sprawled out before him on the gravel of the road.

Before long, he was at his car, and fumbled briefly for his keys that brought the car back to life. As he stomped the accelerator, he felt the man grab at the hood of his car as he sped back in reverse toward the main road. Unable to hold on, the man charged to his truck and got inside.

Kyle's only thought was to get to a place with people. He looked down at the speedometer. 67 miles per hour on windy roads. His car's suspension ached from the force of each swerve as he neared his destination. A liquor store about a mile ahead. The lights in his rearview were still present, but growing smaller with each straightaway on Grange Hall Road. Thirty seconds later, he pulled into the parking lot of the party store, leapt from his car, which he left running, and raced for the entrance.

The radio blared to life yet again, and The Voice came through the receiver.

"This better be good."

"I got into the file. They were coordinates."

"Perfect. The Movement is upon us," The Voice said. Have the others been notified?"

"Don knows, but Liam is taking care of that kid. Said he'd radio us when all is done."

"Where do the coordinates point?"

"I haven't looked up their exact location yet, but I'll have it soon. Call ya back when I know."

"I'll get our passports in order in case it's international."

"Yeah, just by looking at the numbers, I'd have no idea how to even guess, but I'll have it for you in no time."

"Good. Quickly. We cannot waste any more time. As soon as you know the location, call me." The Voice paused for a moment, then continued. "And the girl?"

"With Don. He's driving her to you now," Frank said, his voice sounding odd. "I think that bitch broke my jaw."

"We may have only cleared the first hurdle. She needs to remain the carrot at the end of Jacob's stick."

Kyle ran through the door of the party store and immediately yelled for someone.

"Help! Please! Someone's after me," he said breathlessly.

No response. There wasn't even a clerk at the counter. Reality rushed back into his frontal lobe, the notion of fight-or-flight throbbing behind his eyelids. In a rush of pure adrenaline, he haphazardly began to pick and choose among seemingly meaningless items. Instinctively, his hands landed on a hammer. Good. A weapon if he needed one and a box of black industrial garbage bags. His mind was on auto-pilot, operating in survival mode, his brain not yet reasoning with him as to why he chose the items.

Kyle took the items and sped toward the door, their potential for use now oozing into his mind.

"Hey! You gotta pay for those!" a voice exclaimed. The sound rang in his preoccupied ears, but was muffled, and distant. Alien.

He sprinted out the door to his awaiting car. The headlights of the truck glared into his soul from the parking lot just before he reentered his car. A moment later, the truck smashed into the back of Kyle's car, jarring him forward. He slammed the gas pedal and his tires threw gravel back as he escaped the pressure of the truck pushing on his bumper. Once again, he entered the road. This time, however, he nearly lost control as the truck collided with his car. He felt his car heave, but countered the pending spin with the steering wheel. An action that he found pleasure in during the winter in empty parking lots with friends, but not at all right now.

Once back on the road, he looked back and saw the clerk leaning out the door with a phone in his hands. *Good, he's calling the police*, Kyle thought as he continued past a cemetery and down a slope by Patterson. Moments later, a light in his car caught his attention. Investigating it, Kyle's throat filled with nausea as he looked at a blinking gas gauge on his dashboard.

"Damn it!" he yelled as he sped off, not knowing how far he could get, or more importantly, how far he needed to get in order to once again elude the man.

Kyle knew the area, and realized he had to come up with a plan fast, and lose this guy. Maybe the main roads weren't the best bet. Maybe, he thought, it would be best to lose him on the side streets first.

Moments later down the road Kyle sped through a yellow light. A few seconds later Liam ran through the now red light, nearly causing an accident, his car bouncing awkwardly as it chugged through a dip in the intersection.

Liam trailed closely behind Kyle's car as they both swerved in and out of curves and over railroad tracks.

Although Kyle's car was clearly faster than Liam's truck, Liam was by far a more aggressive and experienced driver. Especially in situations such as this one.

Kyle gripped the wheel and turned hard onto Fagan, followed by an immediate left onto Quick—a dirt road that led to a better arterial road. He did his best to avoid the potholes, but the road was scarred with severe ruts. Some were impossible to avoid. As he sped over them, his car bounced, often bottoming out. After one pothole in particular, his head smashed into his visor. He looked into the mirror and saw the headlights still behind him. Soon after, he arrived at the intersection, and turned right onto North Holly Road. He sped off, the gravel throwing itself from the tread in the tires as he pushed the car to its limits on the pavement.

After a few more S-curves, Kyle sped down the straightaway, putting distance between him and the truck yet again. He looked at his gas gauge. It was almost below the first hash mark. He needed to get away from Liam before he ran out of gas. He stomped every last millimeter out of the gas pedal and looked in the rearview to see the truck still behind him in pursuit. He could see the stop light at Baldwin Road about a half mile farther ahead.

Liam gripped his steering wheel, as his truck bore down on the doomed wildebeest. He was calm, and had been in several car chases in his life. Sometimes fleeing, others chasing. He looked to his passenger seat and saw a .44-caliber handgun that he would use on Kyle tonight. He wondered if it would be a clean shot, or if he would simply wound Kyle first, only to finish him off moments later.

Liam looked back at the road and saw Kyle's brake lights pierce the evening air. Then, his car began fishtailing awkwardly. Liam squinted to make sense of what was happening an eighth of a mile in front of him. He watched as Kyle's car began pitching erratically back and forth, then suddenly careened out of control and off the elevated road. He watched in astonishment as Kyle's car soared through the air, out into a roadside pond just down the steep slope beyond the shoulder of the road.

Liam pulled his car into a service drive adjacent to the pond and watched as the young man's car disappeared into the dark water that mirrored the color of the evening fall sky. The scarlet taillights of the car dimmed as it sank farther and farther to the bottom of the deep pond. He watched as exuberant bubbles raced to the surface, exploding with foam as they were each released into the evening air, Liam's gun held at the ready and trained on each burst of bubbles that reached the surface. To his surprise, however, no bubbles were followed by Kyle's head popping out of the water, gasping for precious air.

He waited longer. Still nothing. Even the bubbles eventually stopped, and perfect silence enveloped the pond once again, as though it were a satisfied monster slumbering after a big meal.

Liam checked his watch. Twenty minutes had passed. No sounds, nor discernible movements from the perimeter of the pond. He began wondering if Kyle had been knocked unconscious from the force of the impact. Liam had faced this situation before, but had never left until verifying his prey was in fact dead. If he radioed back, he needed to be damn sure Kyle was dead.

He waited even longer, visualizing what he would do if he were trapped underwater. Maybe there was a large air pocket in the car that allowed Kyle to breathe. That air, too, would run out soon.

He looked at his watch once again. Twenty-five minutes had now elapsed.

*I'll give it to thirty*, Liam thought as he allowed his mind to land on a number before calling it in.

Thirty minutes came, and still no bubbles or movement had surfaced since minute number fifteen. Kyle's body was forever lost at the bottom of the pond, his car serving as his tomb, the black pond as his eternal crypt.

Kyle's body floated lifelessly in the driver's seat of his car as it plummeted deeper into the water. A diluted cloud of blood hovered above his head, inter-mixing with his wavy hair before dissipating into the pond water.

As the car reached the bottom of the pond, the impact jarred Kyle's body, but otherwise remained motionless.

A moment later his body sprang to life as though it were convulsing; the one working headlight reflect-ing off the bottom offered the only light. He oriented himself for a moment and then swiftly swam out of the window and to the front of the car and held his hand in front of the headlight for several seconds. Immediately following, he looked at his watch to assure its glow fea-ture had been sufficiently charged. Satisfied, he swam back into the car.

He had been holding his breath for almost a min-ute and a half.

His impromptu plan was dangerous, but his brain knew that if this guy caught him he would be dead for sure. The decision to crash in water was made without hesitation, the will to live taking full control.

Once back in the sunken car, Kyle maneuvered to the backseat and grabbed a duffel bag and twine that he had purchased to help his mother tie back some of her tomato plants the previous week.

He had been holding his breath for only two minutes, but the energy exerted during the crash elevated his heart rate, forcing his body to devour the oxygen in his lungs much faster than normal. He needed to open that duffel bag.

Blindly unzipping it, his hand quickly found a small cylinder similar to that of a kitchen fire extinguisher. A personal breathing apparatus, or PBA as Kyle knew them.

Part of his diving practice was built around getting used to the drastic change in temperature experienced deep underwater, and to effectively calm the nerves, rather than simply holding his breath for as long as possible. To do that, the team used rechargeable PBA's to stay underwater for extended periods of time. Each cylinder held enough oxygen for eight full breaths. At least that was how many Kyle could get from one cylinder.

Quickly doing the math, he had enough air for about 25 minutes. More if he could slow his heart rate. Less, if not.

*Thank you, Mr. Cowen*, he thought as he realized the PBA might just save his life.

Two minutes thirty seconds without air, and Kyle noticed the headlight was fading.

Kyle's muscles were starting to ache as they became more deprived of oxygen. He needed more air—fast. His hands hurried to open the box of garbage bags. Fumbling a few times, he finally retrieved one and exhaled into it, effectively capturing the air from within his lungs, and he immediately took his first breath from the PBA, started the stopwatch on his Tag Heuer 500M Aquaracer, and tied the opening of the garbage bag shut. With new air and relieved nerves, he pulled a length of twine and tied the loose end to the door handle of the car, letting the bag drift upward about two feet. He held it for a moment to check the integrity of his knots, then focused on slowing his heart rate in almost pitch blackness.

He checked his watch. One minute and fifteen seconds had elapsed since his first artificial breath, and with the headlight out, he could see dim beams of light emanating across the surface of the water from Liam's car that was still parked at the top of the pond's steep bank.

*Chapter 37 — September 17, 10:52 P.M.*

"I got the location!" Frank's voice screamed through the receiver. It sounded excited, but a trace of the recent trauma to his jaw could still be heard. "Southern Illinois. If we leave now, we can be there in seven hours."

"No. We leave in the morning. There's something I need to do before we go," The Voice said. It too sounded excited, but The Voice was able to hide it much better than Frank. The Voice knew Frank was naive to think he would even be given a small portion of the diamonds for his work. The Voice had his own agenda.

"No problem. How about Don?" Frank abided.

"He's here with me. Got the girl in the basement. Liam's on his way back. Just radioed." He paused. "The kid's dead."

"Well, that's one off our list. What are you gonna do with Reech and his girl when we're done?"

"The girl's seen your face, right?"

"Right."

"That's not good. So, it's either her or you and Don."

"You don't have to tell me twice. Just say the word."

"Once we have the diamond, we'll get rid of her.

Just be at the parking garage tomorrow morning so we can transfer everything to the van. Then we'll all head out together."

The Voice had no intention of keeping either Frank or Don around after he had the diamonds in his possession. In fact, a part of him looked forward to killing them. But he knew he needed to remain patient, even though the sight of either of the foul men disgusted him to no end.

"Golden Dragon?!" a thick Asian voice yelled.

"Seven egg rolls with mustard to go, please," came the order from a man over the phone.

"You want shrimp, chicken, or cabbage?"

"Chicken."

"Okay. Ten minute," the Asian voice replied, and then hung up.

The phone hung up and the man continued preparing for another heist, his alibi the same as always.

*Chapter 38 — September 17, 10:54 P.M.*

A pair of eyes looked on as a man left his house headed back to work. Brent Haley worked at the local big box hardware store and had the late shift tonight. He likely wouldn't get home until after one. The store was less than a mile from his house. He probably came home for a quick smoke on his last break of the night.

Perfect. The disease had been festering, raging within the man looking on, ready to gorge. The poor soul, now taking a bite from his apple, had no idea his house was about to be burgled.

The man in the bushes shook his head hard to each side as he tried to rid his mind of the memory of the man he'd killed a few days ago. The thought plagued his psyche; the disease did not feed on death, but rather writhed and purged the thoughts of the foul act. Time would prove to be the burglar's friend and foe at the same time, like the proverbial angel and demon on either shoulder. He knew time would help to heal the mark his soul now bore, but *that* time, he feared, would not come soon enough.

His head pounded of guilt laced with adrenaline from the heist this night would soon offer. He let out a weighted sigh, picked up his duffel bag from the ground, and watched as Brent Haley's car drove down the road and out of sight.

As he walked to the back side of the house, his mind fought with his body to turn back. The possible threat of another confrontation was something he simply could not face, but his body kept moving forward. Maybe he wanted to get caught. The years of lying and lost sleep were catching up to him, the murder an awful side-effect of his sickening disease.

He compromised. His mind lost the overall war, but won a small battle knowing that this would be quick. One item was all his mind would allow his body to take. The internal compromise fed the body's urge to steal, while assuring it there would be no chance to binge this night.

He entered the garage through a side door and picked the entry door to the house. It was even easier than most; he didn't have to worry about being quiet or clumsy. His movement and sound was entirely entombed within the garage. Before long, he was in the house, the unleveled door to the garage slowly closing itself.

And then he saw it. The one item. His mind joyous at the sight, knowing this would in fact be the quickest heist yet. He approached it without hesitation, grabbed it, and exited through the door he had entered only five seconds earlier. The door had not even had a chance to close. He relocked it behind him and went back into the garage.

The burglar felt satisfied. The one item was securely in tow, and there was no confrontation. He was almost into the bushes when a terrifying thought crossed his mind.

The duffel bag! He'd left it in the house, his lock pick nestled neatly in the bottom of it.

*Oh my God, no! What have you done?* he thought as he looked back at the house.

Without thinking, he raced back into the garage and frantically searched for a spare key.

He looked above the trim of the door, under shoes, and behind shelves.

Nothing.

Panic began to radiate from his veins pumping almost as hard as when he'd killed the man in the other house. He checked more.

*It has to be here!*

His eyes landed on pegs jutting out from a workbench. Nothing. Then they scurried to the track of the garage door. Still no luck. He moved his attention to a rusty grill in the opposite corner of the two-car garage. It caught his attention because right next to it was a shiny one that was obviously the one from which the owner cooked. The rusty one did not even have a propane tank connected to it.

He stormed over to it and began exploring. He lifted the cover, nothing, then he checked the hooks from which grilling utensils would hang. Nothing. He dropped to his hands and knees and checked under the unit, then behind it.

The thought of breaking the door down crossed his wary mind, but he dismissed it quickly.

*Not yet. Time is still on my side.* The thought eased his mind a bit, both for his current situation, and also for the time needed to forget about the man he'd murdered.

He stood straight up and calmed himself as he methodically scoured the garage with his eyes. His gaze turned upward as he saw a light flicker in his periphery. There they were: two fluorescent light fixtures hanging from the ceiling. The fixtures had flat tops that looked ideal for hiding a spare key. He went to another corner and retrieved a ladder, placed it below the fixtures, and climbed up only to see that the tops were barren of anything but dust.

Frustrated, he looked at the garage yet again, but this time he did so from the elevation of the ladder. A new perspective might offer a solution. Nothing new shot into his mind as he descended the ladder. Once down, he realized there was a rug resting beneath about a dozen pairs of shoes that he'd neglected to look under while sifting through the shoes in his initial panic-driven frenzy. He lifted it.

"Dammit!" he said out loud, cursing his bad luck. Then he shot up from his crouched position, turned around, and stared at the rusty grill he so recently searched. One of his eyebrows shot up his forehead as a smirk crept onto his face and a new thought filled his mind.

He walked over to it once again, and without missing a step, reached under it and shook the drip catcher. He heard something metallic clang around inside. He bent down, and looked behind the grill to disengage the tin can from its hook, and tipped it over.

A key tumbled out.

*Finally! Thank God!*

He went back into the house and found his duffel bag. He opened it, and realized he had also forgotten about the print bombs, again cursing himself for his clumsiness tonight.

The disease had progressed profoundly, and in doing so was rendering the aging body and mind of its host nearly useless to continue. He wondered what his life would look like if he could no longer steal. The thought almost made him vomit with fear and disgust for even entertaining such a foul idea.

He placed only two print bombs in the house this time, as he'd only touched the door and never went beyond the kitchen.

After he plugged them into sockets, he grabbed his bag, double-checked everything, and left the house for the second time in what seemed an eternity.

He sped home this time, happier to be there than with previous jobs. He looked at the item he stole and knew that it was nowhere near the value of other catalogued items in the room. But either way, he was relieved to now be the owner of it.

He trudged upstairs and got into bed. His eyes remained open for a time as his mind decompressed. As they began to blink slower and slower, he grew more frustrated with himself, wishing he had taken more from the house.

He was addicted to stealing. And as the kleptomaniac closed his eyes for the last time this night, he wondered if his days of thievery were numbered.

Patrick O'Reilly stood on the shores of Lake Huron taking in the cool breeze of a fall day. His arms spread wide, and he let the unpolluted life fill his lungs. His eyes panned the open water back and forth until he spotted a barge nearly lost in a mirage at the edge of the horizon. He saw a shadow cast on the beach from behind him and turned around only to see a naked woman standing before him. He hugged her.

The two turned back to the water, and the barge that just a moment ago was miles offshore now rested on the sands of the beach, shipwrecked. Its horn blew three times in succession.

Detective O'Reilly, shaken from his dream, picked up his department-issued phone on the third set of successive rings.

"God damn it! Can't I just get a night's sleep?" Patrick blared through the phone.

"Sorry, Detective, but our burglar slash murderer is at it again," a man said. His tone sounded frustrated, mirroring that of the detective's.

"Any prints this time? Did he kill someone else?" he grumbled, still waking up.

"No, and no," the deputy responded without

missing a beat, as though he knew the questions were coming. He gritted his teeth. *Come on, Detective! Give me a chance to fill you in before you start asking questions.* The deputy could have taken two more minutes to answer the questions that he knew would soon ring in his ear. But, alas, he decided to err on the side of proper phone-based conversational etiquette. Back and forth, back and forth. Like a game of tennis. *Oh well. It is what it is.*

"You sure it's the same guy?" he asked, almost hearing the answer before it was even spoken.

"Affirmative. I haven't checked everywhere yet, but I can't find one print so far, just like the last one. And, there were more Glade Plug-Ins, again, just like the last one," he said quite rapidly. *There. How's that for detail, Detective? I'll take that promotion anytime now, thank you very much.*

Patrick sat up in bed as he pondered the lack of prints again. This guy was good, he knew. His method alone was stumping an entire department. "Where this time?"

"Corner of Steubens and Carpenter." *Wait for it. Wait for it.*

"Shit, really? That's three blocks from my house." His voice was crowded with concern.

"Thus, the early morning call." *Ah, that felt good.*

"Don't touch anything. I'll be there in five," he said

as he threw the covers to the side.

"You got it," the deputy affirmed. An appeased smirk grew on his face as he placed his cell phone back in its belt-mounted case.

The detective rose from his bed, threw on some clothes, and headed down the stairs to his kitchen.

Patrick couldn't tell if it was very late, or extremely early. He checked his phone as he grabbed a couple protein bars from his cupboard and a bottle of water from the refrigerator. With rations in hand, he walked out the door to his cruiser.

The car roared to life and before he was even up to speed, he arrived at the corner of Steubens and Carpenter. Only one other cruiser was there.

"What took you so long?" Officer Warren joked.

"I was in the middle of a dream. A damn good one, too." A bit of the grumble found its way back into his voice.

"Guy who lives here says, get this, all that's missing is the rug in his kitchen." The frustration still resounded in his voice, but now it was directed at something different than a promotion. *All this effort for a lousy rug. At this hour? Come on.*

"Are you serious?"

*Back.*

"Wish I wasn't, Detective."

*Forth.*

"Where is he?"

*Back.*

"On his couch, watchin' TV."

*Forth.*

The two officers walked up the driveway and into the house. Just as the officer said, a young man, appearing to be less than 30 years old, sat on his couch watching TV as though nothing happened.

"'Scuse me, sir?" Detective O'Reilly opened as politely as possible as the sun continued to sleep below the horizon.

"Call me Brent," the man said.

Officer Warren couldn't help thinking that his voice sounded like a frat boy. *No, wait. A surfer.*

"You bet. Mind filling me in on what happened tonight?" Detective O'Reilly continued.

"Yeah, um, I got outta work early, and uh, ya know, came right home. No big deal, right? So yeah, I make dinner, catch the news, and head to bed."

*Or was it a stoner? Too soon to tell for sure.*

"Okay," O'Reilly said, nearly following the statement with "*get to the point!*"

"Yeah, so I'm layin' there, and I realize when, uh, I made dinner I was standin' right on my hardwoods. So, I blitzed downstairs to see if I'm crazy, and boom, my damn rug's gone."

*Nope, meathead. Definitely a meathead.*

"Interesting. And that's all that's gone?"

"After I called you guys, I searched this place high and low. He didn't take anything else."

"Did the rug in your kitchen match the other one?" O'Reilly pointed to another, much larger rug under the dinner table.

"Yup. Bought 'em at the same time."

The detective looked at the remaining rug. It didn't appear to have ever been cleaned or vacuumed. Then, he looked at the rest of the house, which was also consumed by discarded debris.

"You don't clean much do you, Brent?"

"Excuse me?"

"I don't mean to be rude, but if you could bear with me for a second I'd appreciate it." He paused to let his quasi-apology sink into the meat grinder of a brain the man seemed to have. "You have any candles or potpourri in the house?"

"No, why?"

"So I guess it's safe to say that those Glade Plug-Ins were not here when you left for work yesterday afternoon?" He pointed to two Plug-Ins located in the kitchen.

"Oh, man. Woah, I didn't even see those there. No, I didn't buy 'em."

*Seventy-thirty ground chuck. At best.*

"Thank you for clarifying, Brent. Excuse us for a

quick moment," Detective O'Reilly said as he made eye contact with Deputy Warren. He raised his eyebrows, saying "tell me about it" without actually saying the words. The two could have been having a telepathic conversation about Mr. Couch Potato and he would have been none the wiser.

The two officers strolled to the other side of the kitchen and began talking in a quieted tone.

"Write up the report, and bring those Plug-Ins back to the station with ya. This guy is probably just a petty thief who got caught up in a job that went bad. What I'm most interested in is the fact that he developed a way to get rid of fingerprints. Can you believe the tool that would prove to be if it were *really* in the wrong hands?"

"I can only imagine." Deputy Warren's hand had found its way to his chin as he listened intently to his boss.

"I need you to track the purchases of Glade Plug-Ins. This model in particular. If we can find where he's been buying 'em, maybe we can catch him on a store camera."

"Consider it done. Go home, and finish that dream you were havin'."

*A firm backhand by Warren right to O'Reilly.*
"Will do."
*O'Reilly follows with a formidable forehand.*

"Just don't tell me about it tomorrow."

*Warren rockets another backhanded missile down the lane.*

The detective chuckled. "Hey, Warren? Great job on this one. You could damn near do this yourself." He meant it too. In part because Warren was an asset to the department, but also because he knew the time was nearing for him to retire. He hadn't told anyone, but needed to make sure that someone capable could fill his position when he left. Detective O'Reilly was becoming more and more confident that Deputy Warren would be that man.

Chad Warren held an ear-to-ear grin at bay after hearing the detective say the words. He'd waited a long time to hear them, and lifted his Styrofoam coffee cup in acknowledgement, as Detective O'Reilly got into his car.

"That's my job."

*Game, set, match. What a spectacle, folks.*

Detective O'Reilly hung on Deputy Warren's last few words. He did want to get home and finish that dream. But what he didn't know was that he wouldn't be able to sleep when he got back home. His brain would throb as he wondered if the petty-thief-turned-murderer would ever be caught.

A weakened hand rose to a plain wooden door. The paint job was all but creative: a mundane taupe. But, nonetheless, it was as effective as paint could be—merely aesthetic. It was shiny in certain areas, but it couldn't be determined whether the glossy smudges were in fact from the sheen of the paint, or the oil from the toll of countless hands knocking on it over time. Either way, it had endured over the years.

The hand fell on the door, frailer than a seeded dandelion held to a box fan. It struggled to steady its owner as the other began pounding feverishly on the door. Or so the owner thought. The sound of the knock resembled a pin dropping during an earthquake. It was impossibly quiet. No one would hear it.

Calista watched TV in silence on her couch. A bag of party snack mix lay beside her, her hand ever moving from bag to mouth, like a backhoe endlessly mining for precious material. She tossed a handful in her mouth, allowing her teeth to pulverize the chunks in an attempt to extract a rare gem from the quarry.

*Oh, there's one. A cashew.*

In mid-chew, her eyes strayed from the screen, growing concerned as she turned off the power to the excavator and listened. *What was that?* She paused the movie, and listened more keenly. Nothing. Silence. *Wait! There. I'm not crazy.*

She wiped the bucket of her excavator clean of a clear and coarse residue. Its presence in the quarry was ubiquitous. Alone, however, it was worthless, but once in a while, she would hit pay dirt and mine an oblong orb with an abundant and nearly sparkling coat of sodium chloride crystals. The rarest and most valuable of all gems.

She got up and went to the door, peering through its peephole. Nothing. Just as she began pulling her eye away from the hole, a solitary foot wearing a Samba Classic came into view at her doorstep. *I know that shoe.* She opened the door in a panic.

"Oh my God! Kyle!"

"They think I'm dead," he moaned.

"That's it, I'm calling the police."

The frail hand, with more vigor now, grabbed her ankle.

"I didn't just walk two miles for you to call the police." He heaved an exhausted breath as he clamored to his feet with her assistance.

Calista took him by his arm and helped remove his wet clothes.

"What the hell happened? Are you okay?"

"I'm fine. Just cold." He paused. "I've been colder."

"How'd you get so wet?"

"Dumped my car in the pond off North Holly just before Baldwin."

"You what? How?" She paused. "Kyle?"

"Some asshole was after me. He was trying to kill me, and I was running out of gas. I didn't know what else to do."

"Why didn't you call me or the police?"

"Lost my phone in the cornfield."

"Wait. What? Who *are* you?"

"Long story, I know. But Cal, we can't call the police. Promise me."

The quarry remained, but all mining operations had ceased for the evening as she sat him on the couch and covered his naked body with a fleece blanket. She sat beside him and helped to return his core body temperature to that of a living human being. As she did so, he filled her in with the details of the long and scary story he had to tell. His first statement, however, assured her that he would be just fine.

"Cal, I was underwater for a long time." He shivered. "There was considerable shrinkage."

*Chapter 41 — September 18, 9:39 A.M.*

As Calista drove, Kyle admired her. She was flaw-lessly average; the temple of every man's dreams. She could track a man around a room without moving a single muscle in her neck. Everything fed off of her eyes; they were like spools of twenty pound test, reeling their prey closer with every blink. Jessica Biel, in her finest hour, came close but still fell short of an equal comparison to the breathtaking Calista. She was magnificent. Men across America wished they could be the sweatshirt that effortlessly hugged her body, consoled her, kept her warm, and caressed her skin. A tattoo seductively peeked out from the neckline of her sweatshirt, placing a carnal pang of desire in the mind of those whose eyes fell upon it, wondering what it depicted and where it continued to carve its mysteriously sexy meaning across her body.

Kyle was never the type to involve himself in these sorts of things. The news never really even appealed to him, but with the victim being someone he held in such high regard, he simply could not turn away from what his heart and mind were telling him to do—find Professor Reech.

"Okay, there's a carpool lot up about a half mile,"

Kyle offered to Calista, who was not from the area.

Calista Jackly, originally from Tennessee where her family owned a horse farm, moved to Michigan two years ago. She'd moved here with the hopes of attending the University of Michigan, but hadn't been accepted yet. Since the move, she's been enrolled at the Flint branch, living in a small apartment, and each day growing more restless to get accepted in Ann Arbor. Her parents had separated soon after she was born. Her mother alluded to the fact that it was all her father's fault, but as Calista grew older, she began believing that her mother—frequently lost in the bottom of an emptying bottle—had made much of this up. She had only seen a picture of her father in an impromptu photo taken during her fifth birthday party. She didn't remember ever speaking with him, but knew he had shown up at her birthday parties from time to time. That had been the last birthday party her father ever attended.

Calista missed her father and found herself growing away from her mother. She had lost all respect for her over the years, due in large part to her mother blowing her entire college fund on late-night runs to the liquor store, which usually ended with a mix of binge drinking and gambling at the local casino.

But she always kept that single picture of her dad tucked snugly in her purse. She couldn't hate what she didn't know, but she could love what she never had a chance to.

"Just pull up close to the back of the lot, where it butts up to the woods." Kyle gestured with his gloved hand to the southeastern-most part of the carpool lot.

Calista abided. "Why all the way back there? Don't we have to cross the entire lot then, to get to where we're going?"

"Yes."

"What do you mean, 'yes'?" Calista challenged.

"Cal, think about it. We're about to trespass on private property."

"Yeah, so what does that have to do with it?"

"If anyone comes by and notices our car, they won't be led to the woods where 'No Trespassing' signs are posted. It's a decoy. Plus, cops can only see us from one direction when we're parked over here."

"Wow," Calista said. "You really are a seasoned criminal, aren't you?"

"No. Just spent a lot of time with the ladies back here." He grinned as if to further instigate her.

Calista punched him in the arm. "Sicko."

Before exiting the car, the two each grabbed a bag that they had packed and checked their boot laces. The car was in Calista's name, and if the police did find her car suspicious, they would be led back to Ann Arbor, where she lived. Plus, parking the car in the lot was not against the law, even though the two intended to break several this evening.

The lot could accommodate about twenty cars, and was kept lit by three streetlights, strategically placed along the center, which bisected the lot into two equal, but separate parts. Kyle and Calista walked onto the grassy slope adjacent to the car, and after only a few steps, their heads were out of sight from any passing car. Before long, the two were indiscernible among the cover provided by the trees and shrubs.

Kyle looked at his watch. "Alright, it's nine forty-five. We need to make sure we're in position by ten thirty."

They were only about eight hundred yards away from the house, as the crow flies. Unfortunately for them, however, a small but awkward pond seated between the lot and the house forced them to walk nearly triple that distance.

Victor opened the front door of his house. A poster detailing the search for Jacob was lying on the porch, cast aside as though it were trash.

"We need beer," a voice called from within. Victor entered the house, and without saying a word, headed for the bathroom. The man lying on the couch paid him no mind, fully engrossed in the rapidly emptying 12-pack of beer sitting on the floor next to him. Before long, Victor was in the bathroom on the main floor. He closed the door and turned on the overhead vent to create a lulling noise, knowing time was of the essence.

Next, he looked toward the shower. Ever so faintly, and only if looking for it, could a tiny hinge be seen in the body of the shower insert. Victor advanced on it, and with one swift press, the shower wall popped ajar, swinging slightly on the single hinge. He opened the makeshift door as wide as he could and entered the pitch-black void.

"Jake, are you here?" Victor whispered with his hands out in front of his body as though expecting to touch something.

"Mmmph!" Jacob struggled, his mouth covered with duct tape.

Victor removed a tiny flashlight from his pocket, clicked it on, and pointed it in the direction of the muffled sound.

Jacob was curled in the corner of the room, eyes wild with fear and rage, both battling to take charge of the other. The rest of the room was barren; the walls were simply a stack of cinder blocks and mortar. Victor approached Jacob.

"Oh my God, Jake. It's me, Vic," he said reassuringly.

Another series of muffled, nonsensical garble escaped Jacob's lungs.

"Jake, I'm gonna get you outta here, but you gotta be quiet when I take this duct tape off, okay?"

Jake's head nodded that he understood.

As Victor gently brought his hands to Jacob's face, an exasperated flinch radiated throughout his body. Soon, the duct tape was off.

"Are you okay?"

Without missing a beat, Jacob blurted back, "Where's Audrey? We gotta find her, she's in danger."

"We'll find her, Jake, I promise. Let's get you outta here first."

The pair headed out of the bathroom door in their attempt to escape the dimly lit house. When the two entered the living room, a burly man was standing in the doorway with a beer in his hand. Victor drew his gun and the man dropped the beer and put his hands out in front of his body, as if to deflect any potential bullets from harming him, instinctively slinking down.

Victor fired twice.

The first bullet entered the man's stomach just above his hip. He crumpled in pain, and in turning his head to avoid being shot again, his lower jaw caught the brunt of a second bullet, shattering his chin and mouth.

"Come on, Jake. Let's go. Hurry!"

Bewildered, and eyes still unfocused from the recent onslaught of blazing natural light, Jacob held onto Victor's hand as he led him toward the front door. Jacob had to step over the nearly dead man; heaving breaths and spurts of blood were the only sounds emanating from his throat; his lower jaw was seemingly nonexistent.

Just as Jacob's trailing foot crossed over the man's chest, he felt the frantic, yet content grasp of a hand clench his ankle. Looking back, their eyes met. For the first time, Jacob Reech was looking at the man who'd held him captive in the trunk of a car. Liam's eyes were vivid blue and pierced into Jacob's soul as if to pass along some sort of message.

The third bullet struck Liam in the forehead, the sudden noise startling Jacob. Jacob had heard guns go off before. He had grown up around them, and never remembered flinching at the booming sound, no matter how unexpected it was. What made Jacob startle was not the explosion of gunpowder—the gun had a silencer—but rather, it was the sound of Liam's head whipping back and smacking against the creaky hardwood floor. It was a sound that was not as unexpected as it was gut-wrenching, like a hammer hitting a watermelon.

The last thing that Jacob looked at were Liam's blue-laced work boots, now just a part of the bloodied mess on the floor. Those boots, Jacob now remembered, were worn by the man who simply delivered him to another, far less humane individual.

"Vic. There's another man. There were two of them that brought me here."

Victor turned around and urged Jacob to flee with him, and not risk staying any longer than he had to, theorizing that if there was another man, he could show up at any time.

"He knows where Audrey is, Vic. I have to find him. I can't give up on Audrey."

"Jake, I haven't heard from Audrey in a long time, and there is another separate search going on for her right now. We can join that search, and the information you can provide will aid the police," Victor pled. "You know firsthand how critical time is during the search for a missing person."

"I know, Vic. But I wouldn't be able to live with

myself if I just gave up."

Victor put the gun back in the waist of his pants and held Jacob's shoulders, looking him reassuringly in the eyes. "Why don't we do this: as soon as we get in the car, we'll call the police and have them send someone out here to keep an eye on any activity. That way, no one gets hurt." He paused. "Jake, keep in mind that if you stay to confront this other guy, you could end up dead. Then what good would you be to Audrey, huh?"

That was the knockout blow. Victor always had a sense of cramming logic right back into Jake when his mind seemed like an empty cookie jar.

Victor turned and descended the front porch toward the car. He began talking about how the police had probably already found Audrey, and that she was home safe. Once he reached the car, Victor turned to look at Jacob at the passenger-side door. Realizing that Jacob was not there, Victor turned back to the house to locate him.

Jacob still stood on the porch, his face contorted in terror and rage.

"How could you, you son of a bitch?!" The words bit the back of his throat as he spoke them.

"Jake? What are you talking about?" Victor asked, puzzled. "Come on, let's go."

"You have no idea what gave you away, do you?" Jacob's tongue was growing thick and dry.

"Gave me away for what? Jake, are you okay?" he said, and could feel his face begin to lose color.

"It's the way you walk," Jacob said. "In those dress shoes." He noticed Victor look down at his own feet. "I've heard that walk before, Victor." His eyes beginning to well. "You're the other man, aren't you? Aren't you?!" Jacob seethed.

Eyes wide with fire, Victor responded. "Jake, how dare you accuse me. I had nothing to do with this. The idea that that thought would even cross your mind makes me sick. I'm here to *help* you."

"So I'm wrong then? Is that what you're saying?"

More calmly now, "Yes, Jake. That is what I'm saying." Victor started walking back toward Jacob.

"True. I have no doubt that you had nothing to do with my abduction, Victor. But you mean to tell me that it wasn't you who disguised your voice and electrocuted me while I was in that trunk? I mean honestly, Victor"—tears were now steadily streaming down Jacob's cheeks—"why else would you have disguised you voice?"

"Jake, you better watch what you're saying. Certain things you may not be able to take back. I swear that I had nothing to do with any of this! Come on. You know me." He paused. "You know me," he pled almost boyishly.

"I'd probably believe you if this happened anywhere else."

"What do you mean, 'somewhere else'?"

"If I took you out to lunch for saving my life and I asked you these questions, you'd probably be able to set my mind at ease. But out here, at this house, it's all so clear."

"Jake, you're in shock. You have no idea what you're talking about."

"Oh really, Victor? Then explain that." Jacob gestured with a nod of his head toward the driveway.

"A person who is coming to save a friend's life doesn't take the time to back his car into the driveway."

Victor looked over at his car, and indeed, it was nestled snuggly against the garage door, as if it had been there for some time. Jacob stared at the car himself, now lost in the raw betrayal he was feeling.

When he looked back, Victor was pointing the gun at him from about ten feet away.

" **A**ll those years, Victor, and you're going to point a gun at me? Over a diamond?" Jacob said after finding what cover he could from a beastly wooden column on the porch. It wore the shallow scars of countless hammer swings that had missed their mark. Whoever built it was by no means a handyman, or was drunk while building it. Most likely, it was both.

"It wasn't supposed to be like this, Jake," Victor spouted, his voice sounding more menacing than ever. "If you just included me in what your grandfather told you, I wouldn't have to do this."

"So you're gonna shoot me? That's it? That's your master plan?"

Victor paused before he answered. His eyes never left Jacob's and began burning, as redness converged onto his sclera. Was he about to cry?

"I will if I have to. Don't make me, Jake," Victor said. He felt the onset of small, seismic tremors reverberating in his voice.

Jacob heard the hitch in Victor's voice. But was it real emotion levitating in his lifelong friend's throat, or was it just another lie? He couldn't tell, but chose to dive deeper into the guilt pool that he wanted so badly to drown Victor in. He composed himself, and fired a nostalgic bullet directly at Victor. "So what about the train tracks, Vic?" *Did it hit anything? A vital organ? Hell, the heart?* "Or, were you a fraud even back then?" *That one had to tear into something.* He emptied his verbal clip on Victor in a barrage. "Ya know, I'm the only one who really knew you inside and out. Or at least I thought I did." *Bang!* "But tell me, was it just a game to you back then, like it is now, or were you truly a troubled young man who gained true respect, adoration, and friendship, as I did with you?" *Bang! Bang! Bang!*

"Stop it! That has nothing to do with this," Victor yelled, his thick Kevlar absorbing everything.

"That has everything to do with this! Don't think I didn't catch you lookin' at those tracks. Would you even be here pointing a gun at me if I hadn't followed you home that day?" he said as he stepped away from the column in defiance.

"I wasn't going to do it. If you really did know me, you would know that."

"Hindsight, right? It's all so clear to you now. But as a teen, you thought happiness, or at least an escape, lay elsewhere. I'm right, aren't I? Admit it." Jacob took a step toward the entry door to the house that was still open, held ajar by Liam's motionless foot. *There was a gun in his waist!*

"No, Jake. You're wrong. I could never do that to

myself." It was an empty statement, and Victor knew it. It wasn't just the train tracks. He'd considered pills. Razors. A gun. He really did have Jacob to thank for standing behind him through high school. He was the only one who actually knew, but without Jacob, Victor would have ended up just another casualty of school bullies.

America would have mourned him for about a week. CNN would have covered a candlelit vigil, and countless people would be seen on camera protesting bullying with banners that might have read: *How many dead kids does it take for the adults to take action? I don't know, go ask a grieving parent.* The bullying epidemic had gained tremendous speed since Columbine in 1999, far too long ago for us as a nation to claim victory. The nation needed some true politicians who weren't scared of losing a vote because the color of their tie didn't match the sound of their voice.

But again, Victor was one of the lucky, lucky ones.

"That's a lie, Victor," Jacob said. *There it is! I can see it in his belt!* "But doing this isn't going to make all those years better. It's only gonna get worse for you." He stalled as he took another step toward the door.

"Who cares? I was fifteen!"

More poised, as though he was about to win a battle, and with a full magazine reloaded in his throat, Jacob responded, "Well, it's just that you seem to think you were the only one to have it hard. You had bad acne." He paused. "Me? I never got to meet my dad. We both dealt with shit. And ya know what? I found a friend I could talk with about these things. A friend who became a role model. I looked up to you, Victor." *Bang! Bang! Bang!*

"We were kids, Jake. Adolescents. Neither of us knew any-damn-thing about life back then."

"For God's sake, Victor." He paused. "College. I was there for you, man. Money, popularity, none of that shit ever mattered to me." He shuffled ever so slightly. *I think I could dive from here and get it.*

"Jesus, Jake! I don't want to do this. If it were any other person."

"Well it's not. It's me. But a diamond is more important to you than the only true friend you've ever had."

"Do you know how many times I tried to think of another way than to involve you with this? I do care about you, Jake. Really." Victor began lowering the gun.

"I'd hate to see what you do to people you don't care about," Jacob said sarcastically—an errant shot at best.

"I know you don't believe me right now, but honestly, this wasn't easy for me."

"Yeah, I could tell by the way you so gently

electrocuted me that you just hated yourself for doing it." *Bang!*

Victor stiffened up as he once again raised the gun. "Jake, the picture here is far bigger than what you can see right now, don't you understand that? Some things just had to be done."

"You could have just told me. I probably would have thought it was cool and helped you, because you were my friend." He accentuated the last part of the sentence. "I had no idea that my grandfather was involved with anything like this."

"I couldn't risk that, and you know it. Come on, Jake, you can't say that a hidden diamond like that wouldn't have piqued your interest. Especially if it were Washington's."

Back to reality. "Enough, Victor. Where's Audrey?" Jacob demanded.

"We found the coordinates, Jake. It's too late. We're on our way to Illinois now."

"Where's Audrey, or I swear to God, I'm gonna force you to shoot me."

"Don't you lose focus, Jake!" Victor yelled, expelling all traces of sentiment out into the cool air. "I'm the one with the gun. Remember that. Now, I want to help you reunite with Audrey. I really do, Jake," he lied. "Just tell me who Franklin is, and I will. I promise," he lied again.

"Where is she?!" Jake exploded, as he took a few boastful steps in Victor's direction.

"Ah ah ah," Victor said as he cocked the gun. "I get Franklin, you get Audrey. Simple as that."

"I don't know who Franklin is, or where he's at, you asshole!"

"Well, you better start figuring it out." He paused. "You have 48 hours, or I'll send Audrey's blood to you in a fuckin' five-gallon bucket."

Victor tossed Jake a cell phone while still pointing the gun at him.

"Consider this Audrey's lifeline. You lose it, you lose her. You don't answer it when I call, Audrey loses a finger. Do it again, and she loses an arm. Oh, and it's untraceable, so don't even try any of that Superman bullshit like last time."

"If you lay one finger on her, Victor, I'll kill you." His voice was more threatening than a hungry alpha lion salivating at an injured gazelle.

Just then, a faint voice came from nowhere.

"Jake?" the shaky and muffled voice yelled.

In an instant, Jake recognized the voice belonged to Audrey, and it was coming from the trunk of Victor's car. Jake noticed out of his periphery that Victor, too, looked over at the car, and in that moment, he heaved his body back inside the house scrambling for the gun from Liam's waistband. He ran back outside in time to see Victor running to his car. Jake fired the gun wildly a few times, but stopped soon after, fearing he would hit Audrey in the trunk.

"Audrey!" he bellowed, tears gargling at the back of his throat as he watched the car speed away.

Panic-stricken, he looked back at the driveway—one other car waited patiently, tucked obnoxiously close to a spruce. He quickly opened the driver's-side door and searched for the keys. Nothing. After a moment of contemplation, he sat back in the seat, defeated. There's no way he could hotwire it. He didn't know the first thing about that.

As his only option, and with gun in hand, he instinctively checked how many rounds remained—never realizing how much of what he saw on his favorite crime-drama TV shows he retained—and began running in the direction in which the car sped.

*Chapter 44 — September 18, 10:18 A.M.*

The two trudged through the medium-thick brush in relative silence for a time. Eventually, they made it to the wood line at the back of the property.

They crept to the south side of the house, staying close to the tree line wherever possible. Ultimately, they ended up with their backs to the siding and faced the tree line from which they had just snuck. As they crouched down with their duffels, the two were stunned by the sound of gunshots echoing from within the house.

After a time, they emerged from their hold and cautiously advanced toward the back-entry door of the house, and heard more gunshots followed by the sound of a car skidding away.

Thankfully, as they entered the house, the door let out a soft whisper rather than a harsh creak. The first room they came to was the kitchen. There were two bowls of chili on the table, both of which were still steaming, the butter on the bread still melting. Then, the two heard voices from the adjoining room.

After a panicked pause, Kyle and Calista each assumed a hold on either side of the entryway to the living room. As they did this, the voices grew louder.

It was not long before they realized the voices were coming from a television. They entered the room and saw a mediocre newscast battling so hard for ratings that an exposé on the dung beetle had landed the top story of the morning.

Kyle turned it off.

While looking around the rest of the room, they noticed the front door was still open, and only when looking a second time did either of them notice a motionless body crumpled mostly behind a nearby chair. Kyle approached the body first as Calista hesitantly followed.

When checking for any remnants of life, there was no doubt as to the outcome of the gunshots they had so recently heard.

Calista let out a bloodcurdling scream as she saw the blood and brains scattered around the body and on the adjacent furniture.

"You okay?" Kyle offered.

No response.

"Cal?"

Calista had never seen a dead body before, and was having what many would call a breakdown. Kyle could tell that it was more than that.

"Calista. Are you okay?"

Sobbing, Calista responded, "That's my father."

Kyle's face went numb, expressionless. His mouth

open, searching for words, but none came out. All he could do was hug her.

As he gripped her body tightly, he noticed the faint smell of gunpowder in the air.

"Shit. Shit!" Victor roared as he looked in the rear-view, seeing only a cloud of dissipating dust dancing behind his car; the dull booming of metal could be heard as Audrey fought to escape from within the trunk.

Enraged at the mishap with Jacob, he slammed an intercom button on the dashboard and let his frustration out on his captive passenger.

"You better shut up back there!" he growled, swerving the car hard to the right, and then left again.

The sound of Victor's voice echoed in Audrey's ear, terrorizing her. She obeyed and all kicks subsided. For now.

"Good girl," he said, more calmly now, as he felt control ooze back into his possession. "Ya know, you and I could have made a great couple. Had some good lookin' kids."

A solitary and deafening boom came from the trunk, in absolute rebuttal to Victor's comment.

Victor smirked at her passionate display of disapproval.

"You just better hope your little boyfriend is smart enough not to play the hero again," he said as he turned up the radio and continued to drive.

The road ahead was no longer as resolute as Victor had planned. He knew one mistake could lead to many. He refocused on The Movement, and smiled at the fact that his name would soon rewrite history.

Kyle drove away from the house, looking straight ahead. "Thank God you knew how to hotwire a car," he said, trying to break the silence, but wished he could retract the statement immediately.

"Yeah, well, I guess crime just runs in my family, now doesn't it?" she said sarcastically, and then doubled back over with her face buried in the duffel bag lying in her lap; intermittent sobs could be heard over the radio. Trying to save himself from becoming a total jerk, Kyle turned up the volume of the radio in an act of kindness, as it offered some semblance of emotional privacy to his passenger in one of the most non-private settings imaginable.

*When's the right time?* he thought, as he pondered the appropriate time to wait before he would offer an even more comforting hand to her leg.

An ambush of successive sobs followed his thought.

*Too soon*, he decided.

The thought quickly left his mind as he squinted through the windshield. A distant figure materialized at the distant horizon.

Jacob looked back as a car approached, and positioned himself in the middle of the road, pointing the gun at the driver.

"Jesus, Cal. That's Professor Reech!" Kyle said, and proceeded to skid the car to an angled stop on the road. He rolled his window down and shouted to his professor.

"Don't shoot, Mr. Reech! It's Kyle," he said, as he took his hands off the wheel and raised them in the air.

Jacob's oxygen-deprived chest could be seen heaving for air as he lowered the gun and ran to the car. His legs felt like their bones were made of lead. He hadn't run more than this in what seemed a decade, if not longer. The occupants of the car could see the rubber surfacing as he awkwardly strode to the driver's side of the car.

"Get in the back, Kyle," Jacob demanded, as his body and mind switched to auto-pilot. Kyle hopped into the seat next to Calista as Jacob got into the driver's seat and floored the gas pedal. The acceleration of the car aided in Kyle's awkward tumbling into the backseat. He settled next to Calista and noticed the speedometer of the car was already approaching 60 miles per hour.

The two sat beside one another in silence, until Kyle's hand instinctively met Calista's leg with a gentle rub and pat. Their eyes met, and Calista shuddered into his sympathetic shoulder.

"They gave me 48 hours," Jacob said, forcing reality back into the gentle embrace his passengers were sharing. "Kyle, I need your help."

"I'm in, Mr. Reech."

"It's Jake, from now on." The leader inside the man emerged as the car sped slightly faster.

"Sure. You got it, Mr. Reech. I mean, Jake."

"They have Audrey. I need to get to a computer," Jake said. He spoke with true clarity. "Can we go to your house?"

"Sure, they shouldn't be after me anymore."

"Anymore? What do you mean?"

"They think I'm dead."

"Wait," Jake said. "They're after you too?"

"Victor lied to me while we were searching for you. I found out he was behind all this. I think he realized that, and sent one of his men after me."

"I'm sorry you got involved."

"The guy in that house…"—he paused, gesturing with his eyes toward Calista—"…her father." Jacob's eyes met Kyle's in the rearview.

"I'm sorry about your father, Calista. I truly am. But they have my fiancée, and they will kill her too. Can you help me?"

No answer. Jacob's eyes once again met Kyle's, who answered for her with a small nod of his head.

"Kyle, do you know how to shoot a gun?" The question just tumbled out of Jacob's mouth.

"Sure do. I'm an Eagle Scout. Grew up hunting."

"Good. How about her?" he continued.

"I can shoot," a muffled, but sobering voice came from Kyle's lap.

"Thank you, Calista. Thank you," Jacob leveled.

Kyle helped Jacob navigate to his apartment, and the three entered as nonchalantly as possible. Jacob wore one of Kyle's hooded sweatshirts that he kept in her car. With the hood pulled over his head, Jacob blended right in.

The sun peeked through the curtains, disintegrating any remnants of morning light. The rays were more vibrant now; the sun was tired, as morning blinks had turned into a radiant stare. Their gaze landed on Lucinda's eyelids, causing her to stir. Her eyes creaked open as the sound of a contented morning sigh danced from her mouth. She rolled over to greet Nick, who lay beside her.

He was no longer there.

She felt the bed where his body should have been. The mattress was cool. He had been gone for some time.

The ensuing sigh was one that carried with it not even a fragment of sanguinity.

"Figures," Lucinda said to herself as she heaved the covers off her fully clothed body. She wore a pair of fleece pajama bottoms and a sweatshirt. "No sex, no guy." And then it hit her. The smell of coffee. Fresh.

She stood from the bed, her eyebrows contorted. And as she approached her bedroom door, she heard a man clear his throat. The sound came from her kitchen. Butterflies leapt back into her stomach, but this time she was also a bit scared.

"Nick?" she said, as she turned the corner to the kitchen. A moment later, she saw the man she'd just spent the night with sitting at her dining-room table, sipping coffee. As soon as he saw her turn the corner, he rose and filled a cup for her too. He poured in some creamer and stirred it, the hot liquid mirroring her skin. He set it on the table in front of her and gave her an all-encompassing hug, his arms wrapped fully around her as delight swirled throughout her body once again.

"Morning," Nick said as he released her from the hug. As he looked at her, a multifaceted smile crept across his face. First, because Lucinda Garrett stood before him in her pajamas. Second, because he now realized the movies had it right, at least for Lucinda. It is possible for a beautiful woman to wake up from a full night's sleep with perfect hair, and no crusties in her eyes. He had always thought that no woman could look perfect right out of bed.

He was wrong.

"Luce, I'm not looking for a sex buddy. I'm looking for a companion. The sex'll come. I couldn't be happier with how last night went."

The smile that exploded onto Lucinda's face was unknown to her. Her cheeks nearly cramped from the use of elationary muscles in her face that had atrophied over time. She hugged him again and gave him a succulent early morning kiss.

The two were accustomed to waking up early to get into the office. They sat at the table and eagerly chatted as they each sipped their coffee.

"All this time I thought you were just a goon."

"Goon? Ouch! Yeah, well, I never thought I'd even come close to meeting your uppity-uppity standards."

"I never knew you had any."

The laughter-filled conversation continued as they migrated to the living room. In one swift and fluid motion, they cuddled up together on the couch as they turned on the TV. A news story filled the screen. The life and times of a solitary dung beetle the reporter affectionately called the Colonel made the couple laugh hysterically.

"As in, 'Corn Kernel'? Nick joked.

Lucinda erupted in laughter; giggles spewed from her mouth and landed softly on Nick's ears, making them tingle with happiness.

"These people need some better material."

"Seriously."

They channel-surfed for a while in silence until they found a good movie to watch on this Wednesday morning. Eventually, a blanket crept its way over their intertwined legs.

"So, what happens next?"

"Well, the kid solves the problem in the hallway,

and the professor begins mentoring him."

"With us, silly."

"Oh." Nick smiled. "First, we gotta stop taking shots at each other at work. Those aren't good for either of us."

"I agree."

"Then, why don't we just start by seeing more of each other. I mean, dinners, movies. You know, all that fun stuff."

Lucinda didn't respond, but Nick could tell she felt the same as she squeezed his arm and snuggled in even closer.

"And I don't want you to think every night has to end with a sleepover. Don't get me wrong, I absolutely loved sharing your bed, but if you ever feel uncomfortable, or we're going too fast, just say the…"

Lucinda cut him off with a kiss and the two did not speak for the remainder of the movie. They were lost in silent contentment, wrapped in each other's bodies on Lucinda's fluffy, oversized couch.

## Chapter 48 – September 18, 10:44 A.M.

The three burst into Kyle's apartment. Calista, the last one in, quickly shut the door behind her, locking it. Without hesitation, Jacob's eyes found Kyle's laptop on a desk located just off the living room. He stormed toward it, almost knocking over an end table in the process. He opened it and requested Kyle's assistance, who was a half-step behind him, as though reading Jacob's mind.

"Kyle, log in to this for me. Quickly."

Kyle swiftly entered his credentials, and a brightly colored home screen appeared. Jacob took control once again. Some might have thought that Jacob was being rude, by practically pushing Kyle aside, but Kyle did not. He knew the adrenaline pumping through his favorite professor's body, and found himself feeding off of Jacob's maniacal movements.

"We need to hurry," Jacob ordered, more to himself than to Kyle or Calista. "I've bought us some time, but not much. They're headed to Illinois."

"What's in Illinois?" Kyle asked.

"The file they found on my computer. It included coordinates. But I changed them. They lead to something. And whatever it is, they want it." He paused. "Desperately."

"What do you think they're looking for?"

"Possibly a diamond. I'm not sure, but I need to get to it before they do. As long as they don't have it, Audrey's safe."

"Whatever you need me to do," Kyle said, as he broke a threshold and placed a reassuring hand on Jacob's shoulder. Kyle could see Jacob was beginning to panic, even if it was all internal.

Kyle remembered a time when he was underwater alone and his foot got stuck in a submerged log. He only had about three minutes of air remaining in his tank. Frantic bubbles escaped from his mouth as he gasped and tugged to release his boot. In a moment of pause, he thought about his options and the best opportunity to free himself. Rather than yanking on his boot and trying to untie his laces, he realized he could just cut the two-inch-thick piece of branch he was stuck on. Within seconds, he was once again bobbing at the surface; a small piece of wood dangled from his boot, but he'd made the best use out of the little time he had.

"We'll get her back. Just try to calm down a little. It'll help you focus," Kyle added.

"Thanks." Jacob heaved off some of the stress-filled worry he had been carrying on his shoulders for so long. He took in a deep breath of fresh air before continuing. "I'm trying to find where the real coordinates point. Should have it in just a minute." His fingers were now doing most of the talking. Keystrokes could be heard throughout the room, but Kyle realized they were far less chaotic than moments before.

After a few more keystrokes echoed within the room, the screen filled with a satellite picture of the Earth. Jacob clicked on an icon used to pinpoint a location. His eyes strained as his brain worked to remember the true coordinates. Eventually, he started typing them in as they rushed back into his mind.

"36, 18, 43 N." He paused, and then promptly recalled the remaining coordinate. "82, 22, 34 W." He hit the enter key.

Kyle and Jacob both watched the screen slowly zoom in to the location he'd just typed. As they watched, their eyes attempted to hurry the zoom process. Before they knew it, they were looking at a ground-level satellite image.

"Shit, that's a cemetery."

"Yeah, but where?"

Jacob manually zoomed out enough to see the state borders and county lines.

"Tennessee."

"Wait," a voice came from behind the two. "I'm from Tennessee," Calista said. "Where's it at?" She, too, was now looking at the monitor.

"Mountain Home National Cemetery, in Johnson

City," Jacob said, not yet understanding the signifi-cance of the location.

"I know right where that is," Calista confidently added. "Who is this guy they were looking for again?"

"Someone named Franklin," Jacob responded, let-ting her take the reins for a time.

"Well, if these guys are after our first president's fortune, I think we're at least on the right trail."

"Why do you say that?" Jacob probed.

"Well, that Franklin guy? Not a guy. A ghost state," Calista continued.

"A what?" Jacob inquired.

"I'll tell you about it in the car. We need to get to Tennessee. Bring the laptop."

With that, the three grabbed their coats and head-ed for the door. Again, Calista was the last to leave.

"Hang on. I'll be right out," she said as she scurried to the kitchen and packed up any food from Kyle's refrig-erator and cupboards. Unfortunately, all she found were protein bars and bottled water. Once she placed as much as she could into a paper bag, she joined them in the car.

"Good thinking, Calista," Jacob said, as the car sped out of the apartment complex.

Calista retrieved a protein bar for each of them. It would be the first food of the day for all three. They ate in relative silence for a time, until Jacob turned onto the southbound ramp.

"So, Calista. Explain to me what a ghost state is."

"Well, in high school we had to take a Tennessee History class. A chapter focused on states that almost were. One of those states was the state of Franklin. I don't remember a whole lot, but maybe enough." She moved to the middle of the backseat, and leaned up toward Jacob and Kyle, who occupied the front seats. "Just after the Revolutionary War, in the 1780s, colonists didn't have too much confidence in the authority figures of their settlements. At least for the most part. And because of that, there was a good deal of political distrust, especially in a portion of land in what was then part of North Carolina. Settlers were furious with how the state was being governed, and it ultimately led to the idea of governing the land as its own state. Franklin," Calista said, feeling a bit better.

The act of talking helped mask the sorrow of her grief-stricken body from just learning of her father's death, and his involvement in Professor Reech's kidnapping.

"Okay. Thanks for the 101. But, how does that tie into Washington's fortune?"

"Sorry, I don't have a 201 version. Maybe just the fact that it's in Washington County might have something to do with it."

"Franklin…is located in Washington County?"

"Yeah, but there's a ton nationwide. Could be a coincidence."

"It's no coincidence. It's a beacon. We're on the right path. When Victor had me in that room, he mentioned something about the Society of Cincinnati. Honestly, I told him I was looking them up, but I pretty much just focused on changing those coordinates," Jake admitted.

"Might have something to do with that society. But *I've* never heard of it."

"Here," Jacob said. "Switch me seats, so I can get on the laptop easier back there."

The two switched seats, and Calista and Kyle once again shared the front seat of the car. Immediately, his hand found her knee and gave it a comforting squeeze. Normally, the act would tickle Calista, but this time she was able to find the true intent of the gesture.

"Why don't you guys alternate and try to get some sleep. I have to look this stuff up before we get down there."

"Ya know, I'm pretty good for now," Kyle said.

"I know, but the biggest help you can be to me right now is getting rest. There's no telling what we'll find in Tennessee."

"I gotcha. Cal, why don't you crash now, and I'll wake you up when we're about halfway there so we can switch."

"Sounds good," Calista yawned.

Calista hunkered down into her seat, resting her head on the window, and began decompressing from all of the recent excitement, however unfortunate it had been. After only a few miles, her eyes were closed. Kyle's hand was still placed on her knee. The faint sounds of intermittent keystrokes could be heard coming from the backseat.

"Dig deeper then. It's got to be there," Victor shouted as Frank and Don continued to dig where the coordinates had led them.

The site was in the middle of an intersection that divided four large fields in southeastern Illinois. The farmland around them was immense. Essentially, they were in the middle of nowhere. No sounds of cars disrupted them, and the only roads around were made of dirt. Their car was off the side of the road behind some thick brush so even if someone did drive by, they would have no idea that three men were digging for a lost and controversial artifact of their great nation.

The sun was fading into the horizon, and Frank and Don had already dug down about 8 feet in the soft and fertile soil, making their effort less cumbersome. Nonetheless, the two were rather winded and paused for a moment to catch their breath and to talk with Victor.

"This can't be right, Victor. Something's wrong," Frank said, his chest heaving.

"Yeah. I mean, how deep you think they hid it? It's gotta be wrong. Just doesn't feel right," Don added; his chest, too, was heaving, but not nearly as much as

Frank, who was visibly out of shape.

Victor contemplated a few scenarios in his mind, until a look of pure anger overcame his face.

"Track that damn phone I gave him."

Frank climbed out of the hole and pressed a few buttons on his phone, accessing the one given to Jacob. He checked the real-time GPS signature.

"They're in Tennessee as we speak."

"Son of a bitch! Get in the van. They're the wrong fucking coordinates!

Detective O'Reilly held a Glade Plug-In in his hand. This was turning into a rather complex game of cat-and-mouse. Many criminals, in part, wanted to be caught. Those, however, were typically of the psychopathic order. His hand throbbed as the pain set in from realizing he was being toyed with. For some reason, he felt that this burglar in particular wanted to get caught. He wondered why a man would steal only a rug, if not doing so in part for the thrill and exhilaration of pending capture. He knew what that felt like. He had experienced the same feeling one fall evening during his senior year of high school.

He and his friends were out late partying one summer night in 1970 when he was in high school. They usually just parked in a field and drank while listening to music. This night was no different, in that it began in the same field as several times before. However, it ended in a much different location.

There were three of them: Nate, Ben, and Pat. They were chatting in the field, sitting on the bumper of Nate's truck, when Ben, between chugs of beer, brought up the idea of stealing a road sign. Nate had a tool bag already in the back of his truck, and they set off with liquid courage to a desolate strip of road about a mile away from the field.

They parked the truck off the road in an adjacent field and raced over to the sign they decided to dismantle. It was a deer-crossing sign. It seemed there were car-deer accidents or close calls every week or so on this strip of road. The three boys didn't care, they just wanted to take the sign because they could.

Nate climbed on the shoulders of Pat with his tools crammed into his pockets. Ben stayed out on the road, and watched for cars to come. Each time a car came, the three would jump off the side of the road and tumble into some high grass that served as great camouflage. They were invisible to the fast-moving cars that passed. That is, if they got off the road before the piercing headlights fell on them. Most of the time, this was not a problem, but one time Pat fell as he was running off the road. The approaching car slowed as it passed him. The driver rolled the window down and yelled at him.

"Hey!" the driver said. "Two feet not enough for ya to walk with?" the voice continued.

Pat looked up to see his other friend Kevin grinning from behind the wheel. Shortly after, Nate and Ben emerged from the grass, and they all laughed together before Kevin sped off.

It was a close call, and Pat could feel the heat from his fear almost melting his heart, which pumped blood harder and faster than ever before. The thought that they almost got caught exhilarated him more than anything else in his young life.

He understood the burglar's desire for adrenaline. But, he continued to think, a *man* was doing this, not a mischievous teenager. He was struggling to grasp why this man was continuing to threaten so much, for so little, especially now that the term *murder* was being used.

"How much time until we're there?" Jacob said from the back. The sudden conversation made Calista wince in her sleep.

Kyle looked at the GPS mounted on the dashboard. On the bottom right corner, he saw an estimation time to arrival. He knew about GPS systems. They were great, except that they were not all too intuitive. They had no idea of traffic jams, and certain construction.

Further, they gave you a time based on the quickest, easiest, most routine path. If a person veered off just a little, the system would have to recalculate. The estimation time displayed 1 hour 50 minutes. Kyle erred on the side of potential delays and recalculations when he gave Jacob a response.

"Just over 2 hours, why?" Kyle relayed.

"I think I figured something out." Jacob's mind was purging from hours of research on the laptop. "Victor said his grandfather created a code for Washington to use to conceal the location of his fortune," he said, almost restating the facts to himself, making sure he, too, understood them.

"Okay," Kyle bit on, offering Jacob the opportunity to continue speaking.

"Well, I asked him how far back the coded letter from his grandfather dated. He said it was 1791," Jacob said, expecting Kyle to make the same connection as he had.

"I'm guessing that's significant," Kyle plainly said, focusing more on the road than the comment Jacob just made. He knew that Jacob was purging, but that the important parts would be pointed out clearly by Jacob as he came to them in the conversation the two were now holding.

"Yeah. That's the same year the plans for Washington D.C. were crafted," Jacob announced, as though the piece of information was, in fact, an important part.

"Who made them?" Kyle inquired, now paying more attention, as suggested by Jacob's change in inflection in his tired but resolute voice.

"An original member of the Society of Cincinnati. A guy named Pierre L'Enfant." Jacob's pronunciation was by no means French and neither of them even cared about the name's country of origin.

Jacob continued. "And guess what? L'Enfant became a member of the Society the same day as Washington. That's got to be important. They must have been close, or at least have known each other pretty well."

"So what's it say about that Pierre guy?" Kyle asked, as he headed down a steep and windy incline in the road. They could all feel him tap the brakes as the car gained speed from the added gravity pulling on it.

Jacob scanned the screen in front of him. "Born in 1754. Hmmm." He continued scanning until he found another noteworthy fact. "Created the emblem for the Society of Cincinnati. That might help us. It looks like an eagle with some stuff in its talons." He dove deeper. A little frustrated now, "Hell, I don't know. That's all I can find. We just gotta get to that cemetery."

"Not too much longer," Kyle said as he looked back down at his Garmin.

"Good. And hey, why didn't you switch with her?"

Jacob quizzed, taking a moment away from the laptop to give his eyes a much-needed break.

"I can't sleep in cars. Plus, she just saw her dad with a bullet hole in his head. She needs this sleep," Kyle whispered while looking at Jacob in the rear-view, feeling as though the act added importance to the statement he'd just made. It did. Kyle saw Jacob in the back slowly nodding his head in agreement that she had a decidedly unknown road filled with grief and unanswered questions ahead of her.

"She's strong, Kyle. She'll be fine, but'll need your help more than you know," Jacob said.

"I know. I'll be there for her."

Jacob added a truth about life that he often injected into his lectures in class. "Death reduces our lives to rubble, but from that rubble greater things will emerge."

The statement resonated within Kyle and as he looked over at Calista, he knew that he would never let her down.

They drove in silence for a time, while each thought about decidedly different things. Jacob, of course, was lost in the myriad of data he'd just gorged on, hoping they would lead to some sort of answer that could help gain more control in assuring Audrey's continued safety. He stared out of the window at the high shoulders of the highway. His eyes kept landing on the rock debris that had collected at the bottom of each cliff. They reminded him of human lives. They looked so strong, but in a moment destruction could overtake them. A crumbled life lay at the bottom, but a fresh face exposes itself. A new view with which to translate the world surrounding him or her. It is with this new view, Jacob maintained, that positivity was able to always prevail.

"We're here," Kyle said as he approached the entrance to the cemetery.

"D on't pull in yet," Jacob said as the car came to the entrance of the cemetery. "Drive past it. Let's take a look around before heading in."

Kyle drove around the cemetery on the adjacent road. It was protected by a wrought-iron fence that stood about four feet high. They all strained to see beyond the fence, but night held too much authority, preventing their eyes from retrieving any usable data from the moving car.

"We gotta get in there. I didn't see a security booth," Jacob said. "You guys sure you're okay with this?"

"You can count on us, Jake. Plus, don't worry about getting caught. If we do, we just tell them the truth. They'll probably help us."

"I hope you're right. But we don't have time to deal with the police if we don't have to," Jacob said as the car entered the cemetery with its lights off.

The GPS glowed in the darkened car, the coordinates ever climbing closer to the plot they needed to find. Eventually, they arrived and exited the car. Kyle got the two shovels from the trunk that they'd purchased on the way down. He handed one to Jacob and they slunk behind some trees to discuss a plan of action. Calista got in the driver's seat and drove out of the cemetery to prevent them from being identified.

Whispering, Jacob spoke to Kyle. "Okay. I need you to dig as fast as you can. Can you do that for me?"

"Don't worry about me, Jake."

"Good. On my go."

Thankfully, the plot just so happened to be located near the edge of a row of trees that offered perfect cover for the two of them.

"Go," Jacob said, and they jumped out and began feverishly digging atop the grave.

They worked like a two-man team of iron workers, taking turns pounding a piece of molten metal, each using their shovel to its full potential. A small mound on either side of the grave grew in size as they labored above it, periodically taking much-needed breaks. Unearthing a grave with only a shovel and deprived of sleep took a lot longer than either of them expected.

After more than an hour, they heard the sound of a thud, as Jacob's shovel struck something solid: a casket. The two worked together to pry it open with their shovels, and after a few attempts, they heard the nails loosen. Another tug and the lid popped open. A small cloud of dust settled as they both looked inside.

A fully dressed skeleton lay inside. He, as the clothing suggested, looked untouched. His hands were clasped across his abdomen, and the bones appeared to be intact, although extremely fragile. This was the first time this casket had been opened since the man was buried. Jacob looked at the gravestone a little closer, and noticed the year of death. *1909.*

As they looked at the skeleton, which neither had ever seen, something else entirely caught their attention.

"A Mason jar," they said nearly in unison, as their eyes focused on a medium-sized glass jar nestled against the man's left arm. It too was covered with dirt and grime, but was otherwise undamaged. Something light brown was inside of it, but they couldn't tell what it was just by looking.

Jacob retrieved the jar and the two once again headed back to the trees and waited for Calista to return. While waiting, Jacob opened the jar and pulled out its contents.

"Holy shit, it's a map!" Jacob exclaimed.

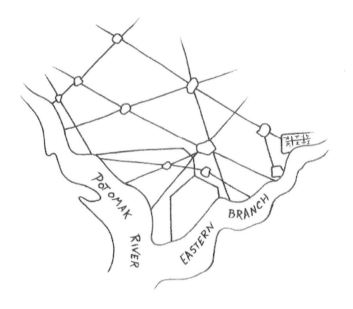

As he opened it, another piece of paper fell to the ground on top of one of the piles of dirt. Jacob looked at it on the ground for a moment, then handed the map to Kyle so he could pick up the paper from the ground. Inside, he saw a series of symbols that made no sense to either of the men.

"It's coded. This must be the language Victor is talking about," Jacob said. "We gotta get out of here. Where's Calista?"

"She's coming around the corner now."

"Okay. Flag her down."

Kyle waved his hands as Calista drove by, hoping she would see him in the dark. She passed them, but the brakes of the car blared to life, and she backed up to the two men waiting at the fence. Kyle arrived to the car first, and opened the door for Jacob, as they both entered the car from the passenger side.

"Let's go," Jacob said as they sped back onto the road.

The on-ramp to the expressway was only about 100 yards up the road, and as they approached it, Kyle noticed a van coming from the opposite direction with its lights off. The vehicles passed each other innocuously. Soon enough, the three in Calista's car were once again on the highway, and Jacob watched as the van pulled into the cemetery.

"They're here. That van just pulled into the cemetery. Shit! How'd they find us?"

Calista pressed down on the gas and sped past some of the cars on the highway.

"No. Don't drive crazy. We need to blend in. Plus, we can't afford to get pulled over. And neither can they."

Calista slowed down to 75 miles per hour and set the cruise control while Jacob scoured the map for a time. It looked vaguely familiar. *I've seen this before. That shape.* He pondered it for another moment, then typed an address into the computer that he had become all too familiar with in the last few days. Almost immediately, his thought was confirmed. On the screen he saw a picture of the same map that was lying next to him. The title of the image from the Society of Cincinnati website read: "L'Enfant's Original Plans for D.C."

As Jacob pondered the screen before him, Calista's voice broke the silence.

"Uh, guys? Don't look now, but there is a cop right behind me."

Neither man looked back, but Kyle glanced into the passenger-side mirror and saw a vehicle trailing behind them about three car lengths back. He clearly saw the silhouette of roof-mounted lights that identified the vehicle as a trooper. What he noticed even more, however, was the fact that the headlights of the cruiser were not on. Apparently, the officer did not want to be seen.

No words were spoken among the three for a time, but Kyle kept his eyes locked on the mirror, and noticed the car continually creeping closer to them. He was only about a car length back when his headlights, and siren, both blared to life.

"**S**hit!" Jacob yelled, as he felt the car begin to slow as Calista started to pull over.

"You think they'll know my face down here?" Jacob asked, almost rhetorically, concerned that the news of his disappearance had crossed state borders.

"Yeah, I don't know," Kyle said as Calista's car came to a stop.

Calista's voice once again filled the anxious air of the car. "Jake, didn't that Victor guy tell you he was in with the police?"

"Oh, man. That's right." The thought scared him, but his mind raced beyond that. *Audrey.*

The officer's door opened, and Calista continued speaking. "Okay, here he comes. Just let me do the talking. Jake, you left your wallet at home, remember? Remember?" she repeated sharply.

"Right. Got it," Jake assured.

A moment later, the officer's flashlight beam landed on the occupants' heads in succession, followed by several taps to the driver's-side window.

Calista looked at the officer through her window and offered a friendly smile as she rolled it down.

"G'Day, Officer. How can I help ya?" she said. Her

voice mysteriously grew a perfect Australian accent out of thin air. Jake and Kyle remained looking forward, silently astonished.

Unaffected by the charm of her accent, the officer responded, "License and registration please." Calista abided and allowed the officer a moment to look at the documents, before he continued. "Any idea why I pulled you over, Miss?"

"Well I sure hope it's not because my dingo jumped out a few miles back." She laughed.

The officer didn't exactly understand if the comment was a joke or an Australian metaphor for something else. *Foreigners*, he thought.

"Uh, your taillight is out." He paused. "Driver's side."

"Oh, dear. Well, we can't have that now, can we? Consider it done. Say, by this time tomorrow?" Her accent remained as thick as ever.

"Just get it fixed. Soon," he finished.

"You bet, Officer. Thank you."

"And hey, one last question, you guys been doing any drinking this evening?" he probed as he shined his flashlight into the backseat, clearly searching the car for empty beer cans.

The question landed on their ears like a ton of bricks. "No sir, Officer. Dry as a rhino's backside." Her chin lifted a bit in a display of pride in the statement.

"You wouldn't lie to an officer of the law, now, would you?"

"Never. Honest. Right, guys?" She looked back at them. "You been drinkin'?"

They both shook their heads, and Jake responded from the back, "Not tonight."

"So where ya headed?" the officer questioned.

"Michigan. Been down here seein' some family over the weekend. A reunion of sorts." She paused, then started right back up. "Want me to call 'em? Ya know, verify my story and all?" The smile grew back on her face as she joked with the officer, who took no part in sharing even a smirk. "Honest. I'm tellin' you the truth." Her smile faded.

The officer looked at all three passengers momentarily. "No. No need for that. Just drive careful, and get that taillight fixed."

"Will do," she said, as the officer handed back her license and registration. "Have a nice night."

The officer tipped his hat and walked back to his car. This time, however, his headlights remained on as he drove off in front of them. Calista reentered the highway moments behind him and accelerated back to highway speed.

Once back on the highway, Kyle was the first to break the silence.

"*G'Day?* Really, Calista?" He laughed. "Or do you

prefer to be called 'Bond. Jane Bond'?"

Calista shoved Kyle in his arm, but a smile grew on her face as she did so. From the back, Jake's voice sounded above the lighthearted giggles coming from the front seat.

"Calista, you did amazing. Thank you. But that whole thing took about five minutes," Jake said.

"Don't worry about it. We're way ahead of schedule. We'll make it, Jake. I promise," Kyle assured, looking back at Jacob.

"That's not what concerns me. It's the fact that Victor and his guys are now five minutes closer to us."

As Calista drove, Jake looked back down to the laptop, directing his attention back and forth from screen to map. After a few moments, his keen eye noticed something. A discrepancy. The far right side of the map on the screen was missing a section, but the same portion on the sketched map was filled in. He noticed more writing on the sketch. Unfortunately, however, the writing was too small for him to effectively read.

"Calista, I need your glasses for a minute," Jacob said, holding a hand between the seats of the center console.

She took them off and handed them to him. She squinted a bit, attempting to gain back some of her vision that was now blurred.

Jacob took the glasses and held them close to the map's surface, just above the area with additional writing. What he saw jump from the page took his breath away.

"Oh my God, it's the cipher." He continued to think for a moment. *Washington's diamond. Washington was president in the late 1700's.* His mind soaked in a realization. *The grave we dug up was dated 1909.* Jacob's mouth chimed in, breaking the silence. "Wait, this doesn't make sense."

"What doesn't?" Kyle responded.

"Victor mentioned the Washington Diamond, as in George Washington."

"And?"

"Well, I'm not sure yet. Hang on," Jacob said, puzzled. He proceeded to type something into the computer without telling Kyle. He spoke up again after a moment. "Okay, here it is. Pierre Charles L'Enfant died in 1825."

"That's the guy whose map we just found. So?"

"So? Kyle, the grave we just dug up was dated 1909."

Kyle let Jacob's statement set in for a time. "Shit." He paused. "What does that mean, then?"

"Not sure, but I'm gonna find out," Jacob said then began typing more into the computer.

After several moments Jacob's voice broke the silence again. "Holy crap." He paused briefly. "I think there's far more to this than what we think."

"So, he gave that map to someone for safekeeping, right?"

Jacob thought for a moment then responded, "Not gave. I think someone took it."

"What makes you say that?"

"Says here that L'Enfant's remains were relocated to Arlington." He paused. "Any idea when that happened?"

"Seriously, you know my only guess is gonna be 1909."

"Bingo," Jacob said. His mind pondered something for a moment. "And you know what? We were so busy digging I didn't even give much thought to the name on the grave," he said.

"Come to think of it, neither did I," Kyle said rhetorically.

"Well, I mean, I *saw* the name, but didn't give it much thought until now. It's not this L'Enfant guy's." His mind was still plunging deeper.

"Whose was it?" Kyle inquired.

He didn't respond right away, again giving his previous statement some thought. "My God, that's it!" he finished.

"What, the code? What does it say?"

"Victor said he found that coded message in his grandfather's things. Well, what if his grandfather told him about a grave that the cipher was placed in?"

"Possible. Maybe that's who he thinks Franklin is."

"You might be right. But we can't count on that right now. I need to know what this message says."

Jacob quickly turned his attention back to the message written in a cipher.

They drove in relative silence for a time as Jacob contemplated the intricate and, he assumed, deliberate format of the cipher. After a while his voice broke the silence.

"There are symbols in this message that aren't on the cipher. This can't be all of it. Something's missing."

He continued prying into the deepest cellars of his mind, referencing long-forgotten Sudoku puzzles and logic problems that his grandfather had challenged him with during his childhood. He chose to place what letters he knew from the cipher—A, T, L, P, Z, and I—into the message. As he scribed periodic letters that matched the symbolic format of each, he noticed something rather peculiar. *Some symbols are completed squares.* He stopped and pondered what possibilities his mind could conjure. After a few moments, he redrew the cipher on the piece of paper.

An eyebrow rose ever so slightly. He was on to something. *There must be a pattern*, he thought. *But what? And where?*

He attempted to dive deeper than ever before, but knew he would soon need to come up for breath. *Pace yourself, Jake. Focus.*

His new focus landed on the unique hash associated to each of the six letters he knew. There were two of each hash mark positioned in the same location of a partial square. He trained his eyes and mind on the A and the I. *Left side.* Then at the T and Z, and L and P respectively. *Right side and bottom. There's got to be something here that I'm missing.*

His air was running out. Soon, he'd have to return to the surface. *No, wait! The first and ninth letters.* He jotted something down and looked at it. He was out of breath, but remained submerged in growing awe. Almost immediately, he began writing in other letters, his speed approaching Mach one. Once again, he admired the ever-changing sheet of paper in front of him, studying his new sketch for what seemed an eternity.

"Holy shit, could it really be that simple?!" he exclaimed as he continued scribbling.

"What?" Kyle asked.

Jacob didn't answer. Kyle's voice came from above the surface. It sounded muffled. Before long, Jacob looked at his page and a relieved smile materialized on his face.

Jacob's voice burst out of the water. "I can read this message."

"What does it say?"

"I have to translate it first, but I'm pretty sure I broke the cipher," Jacob said, still facing the paper. He grabbed a piece of unopened mail from the pocket of the backseat. On it, he wrote down letters as he solved them in succession. More silence filled the confines of the car as Jacob trudged forth with the only weapons he held that could bring Audrey back to him—a dull pencil, a scrap piece of paper, and an unraveled, centuries-old message.

A man stirred in his sleep. He was dreaming. By the contorted look on his face, it didn't appear to be a good dream either. It felt more like a nightmare. His face was sweaty, and the covers had all been tossed from his body, save for a section of the sheet that covered the bottom portion of his legs. The man shot up in bed, and quickly turned on the lamp sitting on the nightstand.

In the low glow of the lamplight, the man buried his face in his hands. In part because he was struggling with a growing case of insomnia, but mostly because of the recurring nightmare he'd been struggling to ward off.

Every night the man dreamt that he was bobbing helplessly in the sea. The sea, however, did not consist of water, but rather words floating as though made of a partially liquefied substance. The gelatinous words surrounding him were those that seemed to describe him. He looked around and saw words like *minuscule*, *breakable*, and *faint* nestled around him, sometimes nudging against his torso as they drifted. The sound they made as they floated echoed the term with which they bore. He looked off in the horizon and saw an infinite number of these words, appearing and disappearing as they climbed to a crest and fell down a trough. Some, off in the distance, were not yet discernible. He tried endlessly to make sense of their true meaning. He looked in all directions only to see more of these words; land was nowhere to be found. Essentially, he was floating in an aquatic thesaurus.

During the dream, he would find himself in this same environment, and would squint to the horizon only to see an approaching tidal wave far off in the distance. The speed with which it approached him was immeasurably fast. Before he knew it, it was upon him, ready to crash over him. The tidal wave, too, was made entirely of words, but these were much different than those feebly existing beside and around him. Words like *abrasive*, *clamor*, and *vociferous* threatened to drown out the man's meaningless and infinitesimal volume of a voice. He would begin to scream as the brash wave would seemingly slow down and taunt him just before crashing onto him with antonymic power.

He could barely hear his own scream as the more powerful words resonated in his eardrums, nearly rupturing them. It was terrifyingly loud, the words changing to all capital letters as they turned to whitecaps after the chaos began to subside. The man would attempt to tread within the scriptous sea, but found he couldn't swim.

Each time calm once again overcame the sea, the words would turn red. They were the color of blood, much darker than a ruby, and thickening in the same way, as though the words had been turned bold, ever scrunching closer together and squeezing the life from his lungs.

He was drowning in his own words.

Before he succumbed to his impending death, he always saw what appeared to be a sign of hope: a handle, rising from the sea for him to grab. Once ahold of the handle, he would catch his breath for a moment, but the handle would always dislodge as two words drifted apart. What was left in his hand was a kitchen knife that he continued to grasp as the overpowering words consumed him.

The man sat in bed crying into his hands. Eventually, he gained composure, and reached for a pill bottle also on his nightstand. He feverishly opened it, almost breaking it to gain entry to the glorious pills he knew he would find inside. He gulped them down with a slosh of a leftover beer from the night before and crashed back into his pillow, praying for God to end the terror that was eating away at his very existence. The terror, that is, that he knew more intimately, as guilt.

Jacob looked back and forth from the completed cipher to the coded message, transcribing the last few letters onto the piece of scrap paper lying in his lap. He finished the last letter and then stared back at the brilliant cipher he just broke. After a moment, he began reading the message to Kyle and Calista, whose ears were perked with pure intrigue and interest.

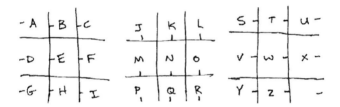

"It says: 'SHOULD ONE INQUIRE WHY ARE THESE HERE THE ANSWER WOULD BE TO STAY TRUE WITH REVERE THEN TO SEARCH THE INTERIOR OF FACES INFERIOR,'" Jacob called out with accomplishment in his voice.

Another riddle.

Just then, the phone Victor gave to Jacob began to ring. Jacob hesitantly placed it to his ear and listened.

"Digging up an American soldier, Jake? How unpatriotic," Victor volleyed over the phone. "Time's a-wastin', good buddy."

"Screw you. But since we're talking, what was your grandfather's name?"

"Pete. Flanten. The third," he said inquisitively.

"Oh yeah. And did he ever tell you anything about a grave?"

"No. Why?"

"Well, I found Franklin."

"You did? Who is he?"

"Not a person, asshole. A place."

Angered, Victor recoiled. "Don, break one of her pretty fingers. Matter of fact, make it the ring finger."

"I wouldn't do that if I were you. That grave had something pretty God damn valuable in it."

"You have my attention. Briefly."

"Ever hear of a guy named Pierre L'Enfant?"

"I'm listening."

"He drafted the original design for Washington D.C. That grave had his original map in it, and something else even more valuable."

"The diamond?"

The sounds of a struggle could be heard in the background. Audrey was proving a worthy adversary to Don, who was still recovering from the failed and very manual excavation attempt in Illinois.

"Call your man off Audrey. Believe me when I say you want what is now in *my* possession."

The statement jarred Victor's memory of what

he'd whispered in Jacob's ear just before electrocuting him in the trunk of that car. After a moment, the struggle seemed to stop. Jacob heard Audrey retaliate in the background.

"Get the hell away from me, you animal!" The sound of her voice terrified Jacob. It had never sounded like that before. It wasn't dainty, happy, and pure. It was wild, feral, and inhuman. Nonetheless, he had never been so relieved to hear her voice than in that very moment.

"Okay, she's fine. Now, what is it? Or I swear to God, I will kill her!"

"The cipher. I have it. And unless she makes it home safe, you'll never know what that fucking letter says."

"Let me enlighten you. When I get that cipher, then, and only then will I even entertain the notion of releasing her. Or, I can just kill her now, and dump her on the side of the road. I mean, do you honestly think you hold the cards here, Jake?"

"Right now I do. The headstone on the grave read 'Pete Flanten.'"

"Still listening?"

"For the moment."

"Good. Now, here's what we're going to do. We'll meet and do an even exchange—Audrey for the cipher. Or I'll just burn it right now, and dump it on the side of the road," Jacob challenged, thrusting a verbal blade through the receiver.

Victor thought for a moment before responding. "Fuck!" he shouted, continuing a moment later. "Where?"

"Four Ponds," Jacob commanded. More power found its way into his voice.

The two were in a battle of words; each blow came laced with razor-sharp testosterone, as they sliced and pierced their way into the opposing man.

"That's all the way back in Michigan," Victor recoiled in defiance.

"Like I said, unless Audrey gets *home* safe, you'll never see this cipher." Jacob twisted his blade, and it tore into the surrounding flesh.

"I know you're in Tennessee, Jacob. I tracked the phone I gave you," Victor followed, annoyed.

"Thought you said it was untraceable," Jacob

countered back, not missing a beat.

"Yeah, well I needed to keep an eye on you. And good thing I did. Plus, I knew you wouldn't dare try anything knowing I had Audrey."

"How do you know I didn't?" Jacob tested the man he knew for so many years as his dearest friend. The depth of his betrayal had not yet entirely sunk in.

"The police are in my damn back pocket. You want to test me? Go ahead. But my phone will ring 30 seconds later." He paused for a brief moment, allowing his threat to land heavily on Jacob's ears. "Ball's in your court, Jake."

"So, then I guess you can trust me." Jacob felt as though he was gaining more power, even if that power came by way of assumed trust.

Jacob began to feel himself emerging as the alpha male in the situation. Victor knew that the tides were turning, and it was evident in the demeanor of his voice.

Victor obviously knew nothing about the note he'd left in the vending machine. There was still a chance, Jacob knew. However slight, it gave him a sense of solace amid the adversity converging around him from nearly every angle. The one angle Jacob knew he controlled was the one straight ahead. He knew the van trailed behind them, but how far remained uncertain. He could not afford to lose this edge. He wouldn't allow it. The diamond? He could care less about it. The cipher? Meaningless. But they were the tools he needed in order to fabricate Audrey's safe return, or if it came to it, her rescue.

"We'll see, but Michigan? We're still hours away," Victor challenged, his voice stern.

"Then you'll have no problem having Audrey there at exactly six this morning, will you, *friend?*" he said, emphasizing the word he'd so recently used to describe Victor. The ubiquity of betrayal continued to cascade over Jacob's heart, but fueled his want for power even more.

There was a pause after Jacob pulled the dagger of control out of Victor's ear, and held it over his head as though it was as mighty and valiant as Excalibur itself.

"Too bad we couldn't share this together, Jake. The world would have been at our fingertips with all that money."

"Cut the sentimental bullshit," he said, honing the edge in his voice. "Do the other guys know that you killed Liam, and'll probably do the same to them?"

No response came.

"I'll take that as a 'no.'" His words stabbed the air as they left his throat.

"Word has it that little butt-buddy college kid of yours isn't doing so well."

Jacob paused intentionally. They really did think

Kyle was dead. "Just be there. And consider this phone deactivated after this call." The hot blade plunged through the phone and into Victor's ear once again. It was the death blow, he hoped, but wouldn't know for sure until he met Victor at the park.

"I'll be there. Oh, and just a reminder, *friend*, I still have that police contact. Believe me, with the cut he's getting, he is definitely on my side."

Jacob pressed the end button on the phone, rolled down the window, and tossed it outside. The phone bounced a few times on the highway before getting run over by another vehicle and breaking into count-less pieces. At the same time, a van entered the high-way a short 30 minutes behind them.

As both vehicles charged north, their respective occupants discussed potential next moves, as if playing an invisible game of chess. Neither group could see the other vehicle, but they both knew they shared the same road.

Audrey looked out of the back window of the van, and stared as the dotted white line zoomed out and disappeared into the black horizon of the night.

The TV roared with action as Lucinda and Nick snuggled closely in bed and watched a movie. It was one they'd both watched during their childhood where a group of adolescents found a treasure map and searched for a long-forgotten pirate's booty, in order to save their neighborhood from being rebuilt as a golf course.

The two chuckled periodically at a variety of memorable one-liners from the movie, and did their best impressions of each.

"ORV. Bullet holes," Nick said as Lucinda laughed, then attempted her own.

"This was my wish, *my* wish! And I'm takin' it back. I'm taking 'em all back." Her eyebrows ascended her forehead as if to say, "Beat that, Bucko."

"Wow. You win this round," Nick said, as the phone began to ring on the nightstand nestled at the side of the bed he was cozied up on.

It was early, and neither Lucinda nor Nick had to work in the morning, and had spent the better portion of the night enjoying a date that was more of a "movie marathon meets pajama party meets all-nighter" than an actual date. Nick rolled over in bed and grabbed

Lucinda's phone on the nightstand. He looked at it as it continued to ring.

"Who's Kyle? And why is he calling so early?" Nick probed.

Without answering, Lucinda took the phone from his hands and answered it.

"Hello?"

"Lucinda?"

"Kyle, it's me. What's going on?"

"Professor Reech is alive. He's with me now. You can't tell anyone, but I need your help. We don't have a lot of time."

"Okay," she said, but it came out sounding more like a question than anything else.

"I need you to do me a favor."

"Um, it depends. What kind of favor?"

"I can't explain over the phone, but trust me on this. Can you meet me?"

Lucinda weighed her options, but knew before contemplating them that she would help Kyle. How could she not? What couldn't he tell her? And why? She was far too intrigued, and that alone was enough to break a few rules. Okay, maybe more like a dozen.

"Hang on," she said into the phone and then continued. "Sorry, Nick. I have to do something," Lucinda said as she held the phone to her chest, and started gathering a change of clothes with her other hand. "I'll be outside in a minute. We can talk more then," she said back into the receiver of the phone.

Before Nick could even process what was happening, Lucinda was out the door.

*Who's Kyle?* Nick thought as the door slammed shut. "That's what I said. You're always contraindicating me. I hate it when you do that," Nick said to himself as he ripped into a fun-size Baby Ruth bar and chuckled.

Calista, Kyle, and Jacob pulled into Kyle's apartment, and Kyle jumped out before the car came to a stop. He was inside his apartment for about a minute, and emerged with two hunting rifles; his pockets bulged from what were likely extra shells.

"Okay. We'll be at the park in just a few minutes. They'll have three guys there. Victor, and two others."

"Got it."

"Are you sure you're okay with doing this? I know what I'm asking of you, but *you* need to ask it of yourself."

Kyle and Calista looked at each other briefly, and discussed their options with facial expressions alone, then went back to Jacob.

"Jake, we're the good guys here. And we're all you have, unless you want to call the police, who you may or may not be able to trust."

"Okay. But, when we're out there, you both need to stay perfectly still on the interior of the tree line until my signal."

The words he spoke, two in particular, forced a thought to rush into Jacob's head. *Stay. Interior.* He thought back to the message he'd decoded. *Should one inquire why are these here the answer would be to stay true with revere, then to search the interior of faces inferior.*

"Why are these here? What are *these?*" Jacob considered the potential meaning of the phrase.

"Why are *what* here?" Kyle said.

"Hang on. Give me a second," Jacob followed, as thoughts began to spew from his mind and mouth.

*'These' is plural.* "Graves?" *Coordinates?* "No. Shit, it doesn't make sense."

Then another idea erupted from his throat. "A diamond?" *Maybe.* "But it's not *here.*" *So what* is *here?*

He dove deeper into his mind. *The page, a riddle, words.* "Words are here," he said aloud. *But which ones shouldn't be? Revere, search, answer...*

Nothing was making sense, but he continued. "...faces inferior." He read the riddle over and over, removing different words each time.

"It makes no sense when the words are taken out." Jacob rubbed his eyes for a moment, frustrated with the riddle. He scanned the words yet again in his mind. *Should one inquire why are these here.* With that thought, and with the energy of lightning, Jacob sat bolt upright in the backseat. "Not words at all. Letters shouldn't be here."

He was on to something.

*Why are. Y and R.* Not the words. The letters shouldn't be there!"

Jacob looked at the decoded message again, and

began crossing out all of the letters representative of the words "why" and "are" found within it. After a moment, only one newly identifiable word leapt from the sheet of paper and out of his mouth.

"Statue. Holy shit, it's in a statue."

"What is?" Kyle said, confused by the rather one-sided and internal conversation Jacob was having.

"The diamond," he said, as he opened the laptop yet again and navigated to the Society of Cincinnati website with a few clicks of the mouse. "I remember seeing a statue of George Washington in one of the banners on the Society's homepage."

He promptly found the banner again, and marveled at it, as it screamed from the screen. He clicked on it and a new screen appeared offering an article about the statue and a caption below the image. He read the caption aloud.

"*Located on the grounds of the Society of Cincinnati, and often compared to Cincinnatus, the Roman model of honor and simplicity, the George Washington statue stands tall, paying homage to the man behind the presidency and the building blocks of our great nation. Made entirely of Carrera marble,Washington is seen leaning on a bundle of rods known as fasces, depicting him as a simple farmer turned president.* That's it!" Jacob said. *Not faces inferior. Fasces inferior.*

His expression quickly turned puzzled as a realization came to mind while looking at the image on the screen. "That doesn't look like marble. Damn, it's a replica."

"We need to go, Jake," Kyle interrupted.

"Okay. I need to find out where the original George Washington statue is located."

"You can keep looking while I drive, just wanted to let you know our timeline. 45 minutes, but we need to get into position which'll take 20 minutes, easy."

Jacob let out a relieved sigh, knowing that he just took a giant leap in the direction of getting Audrey back safely. He did a generic online search for the statue and found that it was sculpted by Jean-Antoine Houdon in 1791.

"Get this, that statue was created the same year that the coded letter was written," Jacob said as he continued to read the article.

He found that the original slab of marble arrived in the U.S. in several pieces. One of the smaller pieces, however, had a flaw in the bottom of it. A chunk had broken off, leaving a distinctive cavity that was not visible while it stood upright, but irritated the sculptor nonetheless. Houdon relayed the imperfection to Washington, who also made note of it. Upon the formal erection of the statue in May of 1796, no one noticed that Washington, the masterful mason that he was, had filled in the cavity.

"He hid the diamond in the fasces! It's in the Capitol building in Virginia!"

With the clarity of a night owl weaving in and out among a forest of trees searching for prey, Jacob approached the abandoned campsite, keeping every ounce of focus trained on the set of headlights farther up the path. A dark silhouette distinctly contrasted in front of the bright beams of a van. As he approached, his insides began to feel like volcanic magma, churning from within. He swallowed hard to quell the sensation, and got out of the car.

The smell of pine assaulted his nasal cavity. Thick and towering pines blanketed the landscape where a campsite once thrived. An old fire pit scarred the ground off to the left of the site, and Jacob could almost see the variety of tents and campers that once populated the area. Kids playing, stacked firewood at the tree line, and happy families creating memories—all appeared in his mind as ghostly apparitions fought to steal the imaginary spotlight.

As he envisioned the scenes in his mind, Jacob couldn't help but wonder if he would be able to create similar family memories with Audrey. He wanted so badly to just give the man what he had, but couldn't. The cipher was the only leverage he held. And it was a far cry to trust that Victor would just let them go if he handed it over, like he said he would. More than likely, he feared, Victor would just shoot them both as soon as it was in his possession.

He couldn't allow himself to think like that. Not now. She needed his every wit. Until she was back in his arms, Jacob would not feel safe.

He shook the ghostly images from just behind his eyes and forced focus back into his exhausted and weary mind. It had all led to this. His best friend, his fiancée, and he had so recently cheered for the Wolverines, and shared childhood stories with one another. How did they all end up like this?

Again, the thoughts were seeping back into his head. He scowled at himself as he slowly continued to approach the middle of the campsite where Victor stood.

When he stood about ten feet in front of Calista's car he shot a glance back to it, where he saw a tiny red light blinking on the dashboard.

Aroom full of men in suits huddled in front of a projector screen that was mounted on the wall of an office. Each stared at the screen as a live feed was broadcast from an unknown location. The men had received direction only moments ago to dial in to it.

"What the hell is this?" one man asked abruptly, as he sipped on his lukewarm coffee.

"Receptionist just gave it to us. Said the caller claimed it was of national security," another man explained. He was still fidgeting with the cords to get better reception and sound from the video feed.

"Quiet," an authoritative, but friendly voice called out. "Someone is coming in on the left."

The men sat and watched a figure appear on the screen. They had no idea who it was, but stood motionless as a conversation unfolded before their eyes. They were as captivated as children watching the first ever cartoon airing on the first ever color television.

"The cipher, Jake. Hand it over," one of the men on screen demanded.

"Where's Audrey?" the other countered.

"She's fine."

"That's not good enough. I need proof," he ordered, as he let authority run rampant in his vocal chords.

The first man looked over his shoulder to a white van parked just behind him, motioning to someone. Two men promptly emerged; one held a woman securely at his side.

"Audrey! Are you okay?" Jacob hollered. Even in captivity, she was radiant. Her sweater draped comfortably around her and fell upon her body, every inch of which he knew.

"Oh my God, Jacob! Yes. I'm fine," the woman called out. Her voice was shaky, but defiant toward the man holding her at bay.

She tried swatting the man's hand from touching any part of her body. Her attempts, however, were entirely fruitless as Frank slung one of his arms around her neck from behind. He tightened his grip and Jacob saw Audrey give in from the awkward stance she was being forced to hold. A moment later, the viper in her struck again. She stomped on Frank's foot. The heavy heel of her boot connected with his big toe.

"God damn it!" Frank said as he pulled back on her long, beautiful hair.

"Get your hands off her, you son of a bitch!" Jacob exploded as he watched the scene play out about fifteen feet in front of him. At this point, he was helpless.

With her hair held tight, Frank whispered in Audrey's ear. "I don't give a shit about your hero-of-a-hubby's cipher. You do that one more time, and you're gonna watch him die. Are we clear?"

She didn't say the words, but Frank felt her nod her head in understanding, and, he hoped, fear.

"See, Jake? She's fine," Victor said. "Now, the cipher, or those'll be the last intelligible words you ever hear your pretty little Audrey say." He was as calm as a goldfish happily perusing a spacious new tank.

"You don't get it, do you?" Jake said, trying a new tactic to buy more time, and to hopefully allow an advantage to make an appearance.

"Get what?" Victor bit.

"The shit that was handed down in your family." He paused. "For one, I think the map I found tonight was handed down to your grandfather. Hell, the name was." A brief silence between the two men followed, then Jacob landed a haymaker. "Your family's real last name is L'Enfant."

"That's impossible," Victor shouted in disgust. *How dare he attack my family's name?*

"Believe what you want, Victor. But I know his real name." He paused momentarily. "Pierre L'Enfant III."

"No. You're lying," Victor shouted.

"I'm telling you the truth, Victor. Think about it.

Pete, Pierre. Flanten, L'Enfant. It doesn't take a rocket scientist."

The water was getting cloudy in Victor's fish tank. There was an undeniable correlation between the two names Jacob just called out. The realization disoriented the goldfish in his own tank. He could barely see the plastic plant among the various rock pebbles at the bottom.

"I don't give a shit what his name was. My great-great-great-grandfather created that language for Washington. Period. It's my diamond, Jake," Victor said, as tiny, errant bubbles rose to the top of his aquarium of confusion.

"I thought you said it was Washington's," Jacob challenged immediately, as though he already had the conversation plotted out in his mind.

"What, you think that diamond would have stayed in the same spot for 200 years if people knew where it was all this time? Bullshit, Jake! Hell, even you would've taken it if you had the opportunity," Victor said, trying to correct his faltering equilibrium.

"Maybe, but don't you think the Society should get it?" he stalled. "I mean, Washington had to have intended it for them rather than to fall into the possession of a raging lunatic 200 years later," Jacob insulted.

To Jacob, the water looked crystal clear. He was able to navigate within Victor's mind without flaw. He knew Victor, even if everything had been a lie up until now. He knew the *man*. Words, beliefs, likes, and dislikes were all things that could be forged. A man's true personality, however, could never be disguised as another. He knew Victor's hot buttons, and hoped he would soon boil over.

"The Society? Are you kidding? They were more fuckin' divided back then than you and I are now. I'm getting that diamond, Jake," he said as he raised a gun toward Jacob and began walking toward him.

Audible gasps could be heard from the group of men watching the scene play out on the screen. One of the men in the room spoke up shortly after L'Enfant's name was mentioned.

"L'Enfant created the original plans for D.C. Shit, that was back in the 1700s." He paused briefly. "My God! They're talking about the Washington Cipher. He used it to conceal a 120-carat diamond," the man said while looking around the room at the other occupants. "Allegedly," he added, as blank stares were cast in his direction. "I'm a history buff, okay? So what?" he concluded, warding off the comments hidden directly behind the other men's lips.

After the man finished, all eyes in the room were once again fixated on the projector's screen. One man near the doorway turned down the lights, making the screen much more vivid. The room kind of resembled a movie theater. All that was missing was a dripping bowl of buttered popcorn in each of their hands. Who knows? Maybe that was coming.

"I'm not disputing that, Victor. But I know where his diamond is. There was a riddle in that grave," he said, as the advantage he was hunting for made its presence clearly known. "I solved it."

Jacob pulled out a Mason jar with a piece of paper in it in one hand, and a lighter in the other. "The cipher is in here." He held the lighter above the Mason jar. "Tell your men to let Audrey go, or I'll burn it, I swear to God," he warned.

A lengthy pause filled the air as thoughts raced through each man's mind.

"Jake, you know I can't do that until that cipher is in my hands. How do I know that's not a fake like your coordinates?"

"Feel free to test me, asshole. You think if you do anything to her, that I'll just give this thing to you? As long as I have this, Audrey stays safe."

"You're right. I wouldn't expect you to be too cooperative if I killed her. But, maybe if I just broke one of her legs? How 'bout then, Jake, would that help?"

he said, as composed and relaxed as ever. Victor could see the water in the tank clearing again as authority filtered through his gills. It almost excited him.

"You wouldn't," Jacob expressed sharply, more as a reassurance to Audrey, who was hearing every word, than in rebuttal to Victor's threat.

Victor turned his attention from Jacob to Audrey for a moment, then back to Jacob. "Why don't we find out?" he toyed, and began backing away from Jacob, toward Audrey.

"Houdon's fasces!" he yelled as loud as he could. "Houdon's fasces!" he repeated, his voice reverberating through the darkened park. The shouting caught Victor's attention, and he turned back to face Jacob only to see him ignite the lighter over the Mason jar.

Several men in the room shouted at the screen as Jacob threatened to ruin one of the nation's most storied artifacts. The search for the Washington Cipher had run rampant for over a hundred years after Washington died in 1799.

"It's The Movement," a man said. "I've heard of them. Small, but ruthless. They've been looking for this cipher for about a dozen or so years."

"Houdon's fasces," another man pondered quietly, then continued. "Shit, I think he just told us the location of the diamond."

The remaining men quieted as he elaborated. "Houdon sculpted the George Washington statue in the Capitol building in Virginia. He's leaning on a bundle of rods." The man looked around as he explained, but no one seemed to be following. He continued as puzzled looks materialized on the faces of the men positioned around the oblong table. "Fasces.

"Initially, no one knew the cipher even existed, and simply included it in stories to their children as legend. It eventually became a staple of American folklore, paving the way for it to become a sort of Holy Grail to treasure hunters, and for American traditionalists to strive to help keep it concealed. They believed that time, if nothing else, would aid in the preservation of one of the last great American treasures. Their strategy lasted over 200 years, but drew fresh attention toward the turn of the century, and the recognition of the 200th anniversary of Washington's death in 1999. A new fellowship of treasure hunters was born, and the hunt for the Washington Cipher commenced once again after almost a hundred years of dormancy. The fellowship referred to the pursuit of the cipher as The Movement."

A plethora of shouts riddled the room that housed what were now about a dozen men in suits, as they watched an unexpected turn take place.

Jacob closed the lighter, extinguishing the flame. Immediately following, two gunshots rang out almost simultaneously and the two men behind Victor fell to the ground, dead.

The weight of one man pulled Audrey to the ground as his lifeless body plummeted to the earth, similar to a horse falling on its jockey. In the same instant, Jake addressed Audrey.

"Run, Audrey! Run!" he yelled.

Audrey scrambled to free herself from under the dead man, and Victor turned to fire at her, but Jacob was already at full speed and tackled him to the ground, fighting for control of the gun. A few errant bullets cut through the air as the two men tumbled toward the ground; one grazed Jacob's stomach, but he barely felt it from the adrenaline surging through his body. More bullets rang out as the fight continued.

Jacob punched Victor in the stomach with all of his might, and grappled for the gun, which was knocked from Victor's hands after the unexpected blow. They each saw the gun now on the ground and wrestled for it on the gravel of the campsite. Jacob was the first to get to it, and bent down for it, but Victor tripped him just before his palm closed around the handle. Instinctively, his hands sprawled out on the ground to break his fall, and he rolled through it back to his feet. Victor was already racing back to the gun, and Jacob pounced on his back, sending both men back to the ground once again. They exchanged blows briefly, until Victor stunned Jacob with a rock from the ground. The sound of it hitting Jacob's head echoed as moonlight peered in through the bases of the surrounding trees. Victor spit blood on the ground as he picked up the gun. Jacob lay disoriented on the ground in front of him.

"The cipher," Victor said, breathless.

Jacob moaned and then responded in a weak voice, "It's not the real one." He, too, caught his breath before finishing, "Real one's not here."

Victor kicked Jacob in the ribs as he lay on the ground. "Where is it!" he demanded.

Still writhing in pain, his head was already throbbing and his rib cage ached. "Not until I know Audrey's safe," he managed, spitting blood.

Victor cocked the gun and leaned down, placing the still warm barrel on Jacob's forehead. "Where is it? I'm only going to count to three, Jake. One."

"You won't do it. You'll never find that damn cipher if you do," Jacob said as he blotted blood from his lower lip.

"Two. Come on, Jake. I don't want to do this, but I will," he warned.

Another gunshot rang out that nearly woke the sun, and echoed throughout the trees. A flock of birds took flight as the echo fell upon their feathers. Jacob flinched, thinking it was Victor's gun that fired, but soon realized it wasn't. His ears were ringing, but he could still hear another sound. Screaming. He opened his eyes to see where the shot came from, and to his left, on the other side of the site, he saw Kyle crouched beside a tree with a rifle at his side.

Jacob looked back at Victor, but didn't see him at first. He scanned the lot, and eventually saw Victor as he climbed back into the van. A moment later, it sped off in the opposite direction, throwing loose gravel toward Jacob.

He struggled to sit up, and on the ground in front of him, he saw Victor's pistol. A hand, severed just above the wrist, still gripped it. Jacob rose to his feet, and headed toward the woods in the direction he saw Audrey run.

On the projector, the men could see Jacob get up and limp out of view as he held his side in pain toward the tree line, calling out Audrey's name.

The authoritative voice in the room spoke up again, even louder this time. "Get the Vice President on the phone." He paused briefly. "You four." He pointed to four Secret Service members. "Put a team together and get to that Capitol building. No one goes in or out unless I say so."

"Yes, sir, Mr. President," the men said in unison, then left the room.

Aside from the men in the room, there was only one other pair of eyes watching the live feed from the camera mounted on the dashboard of Calista's car. Those of Lucinda Garrett. The feed was given to her by Kyle. This whole story would soon unfold, and since she kept his identity secure from the beginning, he made good on his promise of an exclusive since she loaned her camera to him.

"Oh my Lord," she said to herself after watching what was on the screen. She did a Google search for the only two words she did not understand from the exchange. She simply typed in "Houdon fasces." A website appeared, explaining the George Washington statue. It also detailed its location. The Virginia Capitol building. She revved her engine and turned around, heading for I-75 South.

"Jake! Jake, I'm over here!" Audrey responded.

He came over a small swell in the ground and could see his fiancée crouching behind a tree like a turtle. He came to her and the two embraced for the first time in what seemed an eternity. He kissed the top of her head and squeezed her tightly. She gripped him just the same, and turned to face him, not yet entirely believing it was Jacob who was hugging her. Fresh tears of joy flooded her eyes as her hands came up to Jacob's face. She kissed his lips lovingly. When she took her hands away from his face, however, she saw two bright red handprints smeared on his cheeks.

Confused, she looked down at her stomach, and watched as more and more blood wicked into the fabric of her sweater. At the same time, Jacob, too, noticed the sweater's discoloration.

"Oh no. Audrey." The words spilled out of his mouth.

"Jake?" she asked, knowing there was no answer. "It hurts."

"No. You're fine. Here, look at me. You're alright. Keep your eyes on me, sweetie. I'm going to get you out of here." He looked around frantically. "Kyle! Call an ambulance, Audrey's been shot! Hurry!" His attention turned back to his soon-to-be wife. "It's gonna be okay, hon." He took off his shirt and wrapped it tightly around her stomach. Blood began to appear almost immediately. His heart nearly disintegrated inside his chest cavity. "Talk to me, sweetie. Tell me about our wedding."

"I was going to look so beautiful for you," she managed to whisper, her voice trembling.

"Don't you say that. You're going to look amazing. What colors are we going to have?" He stopped and looked up to see Kyle and Calista slowly approaching. Somber expressions were plastered on their faces as they stood, each with a rifle slung over their shoulder.

"They're on their way, Jake." Kyle paused momentarily. "Tell us what to do."

Jacob didn't say anything. He didn't need to as he stared into Kyle's eyes, then Calista's. Tears began to stream down his cheeks as he looked back down at Audrey.

"Tell me about the colors, Aud. Violet, or eggplant?"

No response.

"Come on, babe, don't give up. Look at me. Focus on me."

He sobbed, almost choking on his tears as he felt the love of his life squeeze his hand more tenderly than ever before. A moment later, her hand went entirely limp.

"No! Audrey, I love you!" he said, hoping she heard those last three words.

But it was too late. At the age of twenty-six, Audrey Carlson lay in Jacob's arms, dead.

Kyle sat on the couch in his apartment reading the *Holly Chronicle* as Calista continued to sleep on the adjacent sofa. The article he was reading detailed a variety of crimes that the police were able to connect to her father, Liam, posthumously. As Kyle read, he realized they were mostly murders. He looked at Calista sleeping and felt even more grateful that he had not turned into one of Liam's victims. Not just because he valued the decades of life still bubbling within him, but because Calista already had a hard enough recovery in front of her. He wanted to be there for her during that time, and was happy that she was not grieving for him too, nor would she be left to navigate the dreary catacombs of emotions if she were to find out that her father killed her boyfriend.

Kyle had been waiting for the right time to offer something to Calista ever since she found her father dead on the floor of that house. At the time, all he could think to do was place a hand on her leg. But now, he knew, the time to do more had arrived.

He folded the newspaper, rose to his feet, and walked to the small wooden hutch located next to his compact dinner table. He looked back toward the enchanting

Calista as he slowly pulled open a drawer built into the hutch. He did not want to wake her. Something like this, he realized, was best offered during a time of personal privacy. A time where there would be no misconception of a desired reaction, and would allow the person to bask in the moment for a time found only within the person receiving the offering.

He retrieved an item from the drawer, and looked at it for a moment before creeping over to the sofa where Calista was napping. Her arms were tucked in close to her face, but one hand jutted out farther than the other, almost cascading over the edge of the sofa. Kyle bent down to Calista and placed the item in her opened hand along with a folded piece of paper. He looked at the items again as he rose back to his feet, all the while hoping that she would see and feel what he did in the two items now nestled in her slightly closed palm.

It was a locket and it contained a picture of her as a child. The picture had been cut to size in order to fit into the locket. The most telling portion of the picture, however, was the arm of a man just at the edge with a tattoo of a four-leaf clover on his forearm. The same tattoo he'd noticed on her father as he lay motionless on the floor.

When Kyle found out that the man trying to kill him was in fact Calista's father, he went back inside as she cried on the front porch and searched his body for something to give her. Anything. He was expecting to find a driver's license, necklace, or bracelet to give her as a condolence. He had no idea that he would find something that proved the man who was nothing more than a murderer to most, was also one that kept a deep and unwavering love for his daughter close to his heart, even as he died.

Kyle smiled as he looked at the picture for a moment longer before he left for class. It was the same picture as the one Calista carried in her purse for all those years.

The folded piece of paper, however, was something else entirely.

Less than six hours after Jacob notified the authorities of the whereabouts of Washington's legendary diamond, the Secret Service had fully taken control of the Capitol building in Richmond, Virginia. A media circus sprouted over the next few hours through the lens of one camera, and the scene blared from the living rooms of millions of Americans.

Nick Laslow watched the television in awe as a team of about ten agents warded off eager onlookers.

On the screen, Nick noticed that a large blue tarp had been placed over the building's entrance, making it impossible for piercing eyes to penetrate the heavily protected interior.

The channel was CNN, and the entire nation watched in excitement and speculation. Viewers across the nation were able to take part as news anchors and political experts hypothesized about the breaking story now filling the airways. Their first-person vantage point came from the lens of Lucinda Garrett's cameraman, her red business suit now replaced with a more vivid yellow version as she radiated on the screen.

Lucinda, once a no-name in her profession, was now, in this very moment, the beacon to which everyone looked as this two-hundred-year-old drama unfolded. Hers were the scales among countless fish now shining in the sun. The funny thing is she carried herself exactly the same as when she was at the bottom of that very same totem pole. She had what it took to deliver one hell of a story to the masses, even if a portion of the viewing public only tuned in to admire her looks.

Of course, and no one expected otherwise, Lucinda was only allowed to get so close before the Secret Service turned her away. But, she knew a scuffle such as that made for great television. She also knew that she'd gain support from curious viewers simply for trying, as the Secret Service tirelessly worked inside the Capitol building through the night.

After the initial media-driven commotion, all cameras were forced to leave, and a perimeter was established to assure privacy and that no video or picture was taken. At a certain point, however, the weather took a turn for the worse, and a torrential downpour began, forcing even the diehard reporters to take cover in their vans. No telescopic lens could effectively pierce through the onslaught of magnified raindrops.

There was zero visibility from afar.

"I'll be damned," Nick said as he watched the newscast play out on his screen. "She made national." Lucinda looked more gorgeous than ever as he watched her shine on national television. Now he realized that Kyle must have been a source of hers, and he actually respected her more for keeping his identity anonymous.

Without warning, the Capitol building reopened to the public and Lucinda stormed in with a herd of other people. Amid a circus, she alone stood before one display. The George Washington statue. She contemplated it for a moment. Her cameraman captured her as she did so—a true vision in yellow for America to admire.

From behind the lens, he knew the impact she had made on America. He saw it for himself, as all Americans now did. She had poise, candor, and an intellect far beyond her local-news counterparts, and far deeper than most of her viewers initially gave her credit. America would see that, and she would probably be sitting on the couch of *Good Morning America* before she could count backward from five.

Lucinda stood in front of the George Washington statue, looking at it for a time. She had never taken the time to admire the precision and patience required of a sculptor wanting to purge a three-dimensional masterpiece from his mind. The serenity of the masterpiece now holding her gaze touched her soul at a level she did not know was possible.

Her hand found its way to her chin as she noticed

something peculiar. She took out her 35 mm camera to zoom in closer. Something tiny, almost indiscernible to the naked eye, was lying on the floor at the base of the statue. In the lens of her camera, however, it was clear as day. Plaster residue.

Kyle opened the door to his apartment and tossed his backpack to the floor. The physics exam he just took was brutal. But he was confident that he'd scored well. Passing this test was just one step closer to a career in astrophysics. His interest in the dive team was heavily weighted on the sensation of weightlessness he experienced underwater. But, as time progressed, he'd learned to love the water just as much as the night sky.

He was a sucker for all things astronomical, but didn't realize his true passion until he watched Comet Hale-Bopp in 1997. He remembered seeing its tail stretch out behind it as though it were a million miles long. To him, it looked so tiny, so far away. From his perspective, it soared silently across the summer sky, but he knew it was a violent and alien orb of jagged rock and ice spiraling chaotically. It was similar to life, where an onlooker's perception becomes his or her reality. It was at that moment that he realized he wanted to learn everything he could about planetary bodies.

He walked to the refrigerator and pulled out a bottle of water, taking a few hefty chugs before setting it down on the counter. It was cold, and offered much needed refreshment after taking the mind-numbing two-hour particle physics exam. He turned back toward his kitchen table to sift through the mail, and was startled to see someone standing in the opening of the hallway in his periphery.

"Oh my God, you scared me. I didn't know you were still here," he said to Calista, who still wore the sweatpants and yoga shirt she'd had on when he left her sleeping on the couch about four hours ago.

Calista didn't respond, but began approaching him. Her stride had purpose, and throbbed with sensuality.

"Hey, how ya feeling, Cal?" Kyle inquired genuinely.

Still no response. Kyle could see the locket dangle from her neck, bouncing atop her supple chest as she neared him. My God, he thought as he imagined lying next to her watching another movie. Her warmth, her curves, her equal feelings toward him all tantalized him.

A moment later, he stumbled as Calista collided into him, and into his arms, like converging nebulae destined to share space with one another. Her 6 foot 1 inch frame synced perfectly with his. She looked straight into his eyes and kissed him passionately, thanking him for the locket without ever saying a word. Motion eased back into Kyle's own lips as he returned the kiss, and grasped her more tightly than he'd thought possible. Kyle lost himself in the kiss, and his breathing fell in tempo with hers, as though their chests were magnetized to one another. No fantasy could conjure a kiss this powerful, this enlightening. It overwhelmed him. As Kyle's hands flirted with her shoulder-length hair, he caressed her neck and realized he was falling in love with the woman of his dreams.

A conflicted tear descended Calista's cheek. In time, she knew, her grief would absorb into the overwhelming happiness that now exuded from her heart and into Kyle's piercing eyes.

On the floor of the kitchen, a piece of paper from Calista's hand lay delicately open faced. It was a poem he wrote for her.

### The Midnight Mare
The midnight mare
Dances in the air.
Rearing skyward
While hearing my words.
My mind she sweetly consumes;
A nightly whimsical plume.
Forward she charges.
My psyche she barges.
I want to rein her in.
Though not to feign or sin.
It's her love I cannot lack.
I'm a dove upon her back.
The midnight mare silken, white
Owns my mind, my soul at night.

ADAM J. BEARDSLEE

The midnight mare
Gallops without care.
Dashing so free.
Is she chasing after me?
Burning legs speeding.
Yearning heart bleeding.
She cannot be tamed.
Her eyes cry the same.
But I'm falling for her
Love without borders.
Wanting, waiting;
My love never fading.
The midnight mare silken, whitest
Pulls me from the stable, her beauty brightest.

The ice clinked as the empty glass met once again with the bar top, sending what condensation was still clinging to the vessel of his altered state into a ringed puddle beneath it. Countless years of troubling times for patrons had been eased, though only temporarily and fueled by alcohol, at this open-air bar top. Ring marks had battered the smooth surface over time, mirroring craters on the moon. One area in particular harbored a rudimentary Olympic logo that jumped from the grain, its rings varying in size and width from different mugs taking part in the oddly artistic display of pride in our great nation by patrons.

Jacob sat at Barney's Bar, staring down his fourth rum and coke, as a cold evening breeze patted his back. The letters "B-A-R," after the word "Barney's," were capitalized and blinking, showing just how creative the name really was. As if passersby had no idea that the word "Bar" after Barney's meant just that. A truly creative spirit might have named the watering hole "BARney's" and saved some money on the semi-lit neon sign.

The door of the bar was the only updated piece on

the entire exterior of the building. Jacob remembered hearing about a recent story where a patron was so drunk that when he left on his motorcycle, he drove it back inside the bar, right through the front door, because he forgot his cell phone. According to witnesses who knew the drunken man, he did not even own a cell phone.

The scene kept playing out in Jacob's mind as he drank away the night.

*Her long blonde tendrils cascading down the front of her sweater, drinking up the blood flowing from her stomach. Her face contorted in pain, with fierce eyes that fought for their life while looking into his, silently screaming for help. Her body doubled over in his arms, ever succumbing to the forces of gravity that were pulling her to the earth. Her glazed eyes staring out at nothing. Her head getting heavier with each fading breath. Her chest failing to rise and fall with new and fresh life.*

"'Nother round?" the bartender offered.

The nod that Jacob responded with was as infinitesimal as noticing the Earth tilting on its axis, but Craig, as his name tag displayed, read it flawlessly, as if Jacob had screamed it from the top of his lungs.

Jacob's eyes were lost in the steady wisp of gray smoke emitting from the ashtray in front of him, his eyes mirroring the color of the cinder on his cigarette, and burning just the same.

Craig could always tell which of his customers smoked and which bore a stress they just wanted to smoke out of their lives. The way they held the cigarette, index finger and thumb, or index and middle finger; the type of draw they took, deep or shallow; the rate of exhale, slow and calm, or quick and labored; how often the ash was flicked, constantly or rarely. These were all cues as to why a person was smoking, and for how long they had been dealing with an assumed anxiety. Jacob, Craig could tell, was a very stressed individual looking for escape, or, more dangerously, an answer. Sure, any number of rum and cokes could provide an escape, but no number would ever lead to an answer.

Jacob held the Alcoholics Anonymous eight-year-sobriety token in his hand as he drank. It had lost its luster from years of traveling in the front pocket of his jeans, but it wasn't Jacob who had a drinking problem. The chip was his father's, handed down to him from his mother. He always put it out in the open when he drank to never lose sight that he was in control of the throat-burning concoction sitting before him. This night, however, was different.

*What was in that canteen when you dropped it?*

The alcohol was already taking a toll on Jacob's psyche; visions of ghostly apparitions danced in his mind, screaming for his attention.

*Water. I swear, Jake. I stopped drinking long before your mother even got pregnant.*

He took another swig and heard the door chime, the signaling of another lost soul entering the outdoor bar.

Jacob sat at the bar, still staring at the Olympic logo slightly to his left. He planned to get drunk tonight to erase the images of Audrey's dying body from his mind. There were two types of drunkenness: *unjustified*, commonly displayed by college coeds enjoying themselves far too much, and far too often, and *justified*, found in a locked-away place in the soul of every grieving person. The place where none wanted to visit, but some spent their lives. The place, that is, where a loved one no longer shares the same air, or takes in the same sights. Here is the place where many turn for liquid guidance that inevitably leads to nowhere.

A man took the seat next to Jacob, even though the entire bar top was vacant of customers. Jacob didn't even notice the man sit down. No words were spoken, and the two sat in comfortable silence for a time, until the other man brought his hand to the bar, palm facing down. After motioning to the bartender by raising two fingers from the bar, effectively ordering a double, he removed his hand, leaving behind a polished police badge on the counter. Only then did Jacob realize who took residence beside him.

"I can't imagine that that's just Coke," Detective O'Reilly started.

"How'd you guess?" The friendly-but-firm sarcasm was as thick as the smoke now filling the area. He took another drag on his cigarette—different this time. The bartender noticed it was slower, like his mind was elsewhere, gazing off into the unknown of the subconscious mind. "Or is the grimace of Audrey dying in my arms still written across my face?" Jacob sulked, his lower lip beginning to lose the battle with an oncoming quiver. His mind knew he was speaking, but his face remained lost in grief.

"Don't say that, Jake. She'll always be with you. You know that," the detective counseled, not daring to look Jake in the eyes at a time like this. Patrick knew men were much different than women. Often, a man in an emotionally compromising condition found more consult from his friend looking straight ahead, or down for that matter, as he stumbled around the awkward guise of a successful psychoanalyst, rather than looking him in his eyes. Eye contact at a time like this, Patrick knew, was far more intimate a move than Jacob would likely want to travel.

"Actually," Jacob continued, "maybe it's the fact that my best friend, my best friend since I was a kid, was the one who killed her." Jacob once again dowsed his esophagus with a slurp of rum disproportionately mixed with Coca-Cola. "Or maybe, just maybe"—he paused as the bite of the alcohol dug in—"it's because the love of my life is gone, and I hate everything I've ever known about friendship." His eyes began to burn. "What am I going to do for the rest of my life, Pat?" His lip surrendered to the inevitable. Jacob never knew, but the seasoned ears of the detective next to him picked up every softened sob emanating from the grieving man's olfactory.

Oddly, Jacob now turned and faced Detective O'Reilly.

"I want to kill him, Pat." Jacob began to sob openly.

The double shot of rum in his most recent cocktail provided the tears.

Patrick placed his glass directly on top of one of the Olympic rings, as though he was claiming partial ownership of the piece of art.

"I don't doubt that you do, Jake. Hell, who wouldn't feel like that?"

"It's not just a feeling, Pat."

A friendly silence followed. Patrick knew not to challenge his grieving friend about such a statement. He decided to let Jacob vent, and waited for more pain to surface.

It never came.

"Tell ya what, there's something I wanna give ya, Jake," Patrick posed. "I don't have it with me, but I think it'll help you understand that there are many others in this world who struggle just as you do."

"What is it?" The quivering began to subside in Jacob's voice.

"Well, it's not really something that can be given. Its true meaning has to be seen," the detective continued.

"And you think it can help me?" Vague sarcasm returned as he spoke the words.

"Yeah, I do. Well, I hope." He paused. "Hey, why don't you stop by tomorrow morning after you wake up and shake off the remnants from tonight." He smiled, knowing that Jake would in some way regret losing himself in liquor tonight.

"I can do that," Jacob responded. "Pat? Thanks. And sorry I'm in rare form tonight. It's all just kind of caught up to me, ya know?"

Patrick put his hand on Jacob's shoulder—any male weirdness was now out of the question—and smiled.

"Happy to do it, Jake. By the way, you need a ride home?"

"No. I'm walkin'. Thanks."

With that, Detective O'Reilly threw back the rest of his cocktail, and addressed Jacob.

"Sounds good." He patted Jacob's shoulder, and began walking toward the door. After several steps, Patrick turned around and offered one more truth about life.

"Oh, and Jake? The funny thing about the rest of our lives"—he paused briefly—"is that they're ours. You'll get through this."

Patrick opened the door, and left. Jacob didn't even turn around, nor did he need to. The door sounded as Patrick exited. The ring of the chime brought Jacob's mind back to the present, and he signaled for yet another round.

A man sat at his glass-top kitchen table admiring each and every trinket, souvenir, and keepsake that he had stolen from countless unassuming people over the past twenty-two years. Some items screamed their stories from the confines of their respective material; some hollered from porcelain, others from metal, and some even vied to tell their stories from wood. Each was coated in a variety of different colors, and represented the ability of the man staring at each of them to steal from those who had passed through his life.

The man stared into one room of the many that housed his treasures. In this room, he admired the small items. These were the easiest to obtain over the years, and most of what was in this room was obtained when the disease was still in its infancy. In the adjacent room, he would soon admire the medium-sized objects. These were a bit harder to acquire. Decorative pillows, toasters, and serving dishes, among other things, were strategically seated within the darkened room in which he would soon pay homage.

Like many kleptomaniacs, this man had tediously catalogued each item he ever stole. His ledger—full of names, dates, and objects—proved as profound a token as any one item in his house. As he flipped the pages of his twenty-year-old journal, he looked around his house. Every bedroom—three in all—was packed full of items ranging from the meaningless, like salt-and-pepper shakers and old slippers, to the ornate and valuable, like Samurai swords and antique Moroccan puzzle boxes. In every other second-story room in his house, boxes containing the man's own belong ings were stacked nearly to the ceiling. The disease had overtaken his very existence, forcing him to live a minimalistic life from cardboard boxes.

Without knowing it, the man turned his ledger to a page that he looked at every night, before he went to sleep.

The page haunted him.

At the top of the page was the date, September 14th, and it contained the items the man took from Pete Walker's house, the night he murdered Pete's friend while watching his house. The list included a 35 mm camera, a commemorative spoon collection with each president's face etched into the rounded handle, a digital picture frame, and lastly—the man's eyes stared at the catalogued item—a kitchen knife with a six-inch blade. The man had no idea of the brand, as the logo had been rubbed off from years of use. What he did know, however, was that this was the knife he used to stab Justin Gallecki one time in the heart on that fateful night.

A tear splashed on the page.

He quickly shut the journal, and slammed his fist on the table in guilt.

He had followed the investigation of Justin's murder, and the police had not yet named any suspects in the crime, as no fingerprints were ever found in the house, or on his body, nor, the man knew, would they ever find a murder weapon.

His gaze sleepwalked to his surplus inventory of print bombs that he had spent so much time developing, stacked neatly against a wall in the corner of his third bedroom. So much effort and brilliant thought had gone into their creation, yet they had been so destructive to their creator.

His eyes wandered back to the table and found a brief, handwritten letter on yellow-lined paper cast atop an already mountainous pile of papers in the center of the round table.

He looked at it only for a moment, then rose, got another beer from the refrigerator, and chugged it down with the door still open, throwing the empty can on the visibly dirty kitchen floor. He grabbed another, and duplicated the process—a bit slower this time, burping silently as he finished the frosty brew.

After standing over the sink for a time, allowing

the alcohol to seep into his body even further, he once again grabbed the letter from the table and felt ready to read it in its entirety.

He stood with his back against an adjacent wall and read the words as they were written on the page in their entirety. The letter was short. To the point.

When he finished reading, he turned to face the mirror on his kitchen wall, exhaled powerfully, and then stood on one of the dining-table chairs, placed his head into the noose he had tied, and rocked the chair until it toppled over.

The man swung from his kitchen ceiling, and for his last few moments on Earth, while his trachea collapsed and all life began to expire from within his lungs, he watched his reflection turn from pale to a bruise-like purple. He watched in contorted solitude as his reflection's eyes screamed from their sockets. His eyes noted that their reflective counterparts seemed oddly thankful to soon be rid of the now blurring light that for so long had consumed their retinas.

His last gasp of life was one shrouded in both self-disgust from a life turned wrong and purification for the freedom that lay ahead.

A faint smirk grew across his face. He would soon be free. Free from the torturous life he had let himself fall into.

After only a few more moments, the man's eyes

had all but closed; one eyelid stayed slightly ajar from the recent trauma inflicted on its working parts. His head hung oddly to one side from the force of the rope, and the only movements that lingered were intermittent twitches from his fingertips. Eventually, all life had exited the man's body, leaving the room in perfect silence. The only words that remained were those on the outside of the folded yellow letter. They simply read, "I'm sorry."

The alarm screamed at Jacob, his ears still ringing from the live musical offerings of the local alternative rock group Honey Colmbe, who'd played at Barney's last night. The group got their start in high school at pep rallies, and now played wherever they could, whenever they could. The money was mediocre, but lead singer Austin Colmbe was ever extending the reach of his band's listening net. Often, he would drop copies of their album off at local radio stations, and hand them out at the area county fairs, in hopes of the right person hearing the right song at the right time.

He stirred momentarily. His alarm was one that grew in volume as it sounded until it was turned off by the person struggling to wake up. The alarm clock always won, no matter how badly Jacob wanted to stay in bed, and this day was no different.

Jacob slowly moaned off the edge of his bed, squinting his eyes at the onslaught of light; the action reminded him of his recent captivity where he was lost in darkness. The recollection led to thoughts of Victor. They tore at his heart, and one word came to mind.

*Audrey.*

He clicked off the alarm clock, and stood in silence as his mind reminded him that he would never see her again. He blinked firmly and shook the thought from his head.

"Ugh," he groaned as he held his throbbing head in his hands, eager to rid his hangover.

*Water. Lots of water.*

He stumbled downstairs as he wiped away the cobwebs and fetched a bottle of water from the refrigerator. He chugged it down entirely, and realized that alcohol was not the proper weapon to use when waging war with grief. Maybe for a battle, but casualties would always remain, rendering alcohol useless in combat.

He opened another bottle of water and took it with him as he headed for the door. Even with a pounding head, he was still intrigued by whatever it was that Patrick wanted to give him. Anything to help him deal with the loss of Audrey, or to cope, would be welcomed.

A few moments later, Jacob got into his car and turned the radio off while he drove to the detective's house. There were times when listening to something would set his mind at ease, and allow him to feel relaxed and worry free as he drove. This was not one of those times. He felt an air of uncertainty around him, like a plague was looming over his soul. He tried to strip his mind of the thought, but gave up as a wave of heat overtook him and he began feeling nauseous.

*Liquor. Potholes. Oh God, here it comes!*

Jacob stopped the car, opened the door, and vomited on the shoulder of the road, his body purging the spent bullet casings used during last night's battle. It was hot and burned with the ferocity of lava. He took a chug from his water to flush the vile taste of bile from his mouth. He got back in the car and continued driving, feeling slightly better. An extremely long and white-faced five minutes later, he arrived at the detective's home.

Detective O'Reilly lived in a two-story brick house that seemed to be well cared for, as though the owner took pride in his landscaping—something that is not as common in today's day and age. Many home-owners simply feel that their house is built on ground, rather than a lawn, and end up treating it as such until it becomes entirely barren of life.

Jacob walked up the brick walkway to the front door, and took one hand out of his pocket to knock on the door. However, just before he knocked, he noticed a small note taped to the storm door. He read it. It was a note from Patrick saying, "Come on in and make yourself at home. I'll be right down." Jacob abided, turned the doorknob, and entered Patrick's house. The very first thing he noticed was the smell. Every family has its own smell. The family smell is developed over time, from the frequent consumption of their favorite foods and spices. The spices, especially. The more powerful ones radiated from a person's skin, becoming more pungent when they sweated. This house smelled oddly of nutmeg and ginger. Like a pie.

He began removing his jacket and didn't stop his eyes from wandering in the house. Pictures and vases adorned the walls and shelves. A coffee table was situated in the family room to the left of the entryway; a sofa was matched with it, and faced a bay window that looked into a lush yard peppered with birdhouses.

"Nice place you got here," Jacob said, louder than normal, hoping Patrick would hear him.

He made his way to a hutch that housed a set of china. Each dish was elegantly propped on a holder within the display case. Jacob took note of the brand and slightly nodded his head in approval. Odd, he thought. One man admiring another man's china didn't seem quite right. Not that owning china was a female thing, but that it was difficult enough to find one man who knew a thing or two about fine dishware, let alone two in the same house.

He smiled at his thought, and shrugged his shoulders.

Jacob turned back toward the sofa, and slowly approached it. His jacket was now in his hands, and he decided to sit on the sofa while waiting for Patrick to greet him. The sofa was low, and Jacob had to almost plop down on it, rather than sit into it. It squeaked when he sat in it, and the high-pitched noise apparently got the attention of Patrick's dog, as he could hear him trotting from the other room, its tag jingling with every step. After a moment, the dog appeared as it pushed open the swinging door to the kitchen and approached the visiting guest. Jacob reached down to pet the animal, and got a few good rubs in behind the ears. He looked up and saw the still swinging kitchen door, as it revealed a pair of motionless feet hanging from the kitchen ceiling.

"Jesus!" The word escaped from Jacob's throat as he struggled to get up and clamored his way to the kitchen. His eyes briefly fixated on Patrick's, hoping to see them blink, as though this was some horrific joke. He raced to Patrick's side and lifted the body with all of his might in an attempt to counteract the gravity tugging at the detective's neck. As soon as he lifted Patrick up, he knew he was gone. Rigor mortis had set in, and the body remained stiff even as Jacob lifted it farther into the air; the legs just swayed out to one side, never bending at the knees.

"Patrick!" Jacob called out. "What have you done?! No! Patrick. Why?" He turned around and put his hands on his head as he reeled in shock, and saw his own face in the mirror in front of which Patrick had hung himself.

Detective Patrick O'Reilly swung slightly and silently in the reflection of the mirror, dressed in his finest police regalia complete with white gloves, hat, and his past decorations pinned to the left breast. In the pocket on the right side of his uniform was a folded piece of yellow paper peeking out above the top edge.

Jacob turned around to face the body, and somberly reached for the letter. He gently pulled it out of Patrick's breast pocket, composed himself, and opened it. Written in beautiful penmanship, he read the brief letter.

*Jake, the top drawer of my nightstand will tell you everything. This is my gift to you. An understanding. That many people deal with horrific tragedy. A population of which you are now a part. The road ahead will not be an easy one, Jake. But meet it with positivity, and it'll have no chance of consuming your life, like it did mine. She's with you, and always will be. Believe me. I wish it didn't come to this, but I had turned into someone that I spent my entire career trying to catch. A murderer, because I didn't fight for my life from day one. But you still have a chance, and a good one at that. Let my failure be your lesson. I'm sorry.*

Jacob looked up from the letter. Tears had already filled his eyes. Not because he was close to Patrick, but because he was partially jealous of him. Patrick got to share the same dimension with Audrey. A part of him welcomed death, looked forward to it even. For only in death would he truly reunite with his lost love.

Jacob arrived back at his house after calling the police, who arrived at Detective O'Reilly's house in shock. He turned to see the TV, which continually shouted at him as he attempted to hack away the vines of the jungle in his mind. *Patrick, why? Audrey...*

He looked to the side of the bed and saw the journal he had been directed to in the detective's letter.

In it, he found all of his lab notes that offered the exact method for disintegrating fingerprints. On the last page, there was one sentence written in ink. *In the wrong hands, this is lethal, but in the right, it is a profound discovery.* Jacob didn't know it at the time, but it would take the police about a week to reunite the stolen items from the first box with their owners. In all, there were twenty-seven boxes to sift through. The process would be much easier had Jacob given them Detective O'Reilly's journal, but he held onto it, not yet certain whether or not he should offer such intricate knowledge to someone of power. For now, Jacob decided the journal was best kept in his trusted hands, along with the remaining print bombs Patrick asked him to keep, their use too dangerous for most people. But not Jacob.

A loud knock at his front door broke him of his blank stare at the late detective's journal. He slowly walked toward the door around the corner.

Another obnoxious knock blasted through the hallway.

"Jesus," he protested as he opened his front door a few moments later. Outside, he saw a black Lincoln Towncar with tinted windows drive off. An envelope jutting out of his porch-mounted mailbox caught his attention. He opened it, and two small cards fell to the ground.

He knelt down to gather them from his porch. Looking at the first, less colorful card, he read the name, stumbled back from a kneeling position, and plopped onto the porch. Astonishment grew from his eyes.

"Holy sh…," Jacob said aloud.

He shuffled the items in his hand to look at the second card, slightly larger than the first, and covered in semi-chromatic font and graphics.

The colored card turned out to be an invitation to the Presidential Museum of Natural History Gala to be held next May. The other, with the words "I'm sorry for your loss. We'll be in touch." handwritten in black ink on one side, was the business card of Morton Caldwell, the President of the United States.

*Epilogue — November 24, 10:19 A.M.*

It was Sunday, and Jacob had visited Audrey's grave more than a dozen times since her funeral. This was now his church service. He felt that there was no way to be closer to God than standing over his love's grave and speaking to her, about her, and sometimes, he felt, with her. God was there.

Historically, cemeteries proved to be a breeding ground for apparitions and supernatural activity, from an innocent sighting to the elaborate hoax. Those stories never really affected Jacob. That is, until he saw Audrey for the first time after she was killed. It happened on the third night after her burial.

*Jacob, distraught from the added open space in their bed, turned hysterical and proceeded to layer his clothing with wool and fleece, packed his sleeping bag, pitched his tent, and slept beside her peaceful grave. The night was cold. Jacob still could not sleep, and watched as frost grew from the grass, the trees, and even from the tombstones. It was 1:04 when he heard the first sound. It sounded like odd music. One note, and very quiet. He had to squint in order to gather anything audibly discernible about it. The pitch never changed. It remained steadfast and grew in beauty, as if sung from a child's pure and tender lungs. His eyes strayed from the growing frost, which seemed to only grow when he was not watching it, and focused in the direction of the beautiful sound.*

Jacob stood at the foot of his bed and began shuffling toward his dresser. He heaved open the solid wooden drawer and noticed the scent of raw pine wafting from within.

A day like today required his nicest shirt and tie combo. He continued to dress himself in his Sunday's best—a muted gray suit with a light blue shirt and gray striped tie—and headed for the door. He stopped at the threshold and looked back inside the room to make sure he had not forgotten anything, and then he turned off the bedroom light, allowing total darkness to consume him once again.

*On that third night, Jacob kept refocusing his eyes in the darkness as his night vision amplified. That sound. He'd never heard anything like it ever before in his life, and struggled to comprehend its origin. After a while, he wondered if his ears were simply ringing, questioning whether or not there was in fact a sound at all. Then, his eyes proved him wrong.*

*Like the sun rising from an emerald sea, Jacob watched as a nirvanic vision of Audrey rose from her grave beside him. He had never seen her look so incredibly beautiful. Her hair was waving in a nonexistent wind, her smile immense, and she appeared neither clothed nor naked. She floated before him as pure as an untouched mountainside—lush, fertile, and magnificent. When Audrey looked at him, he could literally feel her overpowering his soul. Memories of their life together—their first kiss, vacations, even their first argument—started to pour into his mind. She was communicating with him.*

Jacob shook his head once again to rid the thought, and headed down the stairs to his kitchen to make breakfast. His previously undying hunger for food—and life, for that matter—had left his body since Audrey's death. He knew he had to eat, but Jacob no longer took joy in the creation of a meal, as he did a short few weeks ago. Today, it was toast and peanut butter. Tomorrow, it would probably be cold cereal or instant oatmeal, whereas with Audrey around he would feast on omelets, homemade pancakes, and sausage patties. His fancy taste buds were no longer present, nor were his skills to cook like Audrey.

He dropped the last half piece of toast onto the paper plate, and threw it in the trash; his anticipation to visit Audrey's grave was too strong for him to eat. Plus, he still had to stop by Flores' Flowers to get Audrey's bouquet. He put his jacket on, headed for the door, and grabbed his keys from the fish dish. He looked at it intently for a time. It reminded him of Audrey. *Jamaica.* How he had to negotiate with vendors for the best price. The memory was priceless to him. He would never know that Audrey, too, recently recollected the emotional effect of such a small, but heavenly item the two purchased together.

*As Audrey appeared to Jacob and bombarded his mind with pleasant memories, he noticed that his eyes were paralyzed. He could not look anywhere but into Audrey's eyes, as if she was now entirely controlling him. He was mesmerized. And just as quickly as she appeared, Jacob's vision of Audrey dissipated into the night. From that point on, he couldn't wait to see her again, and fantasized about what other memories she was going to inject into his mind. It immediately became like a drug. He always wanted more.*

He stood at his car, got in, and revved the engine to life. Since Audrey was gone he never found himself in a hurry anymore, and his car's fuel tank thanked him for that. As he drove, he flipped the radio from station to station hoping to find a song with the lulling rhythmic beat of something acoustic, like Santana or Eric Clapton. He was lucky enough, though, and found himself lost in the reflective contentment nestled deep within the keys of a smooth piano. "November Rain." How fitting, he thought with one hand on the wheel, the other hitched out the window on this unseasonably warm day.

Jacob knew that God frequented cemeteries. From experience. Never haunting, and always welcomed, were his experiences with Audrey's spirit. Jacob did not believe in ghosts, but rather in spirits. Ghosts were thought to evoke fear, and make threats; to stand their ground if bothered. Spirits, on the other hand, were warm, light, welcoming, and reassuring to their visitors.

Before long, he arrived at the place he now called Church. Audrey's cemetery. He turned off his louder than usual car—he had been meaning to get a clunking sound checked out for over two months—and took in the splendor of the surrounding silence, his shoes crushing the gravel beneath them, the only noise to be heard.

As Jacob slowly walked toward Audrey's gravestone, he now believed in only one true certainty in life. Every ending paved the way for a new beginning. One that would offer new questions—for which he now knew many simply did not have an answer.

He placed the bouquet of roses at the foot of Audrey's headstone, nestling it into place among the flags, planters, and pictures that had all been placed in her honor by family, friends, and strangers alike.

The hill where Audrey's grave was located resembled not a cemetery, but rather a nature preserve, with towering oaks, climbing vines, and shrubs sprawling out in all directions. Soon after scaling the moderately sloped hill that led to Audrey's grave, he reached his car. Once there, he took one look back in the direction of the cemetery, effectively saying good-bye to the cherished plot of land where he first saw the vision of Audrey. Whether or not he was hallucinating did not matter to him. Simply put, he was thankful for her appearance to him, and only cared that his heart felt its effect.

This time, however, would be the last time he'd ever look back. Looking back to a gravesite suggested to him that the expired loved one being visited was positioned only in that one spot. That single location. Jacob knew that Audrey did not eternally reside in this sole plot, but rather, displayed her infinite beauty in every tree that swayed, cloud that floated by, wave that lapped against a beach, and flame that licked the air around it. Jacob even knew that Audrey was walking beside him as he got back into his car—listening to his every thought, and bandaging his suppressed pain. Her hand eternally caressed every pulse point on his body, delicately giving his heart the strength to pump another day.

And he did not know it at the moment, but this bouquet carried more significance than any other. It would be the last he would ever leave at Audrey's grave. The vividly red and freshly cut long-stem roses were seated comfortably at her headstone. They were in God's hands now. All fourteen of them.

Coming soon:


"Reech for the Code"
*(Book 2 in the Jacob Reech series)*


An excerpt follows.

## Chapter 4 — May 10, 3:00 A.M.

The door closed quietly behind a man as he entered the room. The action startled Jacob as the quiet *click*, reminiscent of that of the lightweight door of the room he had been held captive in a short few weeks ago, echoed in the library of the White House. The chair he sat in faced a watercolor of Washington crossing the Delaware, but his head pivoted quickly toward the sound.

*A false door!* Jacob realized, even before noticing who in fact now shared the room with him. "Mr. President!" The words erupted out of his mouth.

The President of the United States stood before the face of the wall of books. He was stoic. A sense of pride in his nation could be seen in his eyes, as though their watery retinas bore the pain from countless tears shed by millions of Americans throughout the nation's history.

Even though American troops had been pulled out from foreign soil over eight months ago, the war feverishly continued. And no, it wasn't a war over oil, or terrorism, any longer.

This war raged over something even more powerful, more lethal.

This war was being fought within the catacombs of secrecy, and by the forces of a real Ghost Protocol. Not like the movie, by any means. Team Indigo was far superior to any Hollywood mock-up, and was given their name Indigo—the military call sign for the letter 'I' for that which they tirelessly hunted throughout Russia, China, and North Korea. Information.

"This conversation never happened," President Morton Caldwell said in the calm, but powerful voice of the 62-year-old Vietnam veteran.

"Yes, sir, Mr. President," Jacob followed, still trying to pick up his lower jaw from the floor.

President Caldwell walked over to one side of the room and began pouring a Scotch. Jacob was held in silence, captivated.

"It wasn't my intention to alarm you, Mr. Reech," he said as he walked over to Jacob, his voice much more casual now. He carried two drinks, and handed one to his visitor.

Jacob had never tried Scotch, and didn't know if he should drink. It was only just past nine in the morning. After a moment, however, Jacob realized he wasn't being asked.

He took the glass. "Thank you, sir." The President responded with a brief nod of his head, and Jacob continued. "But you didn't alarm me. I just wasn't expecting that."

"Yeah, I guess I've always been the one to do that to people. Never felt the effect from where you're sitting." A single chuckle left the President's throat as he spoke the words.

Jacob looked around as he merely touched his upper lip to the liquid in his cup, unsure of what his reaction would be. "I'm guessing that's not the only false door in this place."

After a few moments of silence, President Caldwell responded, not addressing Jacob's previous statement.

"Mr. Reech, have you ever heard of the Presidential Book of Secrets?"

The question made Jacob's insides drop to his feet. *Or was that the Scotch?* Jacob set his cup down and shrugged his shoulders. "*History Channel.* That's about it."

"Well, Mr. Reech, I can tell you two things with certainty. It does exist, but we refer to it simply as 'The Book,' and *The History Channel* only covers the tip of a rather large iceberg."

Jacob sat up in his chair. A more serious expression grew onto his face. "Mr. President? Why did you bring me here?"

President Caldwell finished the rest of his Scotch and addressed Jacob once again, also more serious than before as he rose to pour another drink.

"Jacob, this country was founded upon many truths.

Unfortunately, that centuries-old and pride-filled *truth* has bred even more lies. Lies that you can't even begin to comprehend. And they are all detailed in that book. Jacob, these are lies that by taking that oath of office, I also promised to uphold." He paused abnormally long. "But enough about that, most of what's in there would just paranoy the shit out of people. More important-ly, The Book also contains a page penned by George Washington's own hand." The President raised his new glass to the painting of Washington directly in front of Jacob's chair, paying homage to his lifelong idol.

"What he wrote, however, was in a code that every president after him has tried to translate." He paused again.

*Politicians really know how to use silence in a conversa-tion*, Jacob thought admiringly.

"But thanks to your discovery, Jacob, I am the first who is able to. Now, to answer your question. The rea-son I brought you here, Jacob…"

*More silence?* Jacob thought.

"…is as of this morning that page has gone miss-ing." Just as he spoke the words, the President's cell phone began to ring. He put a finger up to Jacob asking for a minute while he took the call, as though a bomb hadn't just been detonated in the room.

Jacob's mind reeled as he sat alone in thought like never before.

*I thought this whole damn cipher thing was over. Jesus, Audrey's dead! I can't just keep doing this. I'm just a prof...*

In mid-thought, Jacob's mind vaguely registered the President's voice.

"Okay. Well done. Good-bye." He closed the phone, and directed his attention back toward Jacob. "Welcome back, Mr. Reech."

*"Back?"*

Source for image on page 278: Library of Congress website, Geography and Map Division – www.loc.gov/item/88694159

CPSIA information can be obtained at www.ICGtesting.com
Printed in the USA
BVOW07s1150060914

365541BV00001B/1/P